All
at Megan's ⸻ done
plenty of da ⸻ man
who was too slick for his own good. ⸻ charm
oozing from every pore. Jim hoped he could soothe
Megan out of her hurt, maybe he could give her a hug
and—

Those thoughts came to a screeching halt when,
over Megan's shoulder he glimpsed Seamus scowling
at him. This time the elf/angel stood, with hands on hips
and his toe tapping, in front of a teeny, tiny gothic
church. The leprechaun looked steamed, and for good
measure shook his head. Jim raised his hand and with
as unobtrusive a movement as possible, backhanded
Seamus off his little tuft of magical grass, mimicking a
fly-shooing movement. Jim turned his attention to
Megan. She stared down at the top of the desk, idly
picking up a file and then letting it drop. Finally, she sat
and took a deep cleansing breath.

"He's scum," she hissed under her breath.

The Wild Mountain Thyme

by

Kathryn Scarborough

The Wild Mountain Thyme

Cover Art by *Diana Carlile*

The Wild Rose Press, Inc.
PO Box 708
Adams Basin, NY 14410-0708
Visit us at www.thewildrosepress.com

Publishing History
First Fantasy Rose Edition, 2018
Print ISBN 978-1-5092-1917-9
Digital ISBN 978-1-5092-1918-6

Published in the United States of America

Dedication

For my brother Bill

Acknowledgments

Many thanks to Gaydrie Browne
for her inestimable help.

Prologue

"Seamus? Seamus!"

The voice was insistent, intruding, and annoying. Seamus sighed and stopped polishing the star he'd been rubbing to a fine luster, straightened his shoulders, and turned to look at the pudgy angel. The little soul had a handlebar mustache and the long ends of it curled and swirled around into infinity.

"Ah, Ignatius, is it? Aye, what is it you be wantin'?" answered Seamus.

Ignatius leaned in and whispered into Seamus's ear, although Seamus hadn't the slightest idea why he bothered, for they were quite alone in this puffy, wispy corner of Heaven.

"It's time."

"Surely not." Anxiety pulsed though Seamus's heavenly veins. What would they ask of him? He'd heard rumors—maybe there was a chance, but he'd have to play it close to the vest. He looked at Ignatius and carefully tried to judge the little angel's demeanor. He looked quite sincere. "I've been here but a little while." He would test the waters to get Ignatius to say more.

"Time to speak to the head clerk himself. If you get this right, you'll be on to the next angel level with St. Patrick's choir."

"Oh, indeed?" Seamus stood and stretched and

then combed his fingers through his long, rather unruly red-gold hair. He straightened his robe and wiggled his back, imagining what it would be like if he had those angelic wings.

"Come, he grows impatient," said Ignatius, grabbing Seamus's arm and pulling him along.

The two heavenly figures passed through one cloudbank after another with bits of fluff wrapping about them and becoming part of their radiant garments. They arrived at a section of Heaven bustling and buzzing with great activity. There was a large table filled with files, an old-fashioned pull arm adding machine, a fax, and a telephone with thousands of flashing lines buzzing and blinking furiously.

The harried celestial clerk shouting orders to harried celestial workers was sitting behind the crowded desk. He had a long flowing white beard covering the front of his long flowing white gown. His fingers and gown and even places on his beard were smudged with ink, and several pencils and a goose quill were stuck behind each ear.

Ignatius held his hands behind his back and solemnly bowed, his little wire rim glasses slipping past the end of his nose.

"Your Honor. We've come. This is Seamus."

The clerk behind the desk looked up, his assessing eyes riveted on Seamus. The fax was faxing noisily, the telephone lines were buzzing irritatingly, the adding machine buttons were clicking resoundingly, and the celestial workers were whispering and nodding anxiously. The heavenly clerk raised his hand and snapped his fingers; the sounds immediately stopped. He looked at Seamus over the top of his reading glasses as he smiled rather grimly.

"I see by your file"—he consulted one of the folders on the top of his desk—"that you've been here quite a while. Hmm," he said under a glowering brow. "I'd say it's time to earn those wings, old bloke." The celestial clerk put down the file and walked around the desk with a frown at Seamus. He clasped his hands behind his back and rocked to and fro while he stared at the little angel, before speaking in a most grumbly voice.

"These are the rules," he said, ticking them off with his fingers. "You can choose to appear as anything you want, or do anything you need to do to get the job done—however, you must stay within the parameters of morality. There will be no lying, no cheating, no stealing…you know, that sort of thing," he said, flipping his hand about idly.

"We have a specific case. Poor fellow is losing his faith. He's disgusted with life, had a terrible time with it." He sighed. "You'll need to find him a wife, and perhaps a child or two. From past experience, we find that should bring him back 'round."

Seamus gaped. "A wife, you say? A nagging woman? A whining child with wet nappies? Now how, by Saint Colum, will that restore the man's faith?"

"Oh dear, dear, dear," said the celestial clerk, shaking his head. "I see your problem." He consulted the file on the table. "Never met your soul mate, did you? Never had the joy of seeing a son grow into manhood? My, my, old bloke, this assignment will help the both of you. Now, Iggy here will give you all the information. I don't know if he has told you, but attached to this assignment is a time constraint," he said, raising his bushy eyebrows. "You have six months' time in which to successfully alter James O'Flannery's faithless attitude. We can only give you six months to finish your task. Sadly, there's no guarantee what might happen with his mortal soul, if you don't succeed, then it's back here to level one for a few hundred more years," he said, scowling. "And if he's lost, then you know where he'll end up, don't you?"

"Ah, Sweet *Jesu*," muttered Seamus. A shiver of fear coursed down his backside. He…well, aye he knew where the bloke would end up.

"Good luck, old mate," said the celestial clerk. "May the blessings of God go with you," said the angel as he waved his hand in a sing-songy, Gregorian chant voice.

In the blink of an eye, Ignatius and Seamus were atop a fluffy white cloud looking down on the Earth.

"And where is this place?" Seamus wondered aloud. He stared aghast at the sleek trains racing through tunnels, the tall glass-faced buildings, and the swarm of people rushing about like ants at feeding time.

"Boston, in the United States of America. It's a grand place. Full of Irishmen and a huge cathedral to boot. Why I think I'd quite like it here; that is if I had to go somewheres, well to be sure, anywhere but where I am." Iggy sounded a little nervous and glanced over his shoulder a time or two.

"And when is it?" Seamus asked.

"Ah." Iggy consulted a large calendar made of curlicue letters and numbers that he drew from his sleeve. "Early it is in the twenty-first century. Quite past your time, eh? And that is your assignment."

4

The angel looked through the end of a long, ebony telescope. Iggy pointed to a man who came into view. "The young, good-looking fellow sleeping on that train. See him, the one with black hair and fair face? Fine strapping lad. Your great-grandnephew six times removed on your sister Maggie's side; your very own grandnephew, ya see. His name is James O'Flannery. He's the fellow who has lost all his faith in the world. Had a fickle woman knock it clear out of him."

"And what did I tell you and His Honor back there about women?" Seamus gave Iggy an "I told you so" smirk.

"Ah, never you mind. There are plenty of good ones about. Now, here is what must be done. You must restore the love in his heart and that will mend it enough to restore his faith. I've done a bit of research. There is a fine pretty Kennedy girl living in Dublin. I believe she is the one for him. You must get the two of them together."

The handlebar mustache flopped in the way of the telescope and Iggy impatiently pushed it aside to watch James O'Flannery sleep on the speeding train. He looked at Seamus and continued in an ominous, much-practiced lecture. "Remember the rules—you can transform yourself into anything or anyone to accomplish this. But you must play fair, no cheating, and no short cuts. I'll be up here watching out for you. And if you need anything along the way, any questions, I'm here to help. Before ya know it, you'll be having those beauteous wings and singing in the choir. I hear you've quite the voice."

Seamus smiled, thinking of the wings, his much missed sister, and singing in the choir, until Iggy's words hit home. "I can be anything? Even the bleedin' King of England?"

"There's a queen now, and I don't know how that would help you." The ends of the little angel's giant mustache flopped and waved in time with the bobbing of his head. "Now be reasonable, Seamus, get on with the assignment."

Chapter 1

James O'Flannery shifted in his seat trying to find a comfortable spot on the Redline, the subway train, speeding into Boston. He yawned, covering up the unmanly lurch from his stomach, and slouched some more. His forehead touched the handrail of the seat in front of him. He pushed the air from his lungs as he tried to clear his mind.

He was…heartsick.

Gad what a word! It was the fiction writer in him coming out in spades. Heartsick. No, how about disgusted, angry—really, really pissed off. No, how about plain miserable, not only miserable, but mad as hell. He slumped farther in his seat and his forehead banged slightly on the handrail in time with the train going over the tracks. Bump, bump, bump: heartsick, heartsick, heartsick. The mantra washed over and over and over him yet again. He groaned as he sat up, forcing himself to look out the window of the speeding train. How could it have happened? The anger came and went, and then the other feelings, like wanting to kick himself in the rear, overshadowed even the anger he felt toward Angela.

He was damn mad about everything, everything; his job, his apartment, his significant other, yeah right! His grandmother had told him not to get mixed up with Angela. She'd told him in no uncertain terms that

Angela was not right for him—and different. Gran said she didn't know Angela's parents, where she went to church, and she was—different. That was ridiculous, bull hockey. She was smart, gorgeous, had a knock-out body that she worked on all the time, *and* she could cook. But she, it turned out, was totally and completely fickle.

Jim's mother and father had grown up on the south side of Boston with their Irish immigrant mothers and fathers. The close Irish ties were strong. But Jim seriously doubted the fact that Angela turned out to be a shallow, bitchy, nagging woman who made it with every guy on the street, and in the next block, and on their new couch in the living room of their apartment, had anything to do with her non-Irish heritage.

She'd broken his heart, but he wouldn't—didn't—have time to think about that right now.

Jim twisted and turned and pushed his shoulder into the unyielding seat. He tried to find a more comfortable position and send his mind back into nothingness. In the middle of the next push, his ear twitched and tingled. It felt like a bug was doing a jig inside it.

"Oh, James, me boy-o."

Jim sat up like a shot. He glanced furtively at the other passengers as he felt the blood run from his head to his feet. His heart hammered in his chest. Had someone actually whispered to him in that singsong lilting voice? He stuck his finger in his ear and wiggled it.

"What?" Jim grasped the seat in front him, stood halfway, and turned completely around trying to find the source of the voice.

There was no one there.

He slumped again in the seat, giving a wry shake of his head. If the voice was inside his head, he really must be losing it.

"Sit down and be quiet. You can't see me unless I want you to." a crisp no-nonsense, but decidedly Irish voice said stridently.

Sweat broke out on Jim's face as a terrific surge of adrenalin rushed through his middle. "Who are you? Where are you?" A whisper pushed through his lips.

It was a ghost. He knew it. He was haunted like those old bedtime stories his grandmother had told him when he was a child. Those stories had totally freaked him out for months on end.

His hands trembled. His knuckles turned white clutching the seat in front of him, but they still trembled. His gaze darted about the train. Nothing seemed out of the ordinary.

He sat down willing himself to relax. Be normal, he told himself. Act normal. Everything else is normal. The rain still poured down and sheeted the windows, the wind still whistled in through the cracks, and all the Bostonians were still oblivious to everything around them.

It must be his imagination running away with him. He had been staying up much too late reading that new Stephen King novel.

"Relax boy-o. I'm your guardian angel. And I've come to help ya."

"My guardian ang—" Jim laughed sharply. The image of a guardian angel sitting on his shoulder whispering to him was too funny and way too weird. "Give me a break, will ya? There's no such thing as guardian ang—" Jim's frenzied voice and whisper stopped abruptly.

Jim had been raised Catholic in a Catholic neighborhood, had gone to Catholic school, and all his friends were Catholic. But his religious training had diminished into a foggy memory long, long ago.

Guardian angel? Jim ran his shaking fingers through his hair and took a calming breath before he closed his eyes. He just didn't believe in angels.

"All right, all right." the voice inside Jim's head said hurriedly. *"You've found me out. I'm really your...your...your.... Oh...bol...well then, I'm your leprechaun."*

Jim uttered a short bark of a laugh. Whatever the voice was must think he was a complete idiot. He tried desperately to keep his head from trying to fall off his shoulders. Jim grabbed his things and got off three stations before his usual stop, Morrissey Boulevard and the offices of the Boston Globe.

Jim climbed the stairs quickly to the street, looking over his shoulder; sure the pressure of twenty-first century life had started to get to him. Once on Morrissey, he turned down DeLancey. He walked rapidly but as nonchalantly as possible and glanced every once in a while over his shoulder. He probably looked like a complete idiot. If he could get to the Globe, he'd get a cup of coffee. Maybe then his life would get back to normal.

"Jimmy boy-o, you can't be thinkin' that you'll run away from me, will ya? It's impossible, me boy. I've no corporeal body to slow me down."

Jim stopped abruptly and flattened himself against the wall of the nearest building. Corporeal, the voice had said corporeal. Now he was completely creeped out. The rain poured over the brim of his hat, sloshing into his eyes as he jerked his head right and then left, ready to manhandle the owner of the pesky voice inside his head. He took a deep breath and closed his eyes.

"Go get a cup of joe and everything will get back on track. It is a figment of my imagination. I am hearing things, but really and truly there is not a disembodied voice speaking to me," he said slowly, enunciating each word clearly, and he hoped, although he hadn't done it in a long time, prayerfully.

"*Oh, yes it 'tis. Indeed, yes,*" came the high-pitched, quick voice. "*Listen, Jimmy-boy, I have been assigned to you, so to speak. To help you, you see.*"

Jim kept his eyes closed and spoke in a relaxed monotone.

"Whatever or whoever you are, I don't want any help. Okay? Now beat it. I am no longer going to listen to voices inside my head. God, I must be going loony. I'm talking to the thin air."

Jim walked quickly down the street whistling as loudly as he could. Losing Angela and then getting on the outs with the editor-in-chief had obviously been too much. His grandmother always said that the human spirit was a fragile thing and too easily quashed.

Well, he decided, his spirit was now on the mend. No matter how he felt, it was mind over matter. There'd be no more leprechauns, or angels for that matter, whispering in his ear. He wouldn't allow it.

He trudged through the revolving door and onto the elevator, empty now except for one young woman. He looked at his watch and groaned. Walking from the Redline stop had made him twenty minutes late.

"Now listen to your Uncle Seamus, you've got to put your faith in me, boy-o. I'll lead you to your great success. I'm on your side, ya know," said a very insistent, very adamant voice.

Jim whistled louder.

"If you can't hear me, I can shout." The voice grew louder and then subsided into a chuckle.

"Cool it!" Jim demanded.

"What's the matter with you?" the young woman snapped as she glowered at him from across the car.

"Oh nothing, sorry, thinking out loud."

The woman snorted in disgust and got off at the next floor. The elevator started again but jarred to a stop suddenly between floors.

There was not a sound. Jim felt as though he'd fallen into a vacuum. He stood very still and tried not to breathe. The only sound was the rapid beat of his heart. A puff of green smoke rose from the floorboards. It wavered through the air and wrapped itself around Jim as it hovered and shimmered. Out of the swirling vapor popped a little man about three feet tall. He wore a Kelly green waistcoat, green breeches, green knee-high stockings, and green shoes with shiny silver buckles. Jim backed against the wall of the elevator as he felt the blood rush from his face and into his feet. His jaw slid south, and his heart hammered painfully from the bottom of his feet to the top of his head.

"I'm not trying to give you palpitations, boy-o, but you must listen. Aye?" said the apparition.

The little man had a long, crooked nose, slightly slanted, pale blue eyes, pointy ears, and a long-stemmed pipe clutched between his teeth. His bright, fiery red hair fell down around his shoulders in soft waves. He had a beard of the same fiery red shade that curled in front of his chin, like he'd used a curling iron to force it into shape. He held his hat, an elf's pointed cap, in front of him, as he stared intently at Jim.

Jim felt the air whoosh out of him as he slid soundlessly to the floor of the elevator. And then he forgot to breathe.

The little man walked up to him, nose to nose and in an undertone, he said very quietly, "Boo."

Jim gasped.

"Grand. I had to get you breathing again. Now listen," said the miniature person wagging his finger under Jim's nose. "My name is Seamus, that's James in the old Irish, and I've been assigned to get you out of your malaise, so to speak. Now if I scare the breeches off you, I can disappear and you will only hear me. Matter of fact, I can do just about anything," Seamus said with pride. He took in a big breath and began to pace. His hands clutched the cap behind his back. "I think a trip is in order. Ah yes, a trip across the sea. It shall give you a whole new perspective on things." Seamus stopped his pacing and turned to face Jim.

"Follow me so far?"

"Where?" Jim voice came out in a very uncharacteristic squeak. He felt he had no other choice but to answer this figment of his imagination.

"Across the sea, boy. To Ireland."

"Ha. How am I supposed to afford that? If you are my guardian whatever. Leprechaun? I suppose you noticed my deficient bank account. Wait a minute. What am I doing?" Jim muttered and shook his head. He looked down at his trembling hands, turning them over and over. He looked everywhere but at the little person. He shook his head sharply. "Am I really talking to a-a-a?" Something occurred to Jim as he spoke; the little *whateverthehellitwas* looked exactly what Jim imagined a leprechaun would look.

"Leprechaun, boy-o. If it's coin you're worried about, don't be. I've it all figured out," the little man said with the grand sweep of his arm.

And with that, the leprechaun put on his hat, clutched his pipe tighter in his teeth, pulled down on both of his ear lobes, and disappeared.

Immediately, the elevator began to rise and stopped when it reached Jim's floor at the Boston Globe. Jim sat with his back against the elevator wall, his legs splayed out on each side and his mouth agape as the doors slowly opened to the bustling offices of the paper.

"O'Flannery? Are you okay?" Karen, one of his coworkers, hurried forward and pushed the open-doors button as she reached in and pulled on Jim's arm.

"It's okay. I felt dizzy," Jim said in a strangled whisper. He stood up and staggered to his desk. With trembling hands, he shrugged out of his rain-drenched coat and hat, and pulled a comb through his hair. His mind raced through the past thirty minutes, re-playing everything. Everything.

What was that thing he'd seen on the elevator? Had it belonged to the voice he'd heard on the train and during his walk? And did he really see it or was he conjuring up scenes from that Stephen King novel? He shook his head. He didn't have time to worry about it now, not with his editor breathing down his neck. It'd all go away. Wouldn't it? Jim took a shaky breath.

Living around the Irish his whole life, he'd heard stories of elves and leprechauns. They'd been spoon-fed to him like babies ate pabulum. No matter what the old tales said, this was the twenty-first century. Those kinds of *things*, those *little people* didn't exist. Surely, they never had except in the fertile imaginations of his ancestors.

Karen came from the suite of editors' offices to find Jim pouring a cup of coffee at the break table.

"O'Flannery, the big guy wants to see you...right now." Karen raised her brows and put her hands on her hips.

Jim shrugged with dejection. *God, what else could go wrong?* He took a quick sip of coffee, hoping to dispel the chill that settled over him, and willed his hands to stop shaking.

Jim knocked on Chief Editor Gray's door once before entering.

"You wanted to see me, sir?"

"O'Flannery, come in, come in. Have a seat. I think I have a great story for you, just up your alley." Fine black powder from Gray's toner cartridge floated in the air when the editor jiggled and knocked on it. Mr. Gray put down the cartridge gingerly and sat with a plop at his desk. He tried to wipe the black toner powder from his hands with an already grimy rag.

"All morning I'd been thinking about Collins for this, but then your name came into my head, and quite frankly, it won't leave." Gray looked surprised by his statement. "And the publishers want this story covered and covered now."

Jim sat across the desk watching his editor's eyes, looking for any hint of Gray's often-used sarcasm. He seemed sincere enough...this time.

Before Jim could take a breath to reply, the

leprechaun, looking like a miniature of the spirit Jim had seen in the elevator, suddenly popped into view and stood on Gray's shoulder near the man's ear. Jim gasped, and then choked; coughing so loudly that Gray came around the desk to slap him on the back.

"Hey, you okay?" Gray asked.

Jim waved his hand, nodded his head, and wiped the tears streaming down his face as the last of the cough sputtered away.

"Now this is what I propose," Gray said as he leafed through a file after he'd returned to his side of the desk. The leprechaun leaned near Gray's ear and whispered something. Gray put his finger up to his ear and wiggled, leaving a large smudge of black toner on the side of his face. The leprechaun whispered again, and again Gray scratched his cheek vigorously, not paying the slightest bit of attention to what he was actually doing. A smear of toner covered the side of his face from his earlobe to his chin and half his nose to the side of his face as he scanned the file in front of him.

"Excuse me? I didn't hear that last bit." The editor had been talking while he scratched vigorously at his face, but Jim had been too fascinated to listen as he watched the antics of the leprechaun on Gray's shoulder.

"I told you that you're going to Ireland," Gray said blowing out a breath in exasperation. "Get your passport and the company's travel agent to get you on a flight to Dublin. Also, get some spending money from accounting and be gone by the end of the day. Here's the file. I want some kind of story over the wire in the next forty-eight hours or so. Got it?"

"Yes sir." Jim swallowed a chuckle. Gray's usual

intimidation tactics were on full bore. The editor's black-streaked face made him look so silly, especially with his pulled down brow and scowl.

Outside Gray's office, Jim leaned against the closed door and scanned the file. Someone in Ireland was killing Irish-American tourists, and the Boston Globe wanted to know all about it. Three were dead already, and the Irish authorities had made no inroads into finding the perp. The groundwork was done and the liaison established. Jim was going to work with somebody named M.E. Kennedy at the Irish Times.

Great, a long tiring trip. Maybe he could catch up on some sleep on the plane. Maybe that pesky leprechaun that Jim was sure his overworked brain had imagined would leave once he got enough sleep.

Chapter 2

Megan Kennedy looked up from the departmental memo she'd managed to read three times, in spite of the haze of fury that clouded her vision. They'd bloody assigned some damn Yank to her loving care. She was now a nanny, shepherding the idiot around when she should be writing the story! Ah bollocks! Perhaps she'd either work him to death or scare him to death. He'd be running back to America with his tail between his legs in no time.

The editors at the Times knew she could write. Hadn't her special interest story on the old monastery won her "The Feature Writer Journalism Award" last year? Here she was with baby-sitting duty, chauffeur duty, and this O'Flannery had the story—with her as liaison. Megan threw the memo down in disgust. She looked at her computer screen and read the e-mail for the fourth time.

To: MEKennedy@TheIrishTimes.ie.co

Arriving Shannon Airport, Tuesday two p.m. Will take next available train to Dublin. Anticipate meeting you at your offices around six p.m.

James F. X. O'Flannery

Ha! Probably begged to come over and touch the auld ancestral home, only a sightseeing trip for O'Flannery—with a byline thrown in!

She could write the damned story for the Globe as

well as the Times. Boston didn't have to send a writer out. She could do it. Megan hit the delete button with a vengeance and watched the screen go blank. She absently reached up to twirl a lock of her hair. Not only was her writer's pride bruised but she was well through with men right now. That bastard Richard had broken her heart, and she'd not let her guard down again so easily.

****

Hoping to find a spare inch to get comfortable, Jim twisted and turned his large frame in the seat. Airline seats were small, and he had another four hours or so to listen to the droning engine as the plane made its way across the Atlantic.

He gave up on sleep and decided to go through the articles he'd found in the Globe's archives—articles that Kennedy at the Irish Times had written. Maybe if the guy's writing was any good, he'd not miss the sleep he wasn't getting. Then again, if the guy's writing turned out to be terrible, Jim would fall into a stupor of boredom. It was a win-win; that is, if that apparition or *whateverthehellitwas* would leave him be.

He hesitated a moment, wondering if the leprechaun would hop out and scare the bejaysus out of him, leaving a few more hairs on his head to turn gray.

Jim shrugged, and leaving his sanity and his sleepless night to the fates, pulled out the first article he found. Kennedy had written about an old crumbling monastery in the west of Ireland and what a tough time the priests and brothers had keeping soul and body together. Kennedy wrote well. The piece was concise and objective reporting. *Maybe it wouldn't be too bad working with the guy,* thought Jim as he yawned. He slowly fell into a deep sleep as the article lay idly on his lap.

****

Megan had met the ultra-cool Richard at a party last spring and thought he'd been the answer to a young girl's heart. Aw bollocks! Not likely. Well, she'd not think about him *now*, not with an American invasion on the horizon.

Megan shoved her chair back, stood, and walked with purpose to the tea caddy. She'd sit and have a cup while she waited for O'Flannery. She'd missed her supper, but that was all right. A few pounds off her hips would suit her well. She looked down at her long, dark brown woolen skirt and boots, and flicked some lint off her tweed blazer.

She glanced at her watch. It was going on six thirty, and almost everyone had left. She didn't fancy meeting this man all alone.

"Lizzy?" She saw her friend, a co-worker, across the expanse of room, still at her desk.

"Oh, aye?"

"Are you going to your supper now?"

"Yeah, soon. My Ned is coming to the downstairs lobby to pick me up in a few minutes."

"Well, cheerio. Have a good evening," Megan said.

"Right. Don't work too late."

"Sure," Megan mumbled under her breath. "This will be a lovely evening. Ah, bollocks."

She wasn't kidding anyone, especially herself. She was lonely, tired, on edge, and irritated with the world—all at the same time. There was a madman out there killing tourists, Irish American tourists, and she was assigned to the story with an Irish American.

Right—

Megan sipped her tea, thinking dark, scary thoughts, and vividly recalled the pictures of the dead Americans as she recited the statistics from each of the killings in her mind. She glanced up. Everyone was gone, cleared off, and she was alone. She'd been deep in her own thoughts. She heard nothing but the constant buzz from an overhead fluorescent light in a nearby hallway, and the sound of distant traffic outside. All the lights were off except a few scattered desk lamps.

The place was deadly quiet. The continuous traffic from Tara Street had seemed to vanish. She sat up and focused all her energies on her surroundings. The hair on the back of her neck stood up as a chill raced up her backbone. She pushed herself back from her desk to cross to the entryway. She cracked open the heavy double glass doors to the hallway and heard footsteps.

Megan's breath caught in her throat. There it was again. Another step. A man's step, heavy and quick. Megan ran back to her desk. Frantically, she grabbed first the stapler, then the fountain pen, then the paperweight, looking for something to use as a weapon. The steps grew closer. She tore open her drawer, her hand feeling and then discarding item after item. More steps. They were right outside the door.

The door swung open and the silhouette of a man in an overcoat and hat was backlit against the glare of the hallway light.

Megan's breath caught in her throat and her heart hammered painfully in her chest. She watched the dark figure as it came closer and closer. Her fingers curled around a smooth plastic handle and she lifted her hairbrush from the drawer.

"Hello," the man called out as he looked about the semi-darkened sprawl of desks. "Hello?" he called out again. "Mr. Kennedy?"

"*Mr.* Kennedy?" Megan squeaked. "*Mr.* Kennedy?" she said again, her voice an octave higher than usual.

The man felt along the wall for a light switch. The dim fluorescent bulbs flickered on, illuminating a portion of the giant floor. Megan was clearly visible to the man now. She stood by her desk, clutching a hairbrush in her hand, poised to strike.

"Yes, is Mr. Kennedy around? He's supposed to be waiting for me."

Taking off his hat, the man walked toward her until Megan could see the deep blue of his eyes, the shining black hair, and the paleness of his skin. God, O'Flannery was Black Irish, and a damn handsome one at that. He had a cleft in his chin and a wide, nice-looking mouth. She'd name him a knockout if she weren't immune to men right now. He glanced down at the hairbrush clutched in her hand and smiled smugly. She saw a dimple appear in his right cheek. He walked up to her desk, his brilliant blue eyes glimmering in the dim light of the room.

"Uh, miss, if you aren't going to attack me with that hairbrush, do you think you could tell me where M.E. Kennedy is? I sent him an e-mail this morning telling him I'd be here about now."

Megan sat down and blew out a great sigh. She threw the brush on top of the desk and swiveled her chair to face him as she extended her hand.

"Pleased to meet you Mr. O'Flannery. I'm Megan Elizabeth Kennedy."

Chapter 3

"You—you're Kennedy?"

"In the flesh, as it were, if you'll excuse the expression."

"See, I told you boy-o, what a fine looking lass would be waiting for ya. Look at that long, pretty ginger hair, will ya?" The voice not only spoke in his ear, it chortled.

When he heard the voice, the *whateverthehellitwas* speaking to him, Jim practically jumped out of his skin. He turned his head surreptitiously, and not seeing the little green man, he muttered under his breath, "Go away."

"I'm sorry?" Megan Kennedy's sandy brows rose up to her smooth forehead.

"Uh, nothing." He gave a cursory look around the room for a little green-clad figure. Not seeing one, he breathed a quick sigh of relief. Maybe the spirit would take off and leave him alone. Permanently.

"I'm sorry, I assumed you'd be a man, since you signed your name with initials." Jim practically swallowed the words as he tried to recover his equilibrium. He'd been startled once again by that…leprechaun. "You know what they say about assuming, sorry." Jim looked up at Megan not quite meeting her gaze, trying not to out and out gape. She was as different from what a man looked like as he'd ever seen.

She tossed her head and her hair swung hypnotically over her shoulder. She stopped and pulled it back as though she thought better of the gesture.

"That's the way Irish writers sign their names, regardless of gender," she said with a tilt of her head.

At this moment she really couldn't remember how other Irish writers, women or men for that matter, signed their names. The only writer she could think of inside her fuzzy brain at the moment was W.B. Yeats. She tried hard to quell the flurry of butterflies crowding about her stomach. Ah bollocks! Seeing this gorgeous man quite made her brain stop. *This is not how a professional writer behaves*.

"And sometimes it helps if you can be mistaken for a man—at least until they can read your piece. Before they reject it," she said very quietly. Being taken seriously as a woman wasn't the problem, not in this day and age, it was the fact that since she was, well, pretty and a blonde to boot that everyone assumed she was an airhead.

"Ah," Jim replied, as he pulled off his overcoat and draped it over a nearby chair.

Megan took her butterfly-filled tummy and thumbed her nose at her silly self as she looked him over. He was quite dapper in a bottle-green turtleneck sweater and gray slacks. Her gaze stopped at his waist and jerked upward, coming to a slamming stop at those eyes, those blue as glass eyes; eyes that could probably cut someone to the quick if that's what he wanted to do.

Megan shook her head, hoping to dispel the hot flush she felt on her neck and cheeks. Now, what had she been doing looking at his…waist? Wasn't it vitally important right now to see through the man, and not really see him? Not drool over him anyway. She cleared her throat and held her hands together in her lap, leveling her gaze somewhere between his eyebrows and the top of his head.

"I didn't think the weather would be warmer here. I guess it kind of surprised me," he said. Jim put his hands in his pockets and looked around the room idly. She was utterly gorgeous, *and* she could write. He'd just have to keep his libido on a leash when he was working with her. He smiled quickly and then focused his gaze at the top of her head, deliberately avoiding eye contact.

"Oh…uh." Megan stopped and started, looked at her desk, and fiddled with the pens and pads, straightening, realigning, picking her little clock up and looking at it, and then her stomach growled. She placed the clock down hard, a little harder than she'd planned and cringed at the sound it made hitting the desktop. She looked up at him. "Fancy something to eat?"

"That would be great! We'll charge it to the Globe. They can afford it more than we starving writers can." Jim grinned at his own stupid joke hoping to lighten the tension. Megan looked as flustered as he felt. Sharing a meal would help them get acquainted with one another. "And while we're at it, can you direct me to the Ramada Dublin?"

Megan laughed in spite of herself as she escorted Jim down the stairs. "I'll show you a better place after we've eaten. The Ramada is clear across town." They stopped at the outside doors as Jim helped her on with her coat.

Jim tried to mask the shock of finding that M.E.

Kennedy was a woman, and what a woman! She was tall, probably close to five feet ten inches, and stood up straight and proud, not diminishing one whit from her height as some women might choose to do. Her long, reddish-blonde hair cascaded past her shoulders in waves. Her face had high cheekbones, and her small chin was slightly pointed with a deep cleft that broke up the perfect oval of her face. Her skin was flawless, and her eyes were deep green.

No wonder she signed her name like a man. No one would take her as a serious writer if they saw her first. He'd like to take her seriously, he thought, as his fingers brushed her arm as he helped her on with her coat.

Now, where had that thought come from?

He would not allow himself to get involved in any way with this woman. His story would stink, and his butt would be really sore when he continually kicked himself for about a year. It wasn't hard to remember the fresh wound that had yet to begin to heal was there because of Angela.

Jim grabbed the suitcase he'd left behind in the office's main entrance check-in desk, and they walked out into the misty, damp night.

"There's a grand little pub not far from here. We can get some hot food and ale there, Mr. O'Flannery," said Megan as she indicated the direction to walk.

"Call me Jim please, and that pub sounds great, Miss Kennedy." Jim said, waiting for the reverse invitation to call her by her first name. He was disappointed when it didn't come.

"Is this your first trip to Ireland?" she asked.

"Yes, I hadn't really planned to come at all," he

said in order to make idle chitchat.

"Not even to visit the *auld sod*?"

"Now how did you guess I'm of Irish decent?" He quirked a smile at her and the dimple peeked out. "No, I'm an American, plain and simple. Glad of it, too. This ancestral home stuff keeps a person from focusing on what's important."

"And what might that be?"

"Anything: wars, kids starving, the latest football stats, anything is probably more important than that to my way of thinking."

Megan laughed as she nodded her head.

"The young woman doesn't want to hear a discourse on political science, me boy-o. Talk about the weather, books you like, anything but that. She'll be liable to turn around and run."

Jim put his finger in his ear and waggled it back and forth. There was that voice again giving him advice, telling him what to do. Maybe it was his subconscious trying to help him stop being such a dimwit. But, his heart chimed in, maybe, just maybe, you'll find your soul mate yet. Jim shook his head and immediately changed the subject telling his heart to go stuff it.

"Gee, the weather is so mild for January. We're usually up to our hips in snow about this time of the year in Boston. We did get a little thaw for a few days. I heard about a blizzard on the way when I left," Jim said and then realized he rattled on like a twit so he shut up.

Megan glanced at him. She had to admit that the man did rouse her curiosity. Writers should not grope about for words now should they? The Globe wouldn't have sent an inept numskull, would they? He blundered on about the weather and then stopped talking as though all the air had gone out of him. Well, if he turned out to be a lousy writer, then for sure she'd get the byline.

Don't count on it, Kennedy, and maybe I should tell him to call me Megan; if he wants me to call him Jim, she thought, walking along in companionable silence. Megan stopped at a building with glassed doors framed in Kelly green-painted wood and huge ornate brass door pulls. They walked inside a noisy, smoke-filled room, and Jim stopped inside the doors and gawked. Megan pulled on his arm to get his attention.

"And here's the pub," she said as she looked around and nodded at a few of the patrons.

The large room had a wooden bar stretching across the width of it, as well as tables and booths. People moved about quickly, visiting from table to table. They drank their ale from huge beer glasses while eating from plates piled high with delicious smelling foods, or nibbled on the pretzels and crisps from bowls strategically placed around the long mahogany bar. The talk and laughter filling the room almost drowned out the background music.

"Miss Kennedy, and how are ya?"

"Fine, Bob," Megan said to the barkeep. The fellow was a tall, thin man with a scant bit of red hair covering all but the very top of his head.

"This is James O'Flannery, just come from America. He's doing a story for our paper and his," said Megan as she took the pint Bob had drawn for her.

"Have a half and half, Jim. You'll like it, I promise."

"Thanks."

She watched Jim sip his beer for a moment and then looked about for several acquaintances. Megan spoke to a few people while they moved through the throng toward a booth near the windows. Jim put his suitcase under the table and helped Megan out of her coat.

Jim pushed up the sleeves of his sweater and looked around, trying very hard not to let his mouth gape open as he absorbed the scene around him. Men and women were talking, laughing, drinking, all quite reminiscent of after work patrons in any bar in the States. "Well, I guess it's a little like I thought it would be. Maybe, except for—"

"What did you think it would be?"

"Old fellows in tweed coats and soft caps, with canes and pipes, talking about their sheep."

"St. Joseph! You've been watching too many Bing Crosby movies. Dublin is as cosmopolitan as any city in Europe. Some people still live on the islands in stone huts with thatched roofs, but I suppose you could find an American counterpart to that in your rural south."

"Well said." Jim raised his glass in a toast to her.

Megan was suddenly conscious of Jim staring at her, giving her a good looking over, and she felt her cheeks redden with embarrassment. He was a man and she was a woman and—wait, what was she thinking? She sipped her beer again, and glancing at him from under her lashes, noted that O'Flannery looked terribly strong and good-looking from where she sat.

Physically strong and…she looked down to stare into her beer and then glanced at him unobtrusively under her lashes. Their waitress came to the table and Megan ordered for both of them. Megan looked at Jim and he shot her a smile, a real smile that started somewhere inside of him and traveled all the way to his very brilliant blue eyes.

Thoughts of that nature will land you in no end of trouble, my girl, said the levelheaded part of her that always tried to keep her out of trouble and zap her back into reality, even though sometimes she wouldn't let it.

In short order, the waitress brought their dinner, and Jim looked askance at what appeared to be beef in gravy with some kind of green mashed potatoes.

"Okay, okay, what's the green stuff?" He looked with apprehension at his plate.

"It's colcannon. Finely shredded cabbage and potatoes are mixed together as they are cooking. It's really good. Try it."

Jim lifted the fork and sniffed before he tried the mashed potato mixture. Hmm, he quite liked it, and in short order, the potatoes began to disappear.

"Tell me something." Jim put down his fork and turned his full attention on Megan. "What was that you told the bartender?"

"Told him about what?"

"You said something to him about me writing the piece for the Times?"

"Didn't you know? You're to write both pieces, and the Times is to give you a write-up and a byline." Megan tried her best to unclench her teeth and smile as she spoke.

Jim put down his beer and leaned forward, his brow pulled down in a frown. "That's ridiculous," he said with a puzzled look. "You aren't a stringer, are you?"

She knew he meant the freelancers who often write

single articles for newspapers. "No, full-fledged, and who the hell knows why I've been excluded from the articles." Her voice snapped with anger and Megan tried not to growl at him. Venting at O'Flannery for the total injustice was easy but hardly productive. Megan shrugged her shoulders. "The powers that be, I suppose."

"I'll talk to your editor. That's crazy to have you do the legwork and then not get credit for it. Don't they have any work support groups with lawyers here? There are all kinds of organizations and unions in the U.S. so that maniacal editors can't run you over. Slave labor, that's what I call it." Jim continued to eat, but his body language gave away his annoyance.

Jim's rant pleased Megan. So he was a pen-waving champion for newspaper journalists. Good. She leaned back in the booth and looked at the strong jaw, and the sexy cleft in Jim's chin. Too bad she wasn't in the market for a man. It would take at least another decade for her bruised heart to heal, so off the market she was. Back to matters at hand.

"Listen, O'Flannery. I appreciate your concern, but I can take care of myself."

"It's a wonder you didn't attack me with that hairbrush when I walked in," Jim said with a chuckle.

Megan dropped her gaze to her plate. Having a pretty face in this business had always made her wary of men offering anything to her. Could he really be different? Jesus, Mary, and Joseph, she hoped so.

Chapter 4

Jim wished that she'd look up at him, but saw only the top of Megan's head. He longed to see those pretty green eyes again. How was he to make things friendly between them? It would be a real drawback to his creativity if he had to stay around a cold brick wall and not an involved and yet friendly colleague. And Megan's attitude right now seemed just like that, a cold brick wall. He'd really like to see that smile.

"Do you have a file I could look at?" Jim hoped to change the subject and get her mind off the last bit of conversation.

"Sure." Megan dug into her briefcase and tossed the manila folder across the table to Jim.

"Now, boy-o—now's the time to tell her how lovely she is."

"What?"

"You want to make her swoon, and her toes tingle, don't ya?"

"Get lost." Jim hadn't meant to, but his jibe to the leprechaun out of the side of his mouth was only too clear and easily understood.

"Well, if that's the way you feel about it," sniffed Megan. She started to shrug into her coat.

"No—no, I wasn't talking to you, I promise." Jim touched her arm, but then quickly withdrew his hand. She gave him a cold-as-ice glare so glacial he almost shivered.

"Listen, we have lots of work to do," Jim said. He felt the blood rush to his face. Damn. Could he ever get this blushing under control? It happened at the oddest times and always embarrassed him, no end.

"Would you direct me to the Ramada Dublin? The Globe made a reservation for me there. We could get to work by nine tomorrow and start in on the groundwork." Maybe if he changed the subject, he could cover up his remark to Seamus and she'd think nothing of it.

"If you weren't talking to me, then who?" Megan had her coat half on and she leaned across the table, one brow raised prettily in question.

"Only myself, I assure you. Maybe it's jet lag." *Good grief, talk about stepping in it.*

Megan cocked her head, looking hard, trying to read right into him. "You know what they say about people who talk to themselves, O'Flannery?" She shrugged out of her coat and took a long draw on her beer, watching him intently over the rim of the glass the entire time.

"Yeah, and they might be right." He pushed his hand through his hair and then sat back and looked hard at Megan. He hesitated for a moment, wondering how weird his next line would sound. He hadn't convinced himself he could talk to anyone about this leprechaun business. They'd probably lock him up in the nearest mental institution. But this woman was Irish. Maybe he could talk to her. It's not like he could ask Karen at the Globe about it. He'd be locked up then for sure.

Jim turned his head slightly and watched the leprechaun's rear end waving back and forth over of his beer glass. The *whateverthehellitwas* had leaned over so far to reach the last bit of beer in the bottom of the glass that all Jim could see was his little behind sticking up in the air. Seamus was sucking away at the bottom of the beer glass with great relish, making all kinds of slurping noises that, it seemed, only Jim could hear. Then Seamus sat on the edge of the glass, crossed his legs, and in a melodious tone, began to sing.

"Oh, the summer time is come,
and the birds are sweetly singing,
and the wild mountain thyme grows around..."

It is so grand to be home*!"* Seamus crowed with delight as threw his arms out wide and hugged himself.

Seamus had no memory of how long it had been since he'd tasted anything so very grand, this miraculous brew that Jimmy boy was wastin'. *"More's the pity, it is."*

"Ah! And don't ya know that youth is wasted on the young! Aye, more's the pity."

Jim stared for a second and then turned his head away from the apparition. He'd ignore that voice. It was probably the break-up with Angela and the long flight that was sending him to the precipice and—hell, he was almost over it. Jim looked into Megan Kennedy's eyes, opened his mouth to speak, and stopped. A warm tingle started somewhere in his middle. This had to stop. No time for women and their nonsensical little games. Maybe if he talked about the apparition slurping beer from his glass he could get his mind off his, well…other parts of him.

"Can I ask you a question?" He paused and looked at her sideways for an instant. "You have to know that I really am not crazy. A little stressed maybe, but not crazy."

"All right, what is it?" Megan sat back and crossed her arms, her face blank, not giving an inch.

"Do you believe in leprechauns?" Jim almost whispered the question. He felt ridiculous, especially since he knew his blush had turned up so high it could be measured in megawatts. "I know that sounds completely insane but..."

"No, no," said Megan, looking at him strangely for a moment. She leaned forward and assessed him coolly.

Something, some emotion played across her face. She restrained a smile, and that little smile made Jim feel the dumber. "You know what they say about the Black Irish."

"Black Irish?"

"Haven't you looked in a mirror lately?" She said it very softly and leaned to him, the corners of her mouth twitching like mad.

"Is that what I am?" This tidbit of news was interesting, although he was a whole lot more interested in looking at that twitching mouth.

"The Black Irish come from the outer islands where there is said to be lots of magic, and if that is indeed what you are..."

"Jeez." Jim sat back and looked at everything but Megan.

"No, really. Druids and fairies and—"

"Listen." Jim turned to her, an all business look on his face. "I have nothing to do with fairies—"

"No, no, the kind with wings and floating fairy dust. You know, like Tinkerbell in *Peter Pan*?"

Megan couldn't believe the look on his face. His slack jaw and rounded eyes said it all. She could pull

35

him in completely. Jim sat back a little and combed his fingers through his hair. He gave her a you've-got-to-be-kidding look. Maybe he was a little smarter than she thought.

"Kennedy, when I've known you longer—well, never mind." Jim let out a great sigh and swatted at the top of his beer glass.

"Do you mind if we call it a night? I've got to get some sleep, or I'll fall into the mashed potatoes."

"Sure, come on. I'll walk you to the hotel near the Times. As I said, the Ramada Dublin is clear on the other side of the city. Since it's January and not many tourists about, they're sure to have a room for you. It's but five blocks."

"The long ones or short ones?" Jim wanted to know.

"I don't—"

"Ah, never mind, I suppose I can walk five blocks. And that's certainly good to know about the hotel. Of course, the folks at the Globe would have no idea where I should stay, though you suppose someone could look at a map. Look, I'll get a cab. You tell the cabby where to, okay? We'll drop you first. That way you'll be safe and—"

"Don't worry about me, O'Flannery. I've been taking care of myself for a long time now."

"But I do worry about you, Kennedy. It's the man's job to escort the lady home. It's in Gentlemanly Behavior 101. My grandma, who's from County Mayo by the way, would smack me but good if I didn't. Besides, the reason I'm here is there's a psycho loose out there, remember?"

"I remember, and it's Megan. If you're Jim, then

you must call me Megan."

"When you use my name, I'll use yours." Jim looked inordinately pleased that she had told him her given name. "Now show me this hotel."

Megan couldn't help smiling. He was a good one, this Jim O'Flannery, and funny. Even if she didn't get her byline, it wouldn't be so bad working with him for a week. Only working with him she reminded herself.

Chapter 5

Jim checked into the hotel with a bar right in the lobby; good for quick night caps. It was a quiet place along a side street. Megan knew what she was doing when she recommended it.

He fished around in his wallet until he found his seldom-used calling card. His cell phone would not work overseas. He hadn't had the time to add the feature before he left. He checked his watch again, making sure it wasn't too late to call home. About five thirty there, his grandma would be making supper. He could almost smell her famous yeast rolls.

"Hullo?"

"Hi, Grandma, it's Jim."

"Jimmy, and how are you?"

"Fine. I didn't have time to tell you before I left, but I'm in Dublin."

"What? In Dublin you say? Why, that's grand. But I thought you decided long ago that you wouldn't bother with going to see my old home."

"The Globe sent me. I'm writing a few pieces with a writer from the Irish Times."

"Oh, aye? And have you met him yet?"

"It's not a him, it's a her."

"A her? And how old is this person, and what does she look like, and is she Irish?"

"Yes, Grandma. She's Irish, she's a redhead, she's

38

real pretty, and she's probably a little younger than me."

"Oh my, oh my. Wait till I tell your mother."

"Listen, Grandma, I didn't come over here to get involved with anyone. I came over here to write some articles on a serial killer killing Irish American tourists."

"Oh my. Is it safe? Because that's what you are, Jimmy, an Irish American. And what do you mean you won't get involved with anyone?" Jim almost heard her tapping her toe at him. "Are you going to live under a rock or like a monk because that high acting woman made you miserable? Is she gone? Has she moved out of the apartment?"

"Yes, Grandma. She moved out two weeks ago. But I am not ready to see women yet. Let this wound scab over first."

"Jimmy, you must listen. You must find the right one and settle down. I'll be gone before you know it, and I'll never know if you've found happiness. It's a grandmother's wish always to see their grands happy and fulfilled. And haven't I been praying to Saint Brigit about all of this commotion with that Angela?"

"Okay, Grandma, okay." Jim sighed. He should have known he'd get the Angela problem brought up again and again. He wouldn't be able to escape it. When he was old and gray he'd still hear about it. But he had to get this other question answered before he made his way to bed. "I called to tell you I've come, but I also called to ask you something. Let's keep the other, about this new woman and me getting married, shelved for now, okay?"

"Yes, Jimmy. I know I nag. But really, I just want

to see you happy and fulfilled."

"I know, I know." Jim pushed his hand through his hair and rubbed his eyes and face hard. He'd been up for hours and hours, and he needed sleep. But he had to ask. And who better to ask than his grandmother: keeper of all legends, stories, myths, and intimate knowledge of pixies, and leprechauns. "Listen, I promise I have not gone off the deep end, but I need to ask you a question, an Irish question."

"All right, lay it on me."

"Grandma, have you ever seen a leprechaun?"

His grandmother's quick answer stunned him. "No, but that doesn't mean they aren't real."

"Okay, yes. But do you know anyone personally that has seen a leprechaun?"

"Yes, my cousin said he saw one. Let's see, that was just before I come over with me mother and father."

"Did you believe him?"

"Of course, and why wouldn't I? Now listen, Jimmy, what is all this about?"

"Do you suppose angels can change into leprechauns?"

"Angels? Leprechauns? Jimmy, one is divine and one is well, one is…they aren't in the same realm. Are you understanding me? Of course they are both spirits but one is of Heaven and one is of Earth. Now what is all this about?"

"Okay, I'm coming clean." Jim shut his eyes for a moment, wondering why he was telling his grandmother about his visitor.

But he had to tell someone. Maybe if he did, the little *whateverthehellitwas* would go poof back to wherever he was from. "Okay, hope you're sitting down. I got visited by a leprechaun. Sounds like I've been working too hard, right? But this leprechaun says he's really my guardian angel. Here's the rub, he says since I don't believe in angels, he'd have to turn himself into what I could believe in. Isn't that a kick? And he looks just like the drawing of that leprechaun from the story book you used to read to me."

A stunned silence reverberated all the way across the Atlantic.

"Grandma, you still there?"

"Yes, Jimmy, I'm here. Now, I don't know about all of this, but I do know I'm going to see Timothy O'Boyle tomorrow. He's been the deacon at Saint Brigid's since before your grandfather died. He's from Kilkenny. Such a lovely wife, he has. He may know a thing or two about, you know who, so and I'll ask his advice."

"Grandma, don't—"

"This is a momentous event, Jimmy, momentous." A few beats of silence bounced across the Atlantic. Jim could hear his grandmother breathing deeply over the phone, as though she wanted very much not to say something that would scare him off and keep him from Seamus sharing. Maybe she wanted very much for it to be true. How often did anyone actually see an angel…or a leprechaun for that matter? "We have to understand why this is happening. You say he said at first that he was an angel?"

"Yes, my guardian angel, to bring me out of my malaise, so to speak," Jim mimicked Seamus's brogue to a T.

"Ah, it's about the girl then. See, I told you. The

human spirit is a thing too easily quashed. Now—"

"Grandma, I'm really tired. How about if I call you in a few days? I'll be recovered from jet lag and we can talk then."

"All right, me boy. You do that. And I'll do the research from this end."

"Thanks, Grandma, I love you."

"Ta ta, lovey."

****

The bed was comfortable and the room tidy with an old European flair. Jim took his clothes off, washed up, and then climbed between the cold sheets.

"You know, Jimmy me lad, she's a fine one, this Megan Kennedy. Think of the beautiful children you'll have and how proud your grandmother will be of you. Open your heart a tiny bit, and all will be well," whispered Seamus into Jim's ear.

Jim's head lay half under the pillow, his arm slung across the top of it. He pulled the pillow aside, opened his eye a crack, and looked at the little man sitting on the edge of the bed, swinging his legs back and forth like a little child on a swing.

Jim sat up, propped the pillow behind his head, crossed his arms against his bare chest, and glared at the leprechaun. "I don't believe in you, you know."

"And what is it I can do to make you believe?"

"Not a thing." Jim watched the tiny green-clad figure march back and forth across his blanket. He continued, "I'm here to do a job with Miss Kennedy, not to have her finish off the mess Angela started."

"Ah, that I-tal-i-an," the little man said, elongating each syllable as he raised his hand to the air in a sweeping, almost sarcastic gesture. He leaned forward, eyeing Jim and wagging his finger. "And didn't your own grandma tell you not to get mixed up with that one?"

"How do you know that?"

"I told you that I'm your guardian angel. I know everything about you. Everything," he said as he waggled his eyebrows at Jim. "I'm here to help you find true love so that your faith will be restored."

"You don't look like an angel."

"That's because I can be anything I want. You seem to believe in leprechauns more easily than angels. A sad state of affairs for your religious training, I might add. Must be the Black Irish in ya."

"And what's in it for you?" Jim asked and then shook his head as he watched the *whateverthehellitwas* eyebrows climb to its hairline. Surely, the reason he spoke to the apparition was that he hadn't had any real sleep in more than twenty-four hours. He felt calm and collected speaking to the leprechaun and *that* worried him terribly. "If you're my guardian angel, how did I break my leg in the fourth grade?"

"Ah, 'tis a touching story it is, and you never told a soul, not your grandmother or mother, or da. You saw a baby squirrel on the ground and tried to put it back in its nest. Then you fell while climbing the tree. You were too ashamed that you'd fallen on the little thing when you hit the ground, so you didn't tell anyone. But don't worry boy-o, I saw that very same squirrel running about an oak tree before I left Heaven. He's fine," Seamus added in a sing-songy lilting voice.

Jim felt the blood drain from his face. No one knew that. No one. He'd grieved over that little baby squirrel for years. He'd felt so guilty that he hadn't even confessed it to his priest at church. He knew his feelings were irrational, even at age ten, but still he'd never told anyone.

"That is so weird. How do you know that?"

"Watched the film of 'This is Your Life,' before I left. The scene made me teary, I can tell ya," said Seamus, hugely wiping an imaginary tear from his cheek.

"This is just too weird," said Jim, pulling his fingers through his hair. He sat up a little straighter. "Do you know why I've come to Ireland?"

"Yes. I arranged it," he said, looking down nonchalantly at his fingernails and then buffing them on his coat lapel.

"Nope. You may have arranged it, but I'm here to write a story on a madman who is killing Irish-American tourists. That's why I'm working with Megan Kennedy. She writes for the Irish Times."

"My, my, murder you say? That's the trouble with murder. A fellow is liable to lose some of his best friends that way. Tsk, tsk, tsk." The little angel stopped his pacing and faced Jim with his arms held out pleadingly. "But really you're here to restore your faith by falling in love with Miss Kennedy."

"You need to do some more research, pal. That's not why I'm here. Maybe you'd better go check it out with the head angel or something. Now, I don't want to be rude, but I gotta get some sleep. Bye. Nice of you to drop in." Jim patted the leprechaun on the top of his head, feeling very strange that there was actually something tangible to pat.

He snuggled back down in the bed, turned off the bedside table lamp, and closed his eyes.

The leprechaun dug into his pocket and scattered some twinkling dust-like material all over Jim's head.

"*Dream on, Jimmy lad, dream of the entrancing Megan.*"

Chapter 6

Megan would speak to her mother. Margaret Kennedy was always sensible and gave great advice whenever Megan asked for it. With that thought securely in her mind, Megan picked up the phone. She thought about Jim and his strange behavior. Perhaps her Mum could shed some light on why this American acted the way he did. Belatedly, she looked at the clock. Bugger, it was already past ten p.m.

"Hello."

"Hello, Mum? Sorry, did I wake you? I'd already dialed when I realized it was so late."

"Oh, Meggie, no it's all right. We've just come in. We went to a grand concert tonight, lovely."

"I wanted to tell you the great news. I got a new assignment today. And I think I'm to get a byline and a big spot on the paper. Have you heard of all the murders of Irish-American tourists?"

Megan heard her mother's sharp intake of breath, but pushed on with her story.

"Well, I've been given the story to write. It will be a three or four parter, and here's the thing; I'm to write it with an American from the Boston Globe. He just came over today and we're to get started straight away. And our articles will be run in both papers. I'll be in an American newspaper!"

"But, Meggie—"

"No, Mother, you mustn't worry. But just think of it, writing for the Irish Times and the Boston Globe is going to be grand."

"So he's already come, eh?"

"Yes, his name is James O'Flannery."

"Ah, and how old would you say this James O'Flannery is? Forty or fifty?"

"No." Megan groped for a quick response. Her mother could drop hints about Megan finding the "perfect man" like a sledge hammer coming down on rocks. And if Margaret knew about Jim's looks and his already ensconced career, she'd be out buying Megan a wedding dress before the morning. "I think he's just a little older than me."

"And what does he look like?"

"I'm sure you can get on the Boston Globe website and see a picture of him. He's all right looking, seems a nice chap."

"Megan—"

"Now Mom, you know I promised not to get involved with anyone again…not for a long, long time." She could hear the wheels turning in her mother's head all the way from Limerick. She wasn't thinking of Megan's news about the articles; she was thinking about Megan getting involved with a man.

"But maybe this is fate? Maybe this is what Saint Rafael has planned for you," her mother said coyly as she spoke of the patron saint of happy romantic encounters.

"Mom! I will not be able to do my job if I get involved with this man. How will I keep perspective and my journalistic flair?"

"Journalistic flair indeed. Oh posh. Sometimes you

sound so full of yourself, when I know really that you are trying your best not to be a scared little girl!"

Megan groaned. "Mom, I just—"

" 'Put silk on a goat and it's still a goat,' as the saying goes. Megan, let's face it. Richard is a louse. No, I will classify him as a paramecium. Lowest of the low. You can't keep running away from life just because that man let you down."

A giggle gave way to a great sigh on Megan's end of the phone.

"You have been angry and hurt for almost a year, and it's time this all stopped. What, have you decided never to have another relationship, find love, get married, or have children because of that awful man? Megan, love, you must put it past you and move on."

Megan listened intently. Her mother was right. Of course she was. Megan was angrier with herself for being snookered in by Richard than she was at Richard. But fool me once and etc.

"Mom, I promise I will keep an open mind. But I must tell you something as well. Here's a strange thing that happened this evening when we were having dinner; he asked about leprechauns."

"Leprechauns? And why is that?"

"He didn't say, but maybe he's a little touched?" If her mother said Jim was a little crazy maybe she could ignore how terrific he was.

"Megan, let's be practical; do you really think a big, all over the world known paper like the Boston Globe would send a man all the way to Ireland if he wasn't all there, so to speak? Really, Meggie, think of the big picture. You have been chosen by the Irish Times to write this story with a big-time journalist from the United States. And your article will be read in America and his here, correct?"

"Correct."

"Then what is the problem, my dear?"

"Nothing." How her mother could change the subject at the drop of a hat. So now, Mother was thinking about the articles, typical. She really had to get her head on straight. Her mother reminded her that her article would be read in the States, and that knowledge had, at last, begun to sink in. "I'll call you in a few days and let you know how things are going. I love you. My best to Daddy."

"Bye love. I'll be speaking with you soon."

****

Margaret Kennedy logged on to the computer within minutes of ringing off with Megan. She Googled the Boston Globe. It took a while to navigate through the pages, but she finally found staff pictures and thumb-nail bios.

She scrolled down until she came to O'Flannery, James F.X. There was a short bit on where he'd gone to university, where he'd grown up, and then his picture. Oh glory be, the man was simply gorgeous. "Imagine my Meggie married to a man like that." She shook her head and tsked, until she closed down the computer and crawled into bed with her husband.

"Frank." Margaret shook her husband gently by the shoulder. "Frank."

"Hmm?"

"Megan is going to write a series of articles for the Times and the Boston Globe."

"Oh aye." Frank woke up a little and yawned before he turned his attention to his wife.

"Yes, can you imagine? And she's been assigned to write with a journalist from the Boston Globe, a James O'Flannery."

"Oh aye, is he Irish?"

"No, he's from Boston; I'm supposing his parents and grands and such are Irish though."

"Yes, I'm supposing as well." Frank chuckled.

"Well, and we'll have to say a prayer or two for their safety."

"And why is that?"

"They are going to write about the serial killer killing the tourists."

"Oh. Bollocks. We'll pray for their safety. Perhaps I'll go to Dublin and just check in with her, make sure she's all right."

"Oh, that would be best. Yes, let's go to Dublin. We can stay with my sister."

"Sounds a good plan. Now, could we get back to sleep?"

"Yes, dear. I love you, good night."

****

Megan paced the small confines of her flat, her floor-length gown and robe entangling themselves in her long legs until she'd have to stop and untangle herself. Teresa, her flat mate, was out on a date and Megan didn't know when she'd be home. She needed to talk to someone. Her mind was more muddled than ever.

The night had turned out to be long, lonely, and filled with thoughts of Jim O'Flannery. The more she did not want to think about him, the more she did. She even fancied that she had heard a voice whispering to her. Something about how wonderful it would be to love him to distraction, have his children, and while away her life in a little whitewashed house with a peat fire.

The thoughts stunned her completely. She'd never in her life thought a smoky, peat fire romantic. A peat fire smelled and grit got into your eyes. Neither was a whitewashed cottage with a stone floor romantic. It stayed cold and drafty even with a roaring fireplace and even in the summer. Her great-auntie lived in one and she'd fought with her parents every time they wanted Megan to visit her.

Where had all these thoughts come from? She was acting like a schoolgirl still in knee socks. No, she was acting completely demented. She didn't care about O'Flannery. She cared about her job. No, she didn't care about her job; it didn't encompass every thought and feeling. But if she did well, it would help her make it in the writing world. Any distraction at all could keep her from reaching her goal in life. She had no use for men right now, especially O'Flannery, just because the man was within her line of sight everywhere she turned.

"Now, I'm thinkin' perhaps you're wrong there, colleen." An ominous voice bounced off the walls of the apartment.

Megan's breath caught in her throat. Her gaze jerked to every corner and darkened cranny around the room. Was there someone there in the room with her? She was paralyzed and she couldn't move. Her feet were riveted to the floor. Dark spots wavered in front of her face. She pushed air into her lungs with her next breath. She forced her reluctant feet to move and she stumbled to the window, grabbed the curtain, and pulled it aside. There was no one there. Megan hurried to the door and checked the locks and then turned them and locked them yet again. In a blur, she grabbed her cat and ran into her bedroom. She jammed a chair under the doorknob and wiggled the latch, making sure it was secure.

Megan huddled under the covers and squeezed the cat until it scratched her, emitted a low growl, and jumped off the bed to hide under a chair. She clutched her hairbrush and held it like a battle-ax. She watched the doorknob, sure it would turn at any second and a murderer would be on the other side ready to pounce. Each fiber of her being focused on each and every sound real or imagined, but for some inexplicable reason, she quickly fell into a fitful sleep.

****

"Don't be talking to the lass, now. You scared her right out of her wits. Some angel you are." Ignatius paced rapidly on a fluffy, white cloud with his hands clasped behind his back and his bushy eyebrows pulled down in irritation.

"Well, I don't have this idea of talking to them in their heads so they think it's their own thoughts yet. I am sorry I frightened the lass," Seamus said, shrugging his shoulders sheepishly.

"You may have to reveal yourself to assure her that she doesn't need to reside in Bedlam, you know."

"Oh, Iggy, I've done a terrible thing. Look at the poor lass, thinking she can attack me with that hairbrush. Tsk, tsk, tsk."

"Seamus, you'll need to mind what you say and do. This is the twenty-first century and people are more likely to think they have imagined us and gone quite daft, rather than thinking we may be real. If you don't get on it, me lad, you're never going to earn those wings. Now, it seems all they need is a little encouragement," said Iggy, as he turned ever so slightly to the side to admire his great mustache that curled and waved and clung to the bits of silver and gold clouds traveling off into infinity. He shrugged his shoulders to watch the ends float into the great wide yonder. Then, seeming to come to himself, he looked sheepishly at Seamus and roughly cleared his throat. "Throw them together in some fashion, and we'll let nature take its course."

"But he says he's here to write a story about a murder and the lass is to help him."

"Seamus." Ignatius put his hand on the little angel's shoulder. "You're a smart lad, and I know you can think of something to get them together.

"Poor Jim lad, he'll die a faithless man if you don't soon fix this up. And you know where *they* go."

Chapter 7

The next morning Megan woke physically exhausted but mentally alert. Her eyes felt raw and grainy as if she'd actually been sleeping in front of that peat fire that had been a dominant fixture in her dreams of the night before. Although she'd been completely terrified, she'd managed to fall into a stupor and fitful sleep. She could feel the fright still in the sticky dried sweat left on her forearms, her face, and between her legs. For the life of her she couldn't remember, no matter how hard she tried, what it was that had scared her so.

"Ah well, get on with it, Kennedy."

She dragged herself into the tiny kitchen and made the strongest pot of coffee she could manage. Ugh, it tasted just short of mud. She heard Teresa taking her shower, and listening to the spray of the water pinging gently against the tiles of the tub soothed her jangled nerves. She sat woodenly, her body not moving, but her mind surging. Thoughts coming and going like the hurried tide of an oncoming storm. Idly, she glanced up at the clock. "St. Joseph, it's 8:15!"

Megan jumped up, knocking the contents of the cup onto the table. She made a quick swipe of the mud-like brew and dumped the rag and the dirty cup into the sink before running to the recently vacated bathroom to jump in the shower.

Ah cripes! Teresa had done it again. The water was barely lukewarm. Hurriedly, she dumped a palm full of shampoo on her head. Of course, the shampoo refused to rinse thoroughly from her hair with no proper hot water.

"Ah bollocks!" She groaned as the frigid water poured down her back. She gave up trying to get the shampoo out of her hair and dashed to her room.

With her comb, she tugged hurriedly on the strands coated with shampoo. She let loose a string of curses and slumped onto the bed in abject misery.

"I'm going to be late, and O'Flannery will think he's saddled with some inept woman," she groaned out into the nothing of the room.

Megan leapt from the bed and ran to her closet, practically diving into it head first, grabbing the first thing that caught her eye as cool, objective, female reporter, and decent enough to wear.

"Not if I can help it," she promised again to the nothing of the empty room. Brushing her hair back, she pulled it into a tight bun and wrapped a scarf around it making sure all the little shampoo-coated hairs were hidden from sight.

"And what were you up to last night?" Teresa stood in the doorway of the bedroom; her arms crossed over her well-endowed self in a dress of navy and lace. One tawny impeccably groomed eyebrow rose almost to her hairline.

"I met that American I telephoned you about last evening. God, he's a nice guy." Megan huffed and puffed like a runner as she hurried to get her clothes on. "Too bad I'm off men for a while."

"Just because that bastard Richard used you for all

he was worth, and such a long time ago I might add, doesn't mean they are all scum," Teresa said from the doorway. She walked carefully into the room across the expanse of floor, dodging the minefield of discarded clothing, kitty toys, hairbrushes, and mounds of wadded up discarded drafts of who knew what, to sit on Megan's bed.

Teresa was already dressed for work. The stunning deep blue outfit complemented her dark, coppery hair. Megan oftentimes envied Teresa for her voluptuous curves. The endless dates Teresa seemed to go on though, were never enough to make her want the same thing. Nothing could dim the joy she felt in their friendship.

"Tell me about this man." Teresa lay back against the bed and turned her full attention on Megan.

"He's Black Irish and so good looking it's amazing that I didn't drool all over him," said Megan as she slapped herself into her pantyhose.

"Will you bring him to the flat?"

"You must be daft," she said with a raised brow. "I'm going to treat him like the plague and so. I already told you, I want nothing more to do with men." Megan quickly checked her hairdo in the mirror and made sure her dress wasn't caught up somewhere.

"Listen, Meggie," said Teresa. She stood, grabbed Megan by the arms, and forced her to look into her face.

"Not every man is a no-good scoundrel like Richard. You must give yourself a chance to love again or you'll dry up inside like an old hag."

The concern registered in Teresa's eyes. She'd put that bit of information away, into the "I'll consider this later" stack. Teresa had always given sound advice, always.

"I'll think about it."

"Do more than think about it, aye?"

Megan hurriedly pulled on a wool coat and boots and waved to Teresa as she ran outside to hail a cab.

Chapter 8

Jim woke the next morning feeling remarkably refreshed. He hadn't dreamt at all during the night, as far as he could remember, and had slept deeply. Maybe he'd have his head on straight before he met with Megan and her boss at the Times.

His mind flooded with thoughts of Megan this morning, instead of the doom and gloom of the last week.

Just thinking about her incredible mouth made him feel a steady but unusual, for him, contentment. He felt the warmth flood him from the tips of his toes all the way to his scalp. What a woman. But what was he thinking? *No more women, remember, you blockhead.*

He'd caught Angela, the supposed love of his life, doing it with a guy he played ball with in the Globe's summer league. The two of them were pumping away, moaning, and groping at one another on the couch in Jim and Angela's happy home, wearing nothing but their socks. Right then, metaphorically, his chest opened up and his heart dropped onto the ground with a resounding splat. Yep, no more women. Maybe not ever. His heart was bruised enough to last a lifetime.

Jim shook his head, trying to dispel the image and began shaving. As he looked in the mirror above the tiny sink, Seamus popped out of thin air and made himself comfortable on the spigot.

Jim jumped at the leprechaun's sudden appearance. He was lucky the razor hadn't slipped and cut his throat. He put his hand to his pounding heart and looked down at the little man with a frown. "I'm going to tie a cowbell around your neck that will announce your presence before you puff your way into the same room I'm in. You scared the crap out of me."

It was such a good idea. A cowbell strapped to Seamus's little pointed head. But Jim had no idea of how to implement it.

The little man straightened his clothes and then looked up at Jim with abject curiosity.

"Don't believe I've ever seen a man with clearer skin," said Seamus, choosing to ignore Jim's comment about the cowbell. "You look like you use that beauty soap the Duchess of Kent always bragged about."

Jim growled and slapped a handful of soapy water at the creature.

"Not now, Jimmy lad," said the leprechaun as he opened his coat and mysterious swirling warm air came out and dried him off. "We must speak of the lovely Megan."

"No, we mustn't. I've got to get to work, and I'm not sure where work is," he said. He continued to shave with half his attention trained on his reflection in the mirror and another half on the leprechaun.

"But, Seamus, me boy-o."

"Hey, don't call me that. Use the English and call me Jim." He put down his razor, wiped his face, and looked around the towel to stare hard at the little man. "Maybe you should just call yourself a figment of my imagination. Because if you are real, you could do something for me, and it's about Megan."

"Oh, aye?" Seamus tilted his head, tapping his finger against his chin, deep in thought.

"Not that I'm saying you are real." Jim put the towel down and leaned on the sink till he was almost nose to nose with the leprechaun. "You could work on that editor of hers. They don't plan to give her a byline on this story, but she'll be writing the story right along with me."

"A byline? What's a byline?"

"Go look it up in the angel encyclopedia, okay? I don't have time now to explain. I have got to get out of here."

"But what about our discussion about you getting married?"

"I don't have time." Jim buttoned up his shirt and pulled a sweater over his head. "Plus, I don't want to get married. I'll be perfectly happy doing a good job on this story and getting back home."

"But ya are home. Don't you know that?"

Jim listened with one ear to the spirit prattle on as he looked in the mirror, trying to decide whether or not to wear a tie. He opted for the professional look, not knowing how the men in this town dressed when they went to work.

"I know one thing, Seamus, if I'm late; they won't look at me the same again. It makes a very bad impression. Now"—he leaned over the leprechaun and pinned him with a stare—"I am not in the market for a wife. I know I've been down in the dumps lately, but you can assure the powers upstairs that no permanent damage was done. As much as I enjoy your company you need to scram and let me get to work. Okay?"

****

The cab lurched through the streets, stopping and starting in the morning traffic. Megan was sure she'd left her stomach on that last corner. She'd tried to put on her make-up during her bumpy ride, but gave up when she'd managed to smear eyeliner down to her cheekbone.

She couldn't be late. She couldn't. Jim really would think she was nothing but a pretty face. Just thinking about those blue eyes gave her chills, in a good way. No, no, no! "Megan, haven't you had enough?" she mumbled under her breath but loud enough for the cabby to give her a strange look in the rear view mirror.

Starting, stopping, lunging to and fro, the cab finally screeched to a halt in front of the Times. She threw some money at the cabbie. "Hey, now then," she heard him grumble as she ran into the nearest ladies' room to finish her face. Finally, she walked through the doors to the offices, and the first thing she saw was O'Flannery sitting at her desk, in her desk chair. Cripes, how pushy. She walked over and looked down at him coolly.

"And what are you doing at my desk?" Just like an American to come in and take over when you were at home. He was here, ensconced in her chair, at her desk, and smiling smugly like he owned the place.

"Good morning," he said in that perpetually cheerful way that puts one's back teeth on edge, to grind just a bit. Just a bit? She felt like the biggest millstone in all of Ireland had replaced her jaw.

How dare he be so smug, so happy, and so American? Well, and didn't he know just how badly she felt about, about, about—?

The steam coming out of her ears dissipated a bit,

and Megan looked at him carefully. She decided she hadn't exaggerated a thing about him in her mind. He was even better looking in real life than she remembered. Megan was disgusted with herself.

"Just looking through the file," he said. "Have any ideas where to start?"

She felt the starch go out of her shoulders literally. Megan grabbed a chair from the next desk. She slumped down and her upper body seemed to deflate. She sighed deeply. *All right now, you, time to get a grip!*

How could the stupid man not notice how badly she felt?

Oh really, Megan, must you act like such a twit? Yes, he does not understand how badly you feel about everything. How could he? Is he a bloody mind reader? Will you ever grow past acting like a silly girl?

Megan slapped her forehead and took a deep breath. So she felt badly. A good cup of tea would get her going again. She took off her jacket, deposited her purse, and without looking up at Jim, went to the drinks trolley for a cup. She looked out of the corner of her eye at him. She realized at that moment that she'd be working with a man who was more handsome than Sean Connery in his prime. He could be on the cover of Gentleman's Quarterly and put all the other male models to shame.

"You look great this morning," Jim said over his shoulder. Megan was not about to let his perpetual cheer nudge her bad mood into a full grump, so she puffed out a disgruntled breath, turned, and smiled at him. And the smile stayed on her face; not an easy task.

"I feel like death, but I didn't drink that much last

night." Megan cringed inwardly; that remark had slipped out faster than she could hold it in. She forced herself to smile, sure that the smile looked vapid at best.

Jim's raised his brow and shrugged those magnificent shoulders. He ignored her remark, making her feel even worse. He looked back down at the file on the desk, dismissing her.

How unprofessional could she be? *Work with the man, get along with the man*, she reminded herself.

"I'm sorry, I didn't mean to take my lack of sleep out on you, and thanks for the compliment." Her smile was genuine this time.

Megan, she chided herself, *act like a professional or Our Mighty Flynn will be more than happy to replace your worthless self.* She ratcheted up her smile a few gigawatts and turned to Jim. "Have you met anyone yet? Why don't you let me take you round and you can meet our other famous Irish writers." Once she'd started, it wasn't hard to be nice to Jim.

"Sure, sounds great."

He turned those gorgeous blue eyes on her and the dimple crowning his smile simply did her in. She felt the bottom drop out, and there she was dangling over the precipice. *Good grief!* She sighed and turned her eyes straight ahead and away, and gestured for Jim to follow her.

She would at this very moment, divorce herself from him in every way, except professionally. She had to keep focused on the job at hand and not her raging hormones that, at this particular moment, threatened to spiral out of control.

They'd made the rounds of the office and Jim shook everyone's hand, smiled, exchanged pleasantries with each person, and generally made himself the poster child for good office relations.

Megan envied his outgoing attitude, his nonchalance, his ease with new people, and what she thought had replaced his over-friendliness with genuine feeling. Perhaps he wasn't over-friendly, she thought wryly. Perhaps I'm under-friendly. Self-realization can be such a bitch.

Years ago, Megan made the decision to ward off all but casual relationships. The decision itself had evolved because of a series of ongoing persistent problems she'd had with other girls. Being the prettiest girl in the class of an all girls' school had set her up for many cruel jokes by her classmates. Like the time several of the girls had written a love letter presumably from a boy at the nearby boys' school. This boy, Liam, was the one Megan had a crush on in a very big way. When the letter had come for her, Megan ran up and down the halls, waving the letter about, crowing, "He loves me." When the time for the next dance came around, she flirted shamelessly with the boy, and clutched at his arm, pulling him toward the dance floor. The young man turned a cold face to her, shrugging her hand away. Megan brought the well-read letter out of her purse and showed it to him.

The young man looked at the letter and laughed. "I never wrote that," Liam said. Then he grabbed the letter and showed it to his mates. They all laughed. Stood there and laughed at her. Megan ran from the dance all the way back to her dormitory. She was mortified, humiliated, and she'd cried herself to sleep that night. After her tears were dry, she vowed to never trust anyone near her heart again.

She'd been in college, years after the dance fiasco, before she formed any close relationships with other women. Even with men, she'd held off the big decision until Richard had come along. And that happened nearly a year before when she was twenty-seven.

Richard was a stock broker at the huge multimillion euro Dublin firm of O'Grady, Halloran, and Penny. He was cunning, charming, and could manage to control everyone with his charismatic ways. He drove a bright red Jaguar and made sure that everyone saw him drive it. When Megan met Richard, it was comforting to be going with a man who was so self-assured. She felt that self-confidence rub off on her a little. He was someone who knew the right things to do, the right things to say, the right places to be, and he took Megan to all of them. Of course, his good looks and the fact that he had scads of money didn't hurt. And for the first few months after meeting him, Megan felt like a princess when she was with Richard. He showered her with little gifts and flowers whenever he saw her, and she perpetually walked about with stars in her eyes and a sigh on her lips. Richard was thrilled to find out that Megan was still a virgin.

She should have known something was off when her grandmother had scrutinized Richard so diligently, and then took her aside to warn her off him. Her granny was one perceptive woman and Megan knew she could rely on the old woman's sixth sense. She could take it to the bank. But that time, she didn't listen, and she lived to regret it.

Later, she'd been mortified to find out that Richard was a little short of dog meat. Richard was romance itself, and like marshmallow cream, he was all fluff, all sweet, and when you bit down, it was nothing but a puff of air with no substance. She'd sold her most secret self for flowers and soft words.

When she'd become suspicious of him, she'd investigated him, as though he were a story she had to write about. She discovered that he discarded women in heaps, piled up like old newspapers in a bin. He threw away more women than even she was acquainted with. It had angered her so. But more than the feeling of betrayal, she'd been angry with herself. How could she have been such a dimwit? Knowing all those other women had gotten the same treatment had made her feel a little less like a typical weeping female. Oh, jaysus how she hated those types! Those clinging, cajoling, manipulative women—

"And right you are, lass, but you're not like them. That I can assure you," said a cheery, chortling voice inside her head.

Megan whipped her head around so fast that her neck popped with a sickening crunch.

"Ow." She grimaced and rubbed her neck vigorously.

Her co-workers and Jim looked at her. "Are you all right?"

"Yeah, sure." Megan tried to hide the flush barreling up her neck to her cheeks. It was the same voice, the one from last night, the one that had scared her half to death. That voice frightened her, but good, and that fright was like a lump gnawing away in her stomach. She looked quickly about, but nothing was amiss. No one was around except O'Flannery and some co-workers. Keyboards tapped loudly, phones rang incessantly, and people ran about doing their level best to get the early edition out on time. She turned to Jim and steeled her voice, hoping it wouldn't shake when the words were finally forced between lips dry from shock. She had to go to the ladies' room and splash some water on her face, get a tea, anything to stay calm and keep the voice away.

"O'Flannery, you finish here and then the editor wants to speak to you sometime during the morning. I think you might as well get it over with. Lizzy can show you where his office is. I still need to finish a piece I'm working on."

"Sure, I'll see you before lunch and we can map out some strategy. Hey, you okay?" asked Jim as he squeezed her hand.

"Fine." Megan turned and walked back to the ladies, dismissing Jim.

Jim shrugged his shoulders and made his way to the other end of the floor.

In a far corner, Seamus stood on a puff of green swirling vapor and scratched his chin. *Now what is it I can do about those two? They are, the two of them, trying so hard not to like one another...but then perhaps...*Seamus paced the puffy cloud. Up and back he strode with his head down. He pulled at his beard, deep in thought. He stopped suddenly and his shoulders sagged in dejection. *No, no, there's something. I must work it out.*

****

The ever-present cup of tea and a biscuit revived Megan, and she worked through the next hour, forgetting about the voice, almost forgetting about Jim O'Flannery, concentrating totally on her work. A chill penetrated her concentration as a shadow fell across her desk. She looked up slowly and felt dread nibbling at the edge of her thoughts before she knew why. It was Richard. He stood there with a smug look about him, leering down at her. She hadn't seen the snake in over six months. She was sure she'd made it quite clear that she never wanted to see him again.

"How's my pretty girl? You aren't miffed are you?"

Her throat tightened and her mind blanked. Her whole body was seized by an uncontrollable anger. Megan came halfway out of her seat, her heart hammering painfully. There was a distinct possibility that she would explode like a bomb.

"Miffed? Miffed?" whispered Megan. She leaned forward on her braced arms. Richard had lost touch with reality if he thought she was just miffed. Megan sat back in her chair as far away from him as physically possible. She stared at him, willing her voice not to tremble and spoke in a deadly calm. "I am not just miffed, Richard. I was not just miffed when I found out what was going on. I was so angry that I felt like clawing your eyes out. Now, get out of my sight. I want nothing more to do with you. I thought I made that abundantly clear months ago. You're disgusting and disreputable." Megan pulled the syllables out slowly and over-enunciated each one. He thought he was a big shot...thought he could do anything, and hurt anyone and get away with it.

"Meggie, Meggie, now I never said I was exclusively yours. You can't blame a fellow for doing what he does best. Can't I tell you how much I love you? You're my best girl. It's just that night—"

Megan slapped her hands on the desk and stood so

quickly that her desk chair flew back and fell over with a crash.

"Get out of my sight, you pig. Now!" she ordered. She strained with the effort not to shout.

"Meggie," said Richard. He reached for her arm. "Can't you see I'm wanting to make things right between us, that I'm willing to make things right, that I'm wishing to make things right despite your stubbornness?" He gave his little speech and a chilling hardness leeched through his voice.

His hand latched onto Megan's arm and pulled her toward him. Megan jerked her arm away and stepped back in an effort to avoid touching him. She trembled with rage. She glanced around the office hoping against hope that no one had noticed her outburst. She turned to Richard and stared at him without blinking.

"Get away from my desk and away from me," she hissed.

"Is this man bothering you, Kennedy?" Jim righted her chair and moved to stand between Megan and Richard as though he could ward off the bad vibes the man sent out by the gigawatt.

She closed her eyes for a second, offering up a prayer of thanks for her rescuer.

****

Her face was ashen when she turned to Jim. It was crystal clear that she was afraid of this smug arrogant bastard. The man turned to Jim and simply stared with eyes colder than death.

Jim stared back.

"Kennedy, would you like me to ask the gentleman to leave?"

Megan let out a king-sized breath. She turned to

look at Jim gratefully.

"No. I think the gentleman will leave under his own power." She made sure the word gentleman had lost any of its niceties.

"It's not over, Meggie," Richard spoke, but his gaze never left Jim's.

"Oh yes, it is, Richard. It's been over for six months. Don't contact me again. Because if you do, perhaps I'll call your father and tell him you're bothering me."

Richard visibly blanched before turning on his heel to leave the complex of offices. He stopped and glared at Jim for a moment more in the open doorway before he stepped through and disappeared from view.

"Charming fellow," Jim murmured.

The man had said, "It's not over, Meggie." Richard's comment was all too ominous. What had he been to Megan? Could you be that angry with someone and not have been a scorned lover?

All Jim had to do was take one look at Megan's stricken face to know that the guy had done plenty of damage. Richard was a type; the sort of man who was too slick for his own good. He had charm oozing from every pore. Jim hoped he could soothe Megan out of her hurt, maybe he could give her a hug and—

Those thoughts came to a screeching halt. Over Megan's shoulder he glimpsed Seamus scowling at him. This time the elf/angel stood, with hands on hips and his toe tapping, in front of a teeny, tiny gothic church. The leprechaun looked steamed, and for good measure shook his head. Jim raised his hand and with as unobtrusive a movement as possible, backhanded Seamus off his little tuft of magical grass, mimicking a fly-shooing movement. Jim turned his attention to Megan. She stared down at the top of the desk, idly picking up a file and then letting it drop. Finally, she sat and took a deep cleansing breath.

"He's scum," she hissed under her breath.

"Hey, I read you loud and clear. And don't worry; he won't bother you while I'm around. He's the type that talks big around women, but is a wimp around men taller than he is, or smarter either." Jim snapped his mouth shut, chagrined. Those were his own words that popped out of his mouth and sounded too, too, too over the top. He was not Sir Galahad, and Megan was a modern woman and would definitely not swoon and fall into his arms when he came to her rescue. That is, if she let him. A knight in shining armor, he was not. He was a man, plain and simple.

"I hope you're right." Megan was too engrossed with her own thoughts to look at Jim. She watched the hallway door close behind Richard. Maybe, he'd escaped her corny meter. Hopefully, she hadn't heard his boast after all.

"Come on," said Jim trying to change the subject along with Megan's mood. "We'll do an early lunch. I got the lowdown from your associate editor, and it's time to travel a little."

"Travel?"

"Yes, a place called Slee-go?"

"Let me see. Oh, that's a nice city on the coast. Sligo? Oh—it's pronounced with a long 'i' as in sli-go. It boasts of being the most Irish of cities. Why are we going there?"

"There was another murder last night."

"St. Joseph."

71

Jim watched Megan's green eyes shrink to mere pin pricks. Murder was too close to home for her. She swallowed convulsively once and then turned all business. Her pretty heart shaped face turned up to him.

"Do they think it's the same man?"

"Yes. The murder closely mimics the ones here in Dublin. The tourist falls where he stands, never knowing what hit him." Jim looked at Megan's puckered brow and wondered briefly how gutsy she was. Especially, since a mad serial killer was out there strangling any American he could find. He knew instinctively she had what it took. He felt it in his gut, that she could give as good as she got.

"There must be a pattern. If we can decipher the pattern, we might be able to decide where he's going next. You don't think it's a woman, do you?" She looked at Jim steadily.

"No, not unless it's a very tall woman with very strong arms," Jim said.

"You know the police have already got something worked up," Megan said. "It isn't likely that they'll let us in on anything. No, we're on our own to figure it all out, I'm afraid. Let's go talk to the editor and make sure that we have an expense account for both of us. And a car. No Mercedes, mind you, but a car nonetheless. He'll send us straightaway. It should take us about two hours, perhaps a little longer."

"Right, let's go in together. That way if he gives you any grief, I can glare at him."

"Hardly think so, O'Flannery. He'll scowl at you, too. Best offense is a good defense."

"Hey, you borrowed that from American football."

"Not likely, me lad. I got it from the real football or

72

soccer, as you Yanks call it." Her look of superiority said it all. "Don't let Flynn think you know more than he does. Even if you do." She gave Jim a playful jab in the arm.

Chapter 9

Megan dashed into her flat two hours before her usual arrival time. She came up short, a little embarrassed to find Teresa and a gentleman caller sitting in the kitchen having a cup of tea.

"Oh, sorry. I need to pack, T. Would you excuse her for a moment?" Megan asked.

The man nodded and smiled as Teresa followed Megan into her room.

"So, what's up?"

"Everything." Megan gave herself the luxury of placing her hands on her hips and taking a huge breath. Her mind was fuddled with this rapid chain of events, events that had caught her up and swept her along. She'd met the loveliest, the best looking, and the cleverest…enough! Megan shook her head, looked up at Teresa, and completely switched mental gears.

"There's been another murder, but this time it's in Sligo. The editor, 'Our Mighty Flynn,' is sending O'Flannery and yours truly. The Times has rented us a car and as soon as I'm packed, we're off."

"You and that handsome O'Flannery stuck in a car together all the way to Sligo and then a hotel, ooh."

"Oh, don't, T," she said with a frown. "I'm off it you know. I can see he's a handsome bloke, talented, very amiable, but really—how on earth can I get involved with him? I have to focus on my career. And," she said, raising her brows at Teresa, "I have to finish this story."

"Very well, find the murderer and finish the story. But for heaven's sake, don't cut yourself off from life." Teresa placed her hands on her curvaceous hips and turned her best and very genuine smile on Megan.

Megan looked long and hard at her best and closest friend; Teresa was such a dear and good person. But her fanciful view of relationships and of eternal love was more like a movie script than real life. Teresa still thought a knight would come some day and sweep her off her feet and carry her off to some crystal palace in the sky. In the meantime, she had as much fun as possible and went out with as many different men as she wanted to. Megan heaved a deep sigh.

"I promise I will keep my mind open, all right. Now, don't let me forget anything. I'm positively fuddled."

****

Much to Jim's dismay, the Times provided them with a car that felt no bigger than a skateboard. He climbed in through the left door, but the steering wheel turned out to be on the other side of the car.

"Oh, I forgot," he murmured, feeling just a bit disoriented.

"Forgot what?" Megan moved behind the wheel. She turned the key and with her left hand put the car into first.

"Left side. I may gasp and my knuckles may turn white from clutching the dashboard while I get used to riding on the wrong side of the road."

"Not to worry." She said as she leaned forward and stared out the windshield with rapt attention. She looked like a Formula One driver, and Jim surreptitiously looked in the back to check for a helmet. She revved the engine once, twice, and the third time, popped the clutch, and tore out into the melee of Dublin traffic. "There are plenty of roads that are just one lane anyway."

"Oh great." Jim coughed and tried to dislodge his heart stuck somewhere near the vicinity of his Adam's apple.

"Oh aye, but it's the loveliest sights in the world this side of Heaven, and I should know." Seamus's brogue was so thick, it was hard to understand him at times.

"Ah jeez," Jim mumbled. He glanced quickly about for the persistent leprechaun.

"Don't worry a bit of it. I'll see to it all." Megan tilted her head and quirked a smile before she stomped on the accelerator.

Jim lurched forward and then slammed back against the seat when Megan tore into second and then into third gear. A driver behind them leaned on his horn, and somewhere, very near, brakes all over the avenues squealed alarmingly.

"Ah bollocks," Megan mumbled. "Sorry. We'll get out of the city soon and be on our merry way. Now, help me with this next bit. It's the turn-a-bout and we have to make the fourth shoot." Megan gave a quick look over her shoulder and attempted to merge into the heavy flow of traffic. She downshifted and the engine whined like a banshee. Again, horns blared and tires squealed, and Jim found himself saying a prayer he'd learned in grade school. He forced himself not to cover his eyes.

"Ah, such a lovely prayer, it is. But it's a bit too childish for such a big strapping lad. Now, of course, you remember the Angelus? In the Latin, don't you know," said Seamus, reminding Jim of a much longer prayer he'd had to memorize in junior high school.

Jim turned his head toward the back seat and glared at Seamus. The little leprechaun was lounging on top of Jim's briefcase, and this time he'd brought a hillock of grass and a tiny sheep with googly eyes. The sheep looked an awful lot like the sheep on the mattress commercial televised in the States. The sheep looked up chewing, and closed his googly eyes, *Baaaaa.* The leprechaun winked at Jim.

"Stay out of this," he mouthed. He was glad Megan concentrated on the traffic and didn't see him talking to Seamus. He hoped. Jim's head whipped as Megan stomped on the brakes. The car lurched and then lunged into the coming fray.

"Only one of two." Megan nodded toward the turn-a-bout and took a split second to smile at Jim.

Jim turned toward the back. Maybe if he wasn't looking out of the windshield, the traffic might not give him a heart attack. He took a peek at Seamus and his livestock. The tiny sheep, oblivious to the traffic outside the car, closed his eyes, took another mouthful of grass, and chewed contentedly.

"Wha—?" Jim said. He wiped his palms hurriedly on his pants. He tried to focus his attention on the sky, the sidewalk, the buildings, the people, the fire hydrant, anything but the car shooting inches from their front bumper cutting them off.

"Turn-a-bout, Jim. Well, maybe that's not it exactly," said Megan. She turned her head, looking for oncoming traffic.

That is, traffic that wasn't already up their tailpipe blaring away.

"I'm not sure. I only know of two, but Dublin is a big city. Do you have them in the States?"

"Yes," Jim croaked after he caught his breath and pumped the imaginary brake in front of him several times, pushing so hard that his foot began to go numb. He squeezed his eyes shut, making his mind focus on Megan's questions and not on his lunch threatening to make a reappearance.

"There's one in Braintree, Massachusetts, that has no rhyme nor reason," he murmured. "The first one there gets in first, that sort of thing. There are lots of accidents. Of course, it's always the other guy's fault," he said, amazed at his quiet, calm tone, because he felt a little frenzied at that moment. He took another calming breath, sagged against the seat, and then opened his eyes a tiny bit.

He chuckled nervously and clutched the dashboard when a huge Mercedes screeched to a stop in front of them.

The little car lurched to a halt and the sudden silence inside was deafening. Jim turned to look at Megan who turned to look at him.

"I feel right at home." Jim noted that his voice was steady and quiet; and he could still hear the sound of the tiny sheep's *baaaa*. "The traffic is worse than this in Boston. That's why I always take the train." Jim grinned and Megan laughed before the traffic again began to move.

Moments later they were on the M4 and drove farther out of the city.

Jim stared at the scenes before him. It was idyllic; green hills punctuated by ancient stone walls and lines of deep trees edging the road side. They passed several huge modern businesses like those found in the States, but by and large, he saw fields, fields, and more fields. He thoroughly enjoyed the beauty all around him. The gently rolling hills that weren't covered with snow were so green they hurt his eyes.

"We'll be going through County Mayo on the way. Here, take a look." Megan pulled out a map and handed it to him. For the first time, he noticed her snug jeans, and wondered what those long, lean legs looked like bare. He shook his head and cleared his mind to look at the map.

"Do you know what city or town she was from?" asked Megan.

"Who?"

"Your grandmother, of course." Megan laughed.

"Can't remember."

"Some grandson you are."

"Ha, she would absolutely agree with you. She left Ireland when she was ten and she's eighty-two now. I guess her birthplace has changed a bit. You should hear her talk. Sounds like she left yesterday. She has more of an accent than you do. For the most part, you sound quite properly British."

"Ah, but, O'Flannery, I haven't got the accent here—you do. After all, where are you?"

"Hmm, point taken." Jim tried again to focus his attention on the countryside outside the car window. His last glance into the back revealed Seamus laying on his back enjoying a nap and two sheep and a goat, all about one inch high, munching on the tuft of "Seamus grass." Seamus popped up and glared at Jim after his last remark.

"'Tis not an accent at all, me lad. Don't you know it was our way of defying the English? They took away our language and made us speak theirs, so we mangled it a bit. Don't you know? 'Twas the Kilkenny Statutes of 1366 that demanded of the Irish that they no longer speak the Irish. Such a terrible thing to be takin' away, our own language as it were. And how can you be insultin' the lass by telling her she sounds British?"

Within a second, Seamus appeared on the dash in front of Jim, sans sheep and goat. He sat and dangled his legs, grinning from ear to ear. He lit his tiny pipe, and Jim was very surprised when he actually smelled tobacco.

The little fellow then made a cradle of his arms and rocked back and forth as though he rocked a baby.

"Thanks for the history lesson," Jim mouthed. *"Now scram!"* The leprechaun vanished in a puff of green vapor, but a tiny wisp of tobacco still lingered near the windshield. Jim watched Megan from the corner of his eye as she crinkled up her nose for an instant as though she were trying to decide if she smelled something.

The car's cramped interior left little room for Jim to stretch, and he and Megan were forced to sit quite close together. Her scent pummeled his defenses, and he forgot about Seamus. She smelled like sunshine or maybe it was lemon and something that he couldn't quite put his finger on. A strand of her hair had come loose from its tight bun and drifted around Megan's cheek. That lucky piece of hair. Then again, look how close he sat to her. Nope, no thinking about her hair.

Jim felt the warmth from Megan's arm seep through his sweater sleeve. He tried to move his arm discreetly, but there wasn't any place to move it to. The feeling began to play havoc with his defenses. Maybe he'd ask to stop and stretch his legs, so he could get away from the temptation of Megan Kennedy.

Jim looked out past the dashboard at the scenery. Despite it being January, the landscape was so green, it was remarkable. He turned his head to look through the rear window and Seamus the Leprechaun stood with his hands on hips on top of Jim's briefcase.

"I can read your thoughts, you know," he said waggling his eyebrows at Jim. *"It's too early for any of that monkey business. You should be thinking about what a fine stew she can make you, or darnin' your socks, or..."*

"If you can read my mind," Jim thought as he looked at the little man, *"then bug off."*

Seamus doffed his hat and bowed deeply to Jim. Jim blew out an exasperated breath and with one hand positioned on the back of Megan's seat, waved Seamus off.

"What's the matter, Jim?"

"Nothing." Jim stared out the windshield and tried to ignore Megan's troubled glances *and* Seamus's presence.

"Do you think people still believe in leprechauns?" he asked suddenly. Man, could he sound like a dork, or what? He had tried to make the comment nonchalant but had failed utterly.

Seamus did a great job of distracting him from Megan. Maybe Megan could distract him from Seamus.

"Le-pre-chauns?" Megan said with each syllable

81

drawn out and elongated with those red-gold eyebrows of hers rising to her hairline. She turned her gaze back to the road. A silence followed. Then more silence. Jim was wondering if he'd said too much and probably really put his foot in it. He tried to slump down in the seat.

"There's a man near here who found a shoe. A hand-sewn, pointed toe, leather shoe, all of two inches long. It was shown on TV on one of these documentaries about the magical world, a really well-done piece, by the way. The writer is a man I've met that works for the BBC.

"At any rate, he said it was an elf's shoe, although I haven't any idea as to how he knew this. There are crags and hills and burrows that are so remote that no one has yet thoroughly explored them. Have I ever seen a leprechaun? No," she said, dragging the syllable out until it sounded like a creaking door. "Do I believe in them?" She quirked him a smile before she again turned her attention back to the road. "I'll reserve judgment."

"Good," Jim said as he snuggled himself down into the small seat. At least she hadn't ejected him from the car or turned herself off to the possibility. That was always a plus. So maybe he wasn't losing his mind entirely.

"Tell me something, O'Flannery. What's all this talk of leprechauns, eh? I think this must be the second or third time you've asked."

Jim looked at her profile. *That old feeling that has me in a spin, lovin' the spin I'm in*, as the song went. His heart began to flutter inside his chest when a strand of her hair played about her cheek in the stir of air inside the car. He sighed inaudibly and searched his mind and heart for a means to distance himself from everything, especially the warmth that started at the top of his head and traveled down to the soles of his feet.

He had come here to do a job, and being distracted by this really beautiful, talented, funny, personable woman would get in the way if he didn't stop it right now. The urge to breathe deeply of her scent and let it surround him became almost too much.

She turned her head and looked at him quizzically. "Did you hear me?"

"What?"

"Did you hear me? I asked you why all this talk about leprechauns."

"Oh—"

He felt so silly asking, but he needed to know. He'd have to disguise the question for sure. What would she think of him if she knew about Seamus, his very own private angel/leprechaun, the little twerp who constantly plagued him to death? Seamus's whole aim, he was sure, was to drive him to distraction and annoy him to death. It was too soon after Angela; matter of fact, anytime would be too soon. Some things in life you just have to keep to yourself. Besides, they didn't know each other well enough for him to talk about Seamus. She'd think he was a total nitwit or worse, a man that needed watching because perhaps he was dangerous. He'd have to make up something. But what?

"Do you think Americans care for that kind of thing?" she asked, still pursuing the topic.

"Oh, yeah no doubt, they'd eat it up. Maybe I'll turn the whole mystical magical thing into a book and sell it on Amazon or Barnes and Noble. Do you like the idea?"

Megan turned and looked at him inscrutably but said nothing.

Glancing toward the back seat, Jim found it devoid of Seamus. Hmm, maybe the little guy really had bugged off. When he wasn't so damnably tired, he'd have to try to figure it all out about Seamus. Why did he actually see him? Why did Seamus have this harebrained idea that he had to set Jim up with Megan to save Jim's soul? Hogwash.

Jim shifted again and found a semi-comfortable position. The effects of jet lag pounded behind his temples. He was so tired and his head might fall off with the pounding it was giving him. If he could catch a short nap, then he'd be ready for anything. He yawned, but the yawn didn't embarrass him at all. He was so very tired. His eyes closed. Soon, he dozed off to the steady rhythm of the tires on the road.

****

Megan glanced over at Jim for just a moment before she drew her attention again to the road. His eyes were closed and his long black eyelashes lay against his cheekbones. The black rough beard on his cheeks and chin showed already, even at three in the afternoon.

If she had eyelashes like that she wouldn't need mascara. He was such a magnificent looking man. And the nice part was he didn't seem to know it.

The things she had believed about getting the proper credit for the piece they'd write together still plagued her. Perhaps Jim told the truth about her byline in America. It would be more than wonderful if it actually did happen. It seemed she'd found a man who was simply concerned about her well-being and not about what he could get from her. Lovely, simply lovely.

Deep in her heart, she wanted more than anything to find out that all men weren't like Richard, out to get what they wanted and leave her flat. How could she be sure? Most of the men she'd met so far in her limited "all-girls school" experience had been out to get what they could from her. Maybe she was too inexperienced to make a call about all men or even most men. She was not using her journalist's objectivity.

Determined to think of something more pleasant, Megan rolled down the window a bit. She imagined she could smell the sea air, although they had another hour to drive before they reached the coast.

"Well, and why don't you open that heart of yours a bit and let the man in, colleen?"

My God! It was the same voice, the voice from last night, the same voice that had whispered to her this morning at the office. Her heart hammered and skipped, hammered and skipped, and she gasped for air. Cold sweat dampened her hands and her grip loosened on the steering wheel.

"No," she shouted.

Jim awoke with a start.

Megan shouted, her head jerking about as she looked quickly from side to side. She clutched the steering wheel and pulled it back and forth causing the car to skitter and weave between lanes. What had just happened? Was she going mad?

Megan's hand trembled on the wheel, and for just a second, the little car seemed to hang suspended in mid-air between lanes. Car and truck horns blared a warning. She had to slow down and get them to the safety of the shoulder, now. She decelerated, making the move smoothly into the slow lane, even though her hand shook on the gear shift.

"Pull over, Kennedy, before you get us both killed," Jim said, his voice deadly calm.

Megan's body shook visibly, but she smoothly turned the wheel over to the left and put steady pressure on the brake. Gravel slushed out behind them ferociously, scattering for yards. Horns honked frantically, blasting in protest from the vehicles behind them. Then the sounds faded away, the eerie silence punctuated by the wind gusting against the little car.

Megan slapped the gear into neutral, put on the emergency brake, and laid her head on the steering wheel.

"What happened? Why did you scream?"

When Jim put a conciliatory hand on her shoulder, she shrugged it away vehemently. She closed her eyes and laid her head back against the seat. What was that voice? Was she haunted? He really would think she was crazy. Crap! Bloody hell! She couldn't let the trip and the assignment go to hell because she heard voices. The editors at the Times would replace her in a heartbeat.

"Megan, what's wrong?" Jim spoke in a calm and reassuring tone.

"Nothing."

"Bull. What's wrong? Why did you scream?"

"*Afraid it 'twas me, Jimmy lad.*" A very small voice came from the back seat. The angel hung his head, his hands clasped behind his back. He glanced up at Jim.

"*Didn't mean to scare the poor girl. Frightened her last evening as well. Don't seem to have this idea about talking to her inside her head perfected just yet. Although, I seem to be doing quite well with you. Know that I've done it good and proper this time. Sorry, Jim lad.*" The little angel's shoulders slumped forward. He was obviously chagrined having put his responsibility, Jim, and Megan at risk.

"*Are you my guardian angel/leprechaun?*" Jim hoped his thought was loud enough for the leprechaun to hear.

"*Well, and haven't I told you as much?*"

"*Then leave Miss Kennedy alone. Got it?*" Jim directed this thought to Seamus in as scathing a tone as he could manage, while never taking his eyes from Megan. The poor woman was still breathing heavily, but in short order had otherwise gotten herself under control.

"Cars can be very dangerous," Jim said aloud, enunciating each word and looking at the leprechaun out of the corner of his eye as he took Megan's hand. "People get killed in cars every day."

"O'Flannery, you aren't helping a bit," said Megan with disgust, slapping his hand away. Neither spoke. The only sounds were cars in the distance and the turn signal's annoying little *tink, tink, tink.*

"Are you going to tell me what the voice said?"

Megan whipped her head around with a sharp intake of breath. Her eyes narrowed at Jim.

"How did you—?"

"Never mind how I know. What did the voice say?" The tone of Jim's voice brooked no argument.

Megan continued to glare at him. Her face was flushed and her green eyes flashed at him with a warning.

"I promise that I will not think you are crazy."

"It said…oh, hell!" Megan glared out the windshield, feeling intense heat radiate from every square inch of her. She pushed a non-existent strand of hair out of her eyes with a still shaking hand. She turned again toward Jim with what she hoped was a look so cold it could have turned bath water into a glacier. She took a breath. *Ah, get it all over with, Megan.*

"It said that if I opened my heart a tiny crack that I could love you," she said between clenched teeth, glaring at him, daring him to contradict her. "Or some such nonsense," she added, carefully drawing out her words for emphasis to cover up feeling totally foolish.

"Seamus!" Jim expelled a breath. Now, he was angry.

"Who?"

"My guardian leprechaun."

"Your *what*?"

Chapter 10

Jim looked about, sizing up the hotel as they entered the large lobby of the Sligo Arms. It seemed a nice enough place. The hotel was perched on the bustling strand of Sligo and sported a terrific view of the harbor. It was clean and thank goodness, to his overly sensitive olfactory nerves, smelled okay. There seemed an unusually large group of people milling about the lobby: artists, boisterous impresario-like men, and some really great looking girls probably signed up for the annual beauty pageant. The concierge's desk backed against a wall filled with old-fashioned cubbyholes for guests' keys and several computer stations on the long counter. Potted palms, huge ornately framed mirrors, red velveteen sofas and overstuffed chairs graced the lobby, reminiscent of the 1920s. Mouthwatering aromas of roast beef and potatoes wafted from a doorway nearby, accompanied by the subtle sounds of cutlery against china. The hotel's review in all the tourist pamphlets was four stars. It was also one of the largest on the strand and some distance away from the city's center.

"Well, and it's as I have said, Miss Kennedy. With the competition and everything, we've no rooms at all." The little man dodged quick glances at the large American as he spoke.

"Mr. Smith, this is ridiculous." Megan felt herself

flush as a thousand thoughts of her and Jim being forced together in a hotel room, and not all of them wholesome. And wondering not for the first, but perhaps for the thousandth time, if he were a bit daft and just how safe would she be after all?

"Surely, you can find the two of us a room. This is the largest place in town, and all of the other hotels are full as well. The Times would have made us a reservation, but we came on such short notice."

"And what do you think, Kitty? Is there a place we can send these two?"

A small red-haired, crone-like woman came over to the clerk and whispered in his ear, never taking her beady blue eyes off Jim. The man nodded.

"Ah. Kitty has just reminded me. We do have something, if you won't mind a bit small," he said, demonstrating by pinching his forefinger and thumb together.

"No, no, we'll take anything at all. I'm sure it's lovely," said Megan anxiously, forcing the thought of Jim in his underwear or maybe Jim out of his underwear from her fertile imagination.

The man nodded his head, took a key from a nail near the doorjamb, and gestured for them to follow him.

Jim tried to take Megan's suitcase, but she jerked her arm back and hissed. "Leprechaun, indeed." She gave him a quick but icy glare.

Jim muttered something about Seamus and carrying the bag, and then nudged the handle from Megan's clenched fingers.

"I'll carry the bag, Megan," Jim said through his own clenched teeth.

He shouldn't have mentioned the leprechaun. Of

course, when he'd spilled the beans, the little guy had disappeared, and no amount of cajoling or begging on his part could make Seamus show himself. The little weasel! Jim had egg all over his face, and could see no way to reclaim his short-lived respect from Megan. What lousy timing. She hadn't spoken to him for the rest of the trip, over another hour, but had just glared at him every once in a while, with her face flushed a bright pink, and this after she'd insisted that she'd not have him anywhere near or in the driver's seat.

"Seamus, you'd better move to parts unknown, because I am going to decidedly punch your lights out if you ever show your face again."

He'd have to decide how best to punch out an elf that was four inches tall, first.

"You told me you came here just for me. Hadn't you explained at great length that your assignment was to help me and that would earn you your wings or some such nonsense?"

The leprechaun had kept Jim's mind teetering on the edge of sanity for the past few days. Surely, Heaven couldn't condone that? *Or,* thought Jim darkly, *was it Heaven at all?* He'd find a moment to call Grandma. Maybe the deacon, O'Boyle was it, had given her some insight on the angel/leprechaun phenomenon.

Jim's thoughts whirled together as the two followed the man up the staircase. Jim noticed that they had stopped when he ran into the clerk with the keys. They had reached their destination and Jim turned around in surprise. They were pushing against each other on a tiny landing perched, it seemed, at the very top of the inn, and trying mightily not to make like the Three Stooges and tumble back down the stairs. The hallway was sparse, barely big enough for the three of them to stand by the lone door. Perpendicular to the landing was a grimy garret-like window looking out on the front of the hotel. The clerk produced the key, unlocked the shorter than normal door, and ushered them into what appeared to be an attic. The ceiling was made of exposed beams and slanted with the slope of the roof. Jim had to duck quite low to get into the room and could only stand completely upright under the centerline of the roof. There were two beds, more like cots, braced against opposite walls, and an old gray metal desk sat in the center of the room. The place reeked of dust and mold. Jim looked around in dismay and promptly sneezed.

"This is it? You've got to be kidding."

Megan glared at Jim for a split second before saying, "We'll take it, and I thank you."

The man shook his head and mumbled as he moved to the door. He opened it, looked at the two of them, and shook his head once again.

Jim and Megan stood motionless for a moment. Megan was so angry that it hadn't occurred to her until she'd taken a full turn around the room, that it was *one* room. When the realization dawned on her that she would be sleeping in the same room with him, he'd be willing to bet that he could smell the smoke leaking from her ears. Promptly, he sneezed again. He could be put upon, as well as Megan.

"Jeez, can you at least get somebody up here to dust the place?" Then Jim realized he sounded petulant, but still he added, "The Boston Globe is paying for the room."

"Yes sir, we'll have someone to clean it and put on

the fresh linens. Perhaps you and the young lady would like to wait in the bar and have a pint while we get the room straight."

"Is there even a place to plug in my computer?" Jim asked, forgetting about the room and then thinking about work. Hopefully, there was still plenty of available juice in the battery of the laptop he'd rented back in Dublin.

"Ah, I believe you'll have to use the outlets in the bar, sir."

"In the bar?" Jim raked his hands through his hair, gave one more look at the room, turned on his heel, and whacked his head against the doorjamb. He uttered a healthy curse and rubbed the offending spot vigorously.

"We thank you, and we will leave now for a bit, if you could see to the room. Come on Jim," she said, giving one tug on the arm that was already halfway out of the door.

"But, Kennedy—"

"Come on so the girl can clean the room." She practically growled at him. Jim nodded, and followed her down the stairs into the bar. They scooted into a booth, arranging themselves on opposite sides and avoiding eye contact as they set up their computers. Jim looked up and found Megan's finger pointing right at his nose, as though the thing weren't attached to her hand but looking like the "fickle finger of doom."

"Now, you'll be listening very carefully, O'Flannery. We'll have no more of this gibberish you came up with on the trip here. I won't and I can't hear another thing about"—she leaned forward and whispered—"leprechauns." She sat back, patting her hair in place and smoothing the front of her sweater.

"What we will do"—she glanced around the room, at her computer, the notes, at her silverware, anywhere but at him—"is simply get some supper and make a goals sheet for tomorrow." Finally, she gave him a hard look.

"That's just fine, Kennedy." Jim was resolved for the moment that he'd looked like an incompetent dweeb to her. Seamus was the little troublemaker and had caused no end of frustration since the trip began. Maybe Seamus would see what a mess he made of this trip and take off.

Jim looked up. They were there to work on a murder case. The insanity of the trip and Seamus, all of it faded into the background when he looked at her. Megan's quick bout of anger put a classic redheaded flush on her face and neck. The flush slowly intensified into a glowing and persistent red. Obviously, her whole body got into the act when she was angry. At least the all of her he could see...now if he was to use his imagination. She'd have a fit if she could read his thoughts. Even after such a short acquaintance, Jim knew that Megan was not the type. She'd never be a pushover and she'd never let herself "go all gaga" for any man. Megan would take nothing less than being treated as a colleague and journalist.

"There'll be none of that, I'll thank ya. My God, man—and where is your mind takin' ya to?" a disembodied voice said just over his right shoulder.

"Probably someplace you've never even imagined, Seamus," he said out of the side of his mouth after ducking his head.

"What?" Megan looked up at him.

"Nothing, Kennedy, nothing. Let's order dinner.

I'm starving."

As unobtrusively as possible, Jim looked first over his right shoulder and then over his left, trying to catch a glimpse of the elusive angel.

Seamus was no dummy and probably knew better than to show himself after what he'd pulled during the trip. Jim glanced up again from under his lashes and gazed at the top of that red-blonde head bent over the menu. Tiny red embroidered hearts were stitched around the neckline of her navy blue sweater. If he started kissing at that little heart there, he'd move slowly up to her ear within three kisses. His gaze stopped there. Maybe he'd take his time and it would take him more than three…

"Take your order, sir?"

Jim started and then felt the blood rush into his face. He looked down quickly trying to read the menu but managed to see nothing but squiggles.

"Ah, yes, I'll have the roast beef with the roasted potatoes, the roasted carrots, and the roasted, um…well, and a nice cup of tea," he finished off, trying not to sound too lame.

"And you, madam?" the waitress inquired.

"The salmon, please."

The waitress nodded and hurried off to the kitchen. Megan looked up at Jim. Her eyes were as cold as her expression was closed.

"I think it imperative that we contact the police station after we eat. You can take your computer, and I'll bring the notes we've already compiled. The goal sheet can wait until we've got a better idea of where to start."

Jim shifted restlessly in his seat. She could be very

authoritative. He had to get back on some kind of even footing so that they could at least work together. The other—the fascination with her—would have to wait until the story was finished. Oh well, no time like the present to get everything back under control. He shrugged his shoulders slightly. "Sure, that sounds fine. Can I see your file?" he asked, holding out his hand.

Megan stared at him without blinking and then tentatively held up the manila folder. He grasped the edge and pulled it forward, but she held on. He pulled again, and still, she held it.

"Promise me." Her face was grave, and her eyes glowed out of her still flushed face.

"What?" He was almost afraid to ask.

"There'll be no more talk about you-know-what," she said, drawing out each syllable while her eyes bored into him. She never blinked, completely focused on his face. She did not release the file. Instead, she kept looking at Jim like a schoolmarm chastising a recalcitrant child. "We need to investigate a murder, and I can't do that if I have to crate you away to Bedlam."

Jim sighed, trying hard to keep the blood from rushing to his face even more than it already was. "Okay, I promise. Don't blame me if you hear voices in your head again. It's not me that put them there."

He'd have to be smug to save face, but he was really out of luck unless Seamus showed up and bailed him out. If not, Megan wouldn't believe anything he said.

"Ri-ght." Megan drew out the single syllable word. Jim tugged on the folder again and when she finally let go, the added momentum threw the papers out of the folder, all over the tabletop and onto the floor.

"Ah, jay-sus, sorry." She ducked down to pick up the papers.

At the same moment, Jim ducked down as well and they collided under the table. Stunned, they rubbed their heads before they straightened. Jim glanced up to see the grimace on Megan's face. He reached for her free hand and kissed it.

She looked up at him; he still held her hand.

"Jim, I—"

"Megan, I promise, no more Seamus talk. We will get this story written, and it will win a Pulitzer Prize, I promise."

Megan gave him a tiny smile and a tingle coursed down Jim's spine as she pulled her smooth hand slowly out of his.

"Harrumph, excuse me. Your dinner's come," said the waitress, her arms loaded down with food.

"Sure." Megan pulled her hands away.

Jim watched Megan while the waitress put his plate in front of him. He was glad to see her blush. Maybe that meant something. Maybe she did have feelings for him. Maybe that little pest Seamus hadn't scared her away…yet.

Remember O'Flannery, your vow, no more women. He did not need entanglements from all the way across the Atlantic. He did not need entanglements period. He wouldn't be up to the task for many, many moons to come.

Remember O'Flannery, no more women for a long while.

He looked up and sighed inwardly when he saw Seamus sniffing his food and then jogging across the table to sniff Megan's plate. The salmon did it, because he put his elbows on the edge of the plate and breathed in happily.

Jim tucked into the mountain of food in front of him, getting his brain back on track. He peeked up near his teacup and saw that Seamus had positioned himself on the saucer. He half expected Seamus to say something, but the little man seemed to be in the throes of ecstasy. Jim supposed they didn't have a lot to eat in Heaven. Jim glanced quickly at Seamus, hoping the angel would take the hint. *Please,* he thought loudly, *leave already. I need no more bull-shit in my life at the moment!* He gave another surreptitious glance about the room; sure that Seamus had heard him. He hoped Seamus had heard him and would bug off.

****

Moments later, Megan saw a movement out of the corner of her eye. She ignored the niggling feeling and tucked into her salmon. But a wisp of memory triggered something in her mind. She snapped her head around, drew in her breath, and looked quickly over the sea of faces in the bar and restaurant.

"Kennedy, what's wrong?"

"I thought I saw…I thought I saw…Richard," she muttered, and the sound faded slowly away in the back of her throat.

Jim saw the subtle quiver run across her shoulders. Her skin took on an ashen tint, until she inhaled deeply and the breath slowly vented through her front teeth. "Did Richard upset you that much?"

Megan took another breath, pulling in the oxygen that had become a rare commodity, and then looked at Jim. "There's something about him that's so sinister. I never really saw it until it was too late. I don't know." She waved her hand about dismissively as she looked around the room again. "It's silly. I suppose I just don't want him to bother me, and then…well, I think it's something more." Some emotion triggered a feeling deep inside her. At first, it had been typical jealousy, but now—perhaps, if it was only jealousy, she'd sound as ready for Bedlam as Jim was with his leprechaun.

"I'll make sure Richard won't bother you." *Good God, was the Tarzan attitude in males hardwired or what?* He leaned forward and patted her hand. "Wait here, I'm going to check out the lobby."

He was almost to the entryway when a blast of cold wind blew in through the opened door.

He moved to the door, held his hands up to the pane of glass, and tried to look through the glare. There was nothing to see save a pool of light spilling across the steps that led out into the darkness. Jim stepped back from the glass and slowly walked the perimeter of the lobby. He saw neither Richard nor anyone that looked remotely like him. He was in the mood to clean the guy's clock. If Richard had come around to harass Megan, the guy had bought major trouble.

"Coast is clear," he said as he seated himself in front of his now cooling food. He saw a tremor run down Megan's arm.

He reached over and gave her hand a squeeze, pleased to see her smile. "Hey, it's okay. I won't let the puckas get you," Jim said. All Irish children were warned by their frazzled mothers about puckas, bad Irish spirits ready to take naughty youngsters to their lairs. Megan giggled into her napkin and Jim took her hand and raised it to his lips. Her alabaster skin shimmered in the light of the bar. He felt a tingle when he touched her, and he didn't mind it too much. He didn't mind it at all. She looked him in the eye, her gaze unfathomable. Jim shook himself.

"You are quite a man, O'Flannery."

"Yeah, well, when ya got it, ya got it," Jim quipped.

They finished their meal and Jim asked the waitress directions to the constabulary, the police station. He paid the bill along with a generous tip. They braved the cold outside and huddled under umbrellas. The few passersby they asked along the way helped finding the address the waitress had given them.

They climbed into the little car and before they could buckle up, Megan looked over her shoulder with a sharp intake of breath.

"What is it, Kennedy?"

"I can feel it. Feel someone watching me."

Jim looked through the windshield sheeting rain and saw no one. Jim patted her hand doing his best not to sound like a dweeb. "You're likely spooked because of these murders. Don't you think? Don't worry; I've got your back."

"Oh really, O'Flannery, you are full of yourself, aren't you? You patronizing so and so."

"Sorry, I sounded a bit pompous, huh?" Jim laughed aloud and Megan joined in. The ominous feeling of doom dissipated and floated away.

****

He leaned slightly toward the right and watched the car putter down the street. So she was sharing a room with the bloke. But she couldn't be. It had taken him too long to get into her bed. She couldn't be in love with that Yank. No, she still loved him. Yes, he knew she did.

He'd show her in every way he could how much he loved her. He'd be famous and then she wouldn't be able to help herself, she'd be so much in love. Richard's rushing thoughts slowed to a crawl.

First, he'd take care of that Yank. He'd have to be careful, though. If he was caught too soon, then Da would be very upset. Very upset. His father would hit and yell and snarl. The things he said, the demeaning slurs, hurt more than the beatings.

And then the expectation of horror, the angst, more horrible than the horror itself, would overwhelm him.

He wiped his face covered with nervous sweat despite the frigid, rainy night. The thought of his old man, just the thought of him, made him shiver.

He turned toward the hotel. He still had his room. He'd keep a watch. Maybe he could get to the bloke later tonight, and then Meggie would be his forever. Yes, they would be together forever.

****

"And I'll give you the statement again, miss, 'We have no statement.'" The gnarled-up old man leaned forward over the desk, using his body and the finger of his right hand for emphasis.

"But, Sergeant, surely you can give us at least the location of the murder and the names of a few witnesses?" Megan persisted. The tiny police station was a long, narrow room, with benches on each side. Above the benches, bulletin boards crowded with memos, pictures, and handwritten ads of all types hung from the walls. One door behind the sergeant's chest-high counter led to a hallway. Several doors, offices

Jim supposed, fed off the hallway. The jail itself was a separate building accessed by a covered walkway from the station. He and Megan would no doubt be kept from that area.

The officer's three gold chevrons vibrated just a little with his level of annoyance and the handlebar mustache he sported was so dotty and old fashioned, that watching it took the sting out of the glare he gave Megan. "Sergeant, Mr. O'Flannery has come all the way from Boston, in America, to do a story on this killer. There must be something you can share with us that won't compromise your investigation."

"Aye, there is," the sergeant said with a scowl. He stood and extended his already extended arm and pointed at the door. "But I'm not giving it to you. Goodnight."

"Come on, Kennedy, we Americans have our ways. They call it American ingenuity." Jim smiled at the sergeant and pulled Megan from the room. He glanced around when they reached the outer lobby. He saw a boy of about sixteen lounging near the washroom and nonchalantly moved up to the boy.

"Hey, kid," he said quietly, looking away from the boy. The boy tensed. Jim knew he was listening. "Ya wanna make twenty American dollars?"

"Jay-sus, too right, mate."

"Take us to where the murder was committed last night and give any information you know."

"Is it all then? Foller me." The boy latched onto Jim's top secret mode of behavior, and practically slithered out the door ahead of them.

"O'Flannery, I don't think—"

"Never mind, Kennedy. This is how an

investigative reporter works."

Jim and the boy moved quickly down the rain-slicked sidewalk, and Megan scrambled to catch up.

The teenager led them two blocks in the rain that had by now turned into a wringing mist. They turned down an alleyway next to a noisy bar.

The upper end of the alley, deserted and silent, was cordoned off, but no policemen were standing guard. The area was dank and gloomy, and even the leaves, sodden with rain, made no sound.

Jim took a small digital camera out of his pocket and took a few shots from different angles. He concentrated on his picture-taking, successfully blocking everything else out.

Megan looked about anxiously, sure that the police would come any minute and throw the two of them in jail for obstructing an investigation.

She rocked from one foot to the other as she wiped away the drizzle dripping into her eyes and nervously muttered to herself. What exactly was she doing here?

The silence began to press in on her, so Megan turned her attention to the boy. She'd have to get to work. Maybe talking to the teenager would help get her mind off her nerves. "Can you tell us who the murdered man was?"

"Ah, no. He was a big chap and talked funny like one of those, er—" The boy ducked his head in thought for a moment. "Oh yeah, one of them American southerners."

Jim looked up and grinned at the boy. The boy's thick accent kept Jim wondering what exactly he had said.

"Lots of actors and musicians around, huh?" Jim

asked between shots.

"Cor, yeah. This time o' the year ya can hardly take a piss without it being on an arteest," the boy said, tilting his head up dramatically. The kid looked at Megan and then shrugged his shoulders, obviously not caring if he offended by his language or not.

Jim laughed to himself and shook his head while he finished shooting the pictures. He came back to Megan and their "informant." "Come on, we'll walk you back to the station."

"What are you doing out, anyway?" Megan asked, knowing it was none of her business.

"Me da's a policeman, and I just brung him his supper."

"Isn't your mother expecting you?"

"Oh, aye, I suspect I'd best get on home. I thank you for the quid. Easiest money I ever earned."

"Hey, kid, what's your name? In case we have to get in touch."

"Freddy, Freddy Nolan," he said and then sprinted away in the dark.

"Two hours in town and I already have a paid informant. Sometimes I astound even myself," said Jim, rocking back on his heels and looking decidedly pleased.

"Well, if your head's not too big to fit inside the car, shall we go back to the hotel?"

"Right."

****

They made their way back toward the strand in the car. The tires slushed against the sopping wet pavement in the heavy mist. Within minutes, the light drizzle that had been with them for the afternoon turned into a deluge. Megan slowed the car to a crawl until finally they reached the hotel.

They sat watching the rain sheet the windshield after the sound of the engine died into nothingness. The sound drummed on the top of the car so loudly they didn't even try to make conversation. Megan looked straight ahead; what she was thinking, Jim couldn't even begin to guess. He put his arm around her and drew her closer. She fit nicely in the crook of his arm. His thoughts raged as violently as the rain hitting the car, and his body reacted to her nearness.

Jim lightly cupped her chin in his fingers and turned her head. He gazed at her, trying to read her expression.

The rain poured down as Jim's mouth slowly descended on Megan's. Her lips were warm and soft and the chaste kiss sent a thrill through him like he had never known. His arms pulled her closer and his lips moved with increasing pressure. He could feel her resistance, and then slowly, her compliance. His hand moved to tangle in her hair. He drew his fingers through the softness of it. Then his hand moved down her arm and onto her thigh, pulling her closer, feeling the heat of her zap him like an electrical charge. He—

"There'll be no patty fingers, if you please. We'll wait at least for the Banns to be read. No patty fingers."

Chapter 11

Jim's eyes shot open and his mouth froze in mid-smooch. He pulled his head back from Megan's and slowly withdrew his hand. She sat with her head poised to one side and her eyes closed. She opened them slowly, looking dazed, and then almost immediately, she sat up, straightened her clothes, and patted her hair into place.

"Wha—what happened?"

Jim cleared his throat and looked out of the corner of his eye for Seamus. The very sneaky little angel had chosen to be conspicuously invisible.

"Umm, well, I didn't want to get too carried away with us being forced to share a room and everything."

Megan looked properly embarrassed and hurriedly turned away to look out the window.

I thought you wanted to restore my faith by making me fall in love, Seamus. His mind reverberated with the thought. *Well, I think it's about time you high-tailed it back from whence you came. I am not going to fall for this woman and earn you your wings. You'll just have to find another way. Go find some other poor stooge to pick on. I refuse to get involved with a woman who lives an ocean apart from me. I refuse to get involved with a woman. Period. I must have taken leave of my senses, so blast off, ol' buddy.*

Jim pulled his arms down by his sides and sat for a

moment, feeling the palpable tension inside the car.

What could he say to her? What should he say to her? He'd acted on impulse. This over-powering impulse was just the sort of thing that always got him, and every other man on the planet, into trouble. But this was different. There was something so electrifying about being near her. She was more than a little desirable, much more. He had to say something, anything, or she'd think he had no control over keeping his hands to himself.

"Megan, I'm sorry." He looked down at his hands and then tried to look anywhere but in those lovely green eyes. "I seemed to have gotten carried away with the moment." He sounded lame; he was lame, and he was acting like a complete dweeb. It would be comforting and convenient to blame it all on Seamus. But he just couldn't. He was responsible for his actions, plain and simple.

****

Megan turned and peeked over at him, but just for a fleeting second. She was the one who'd gotten carried away. She'd been carried away by a knight on a white charger right to the hilltop. He'd laid her down in a field of wild flowers and then—and then—he'd thrown a bucket of cold water on her. Megan expelled an exasperated breath and leaned her head against the seat back. She'd obviously taken leave of her senses. What was she doing being overwhelmed by this man's phenomenal kisses? She wouldn't have it. She was much too levelheaded for all of this nonsense. Megan released another pent-up breath. No use letting him in on her frustration.

"Well." Jim straightened in the seat. "I think the

rain's slowing down. Shall we?"

"All right."

They both dashed from the car and raced into the lobby.

"Why don't you go on ahead and get ready for be—um, and use that little bath near the stair. I'll be up soon. There are a few things I want to e-mail to Boston." Jim looked at her, but he could feel the tell-tale signs of blood rushing to his face, so he ducked his head as he backed away, waved quickly, turned, and headed into the bar.

Megan watched him retreat into the pub. He was such a beautiful man; she could sit and look at him all the day. Good grief, ah bollocks! Had she quite taken leave of what senses she still possessed? His kisses had the power to drive her to absolute distraction. She shook her head to clear the thoughts from her mind and trudged up to the attic, hoping to find a bath near the stairs.

Perhaps the bath had a cold shower she could use.

****

"Iggy, I'm worred out. These stupid children have no notion of love and commitment to God and Church. Ah, no, they don't. It's grand to act out the marriage with no priest. I tell ya it makes me blood run cold, it does," said Seamus, watching the two "children" from his vantage point on a cloud. He shook his head and felt like the entire world weighed down on his shoulders. Had he failed? Had he been too flippant, too arrogant in his posing as a leprechaun to keep what mattered— what was most important—in the foreground? He slumped down into the cloud, bits of the swirling mist settling about his face, hiding it, he hoped, from Iggy.

Too ashamed he was to admit defeat.

"But Seamus lad, it's the modern times, it is, and things like those aren't thought of as rebellious as they once were. And yes, I've read your thoughts; you have been arrogant to think that all you had to do was snap your fingers and Jim would fall in line. Human beings are a complicated lot. You've been in Heaven so long you've quite forgot."

"But I think all of this patty fingers business will cloud the boy's judgment."

"Nay, nay. It is a dance that is as old as time itself. Really Seamus, you must let nature and the affairs of the heart take their own course. You needn't orchestrate everything.

"Now, my next idea for you is to show them a movie of the future. Show them each what an idyllic life it could be—trusting their hearts to one another." The little angel held his hands over his heart and fluttered his eyelashes in fake rapture while Seamus stood in a fuddle. He tapped his toe and sent bits of cloud floating off into the great chasm at the silly Ignatius. "Now, here is the projector, and the boys in the ad department have made a beautiful little movie to show them. Wait till they're asleep and then have at it, so to speak. Well, Seamus, good luck to ya."

Ignatius hopped a quickly moving cloud and waved. Seamus waved back and then turned to gaze at the boxy-looking contraption. The sign on the end glowed. "Touch me," it said. Seamus did.

"You may start the film at any time," said a mechanical voice creaking from inside the contraption.

"St. Colum! What will they think of next?"

****

Jim sat in the enclosed phone booth fingering his long distance calling card. If his grandma had managed to get in touch with her deacon, maybe she had some news. He quickly calculated that Grandma was in the middle of watching her evening quiz show, and hoped she wouldn't mind the interruption.

"Hi, Grandma, are you watching Jeopardy? I hope I'm not interrupting."

"Oh, Jimmy. So grand to hear your voice. Never mind about the silly show. It comes on again at ten thirty just before the news so I can catch up then."

"Good. Have you spoken to Deacon O'Boyle? I could use some help in this angel business."

"I did speak to him the very next day after you called. I tried to explain to him all that was going on and what the little leprechaun said about helping you out of your malaise and that he was there to save you. I hope I got that right?"

"As far as I can figure, he has come because: a. helping me will help him earn his wings; b. he thinks I'm going to go to Hell if I don't straighten up and regain my faith by falling in love; and c. he's decided that Megan Kennedy is the one that I should get hooked up with. That getting married is supposed to save me. Kind of black and white, don't you think? Human beings are a little deeper than that. Me falling in love and getting married to some Irish journalist is going to save me from Hell? Now, how could such a generalized and generic statement actually have originated 'in the great beyond'?"

"I think that's the crux of what I told him, the deacon, that is. He said he's never heard of such a thing before but that it could theoretically happen. Now, what book he gets all those notions from, I'm sure I don't know. 'There are greater things in Heaven than can be dreamt of in your philosophy,' or some such thing. At any rate, he said he's going to contact a friend in the Bishop's office that is supposed to be well read on personages from Heaven. But as I said, during our last call; leprechauns are spirits of earth and angels are spirits of Heaven. How the two could be one and the same, I'm hard pressed to figure out."

"Oh brother!"

"Aye, so here's the plan. Deacon O'Boyle will be contacting his friend, but in the meantime, he says I must say a novena for the safety of your soul. But I think I shall be adding some prayers about you and this nice young woman. Now wouldn't it be grand to have a Kennedy in the family?"

"Grandma, please don't get ahead of yourself. We like each other, sure, we respect each other professionally, but I don't know if it's going to go past that. She is very pretty, that's certain. But I don't want to set myself up for another fall. I just got out of the world's worst relationship with Angela. I've been asked by my editor to write these articles with Megan, and I can't let anything get in the way of my concentrating on that. Angels and love and all that is grand, but I sure can't eat it or pay my rent with it."

"It's true, Jimmy, that it is. But the matters of the soul and heart are a part of you as well. You are made up of three parts, intellectual, spiritual, and physical. If you ignore one, then the others parts suffer. All three must be in balance to keep you happy."

"Okay, Grandma. Please let me know what you find out. I'll call you in a few days. Give Mom a big

111

kiss for me and tell her I'll bring her something nice from Ireland."

"Grand, grand."

"But, Grandma, besides Deacon O'Boyle, I think maybe we ought to keep all this leprechaun business to ourselves. We don't want anyone to think the O'Flannery's are any crazier than usual."

"Right you are, Jimmy," his grandmother said with a laugh. "I'll talk to you in a few days. I love you, sleep well."

"Night, Grandma, love you too."

Jim hung up the phone and rested his forehead against the receiver. Maybe he'd make a trip to a church here in town himself. Couldn't hurt to flex those spiritual muscles every once in a while. But now, sleep.

Jim climbed the stairs wearily and warily. The conversation with Grandma was helpful. Maybe Seamus hadn't come from Hell with plans to pull him into the fiery pit. Jim shivered, but then he thought about Megan. He hoped he could keep his hands to himself and just get the much needed sleep his body craved.

Those kisses, as chaste as he'd wanted to make them, just didn't feel chaste no matter how hard he'd tried. And they wouldn't have been chaste for long.

Chapter 12

At the head of the stairs, Megan found the bath while Jim was still safely at the bar. She closed the door, sat on the edge of the tub, and turned on the tap. While the tub filled, she pulled out her cell and called her mother.

"Mam? Am I calling too late?"

"Meggie, so good to hear from you. How is the article coming?"

"We haven't uncovered much information as yet, but we will. Jim O'Flannery has such a great way of finding information and then piecing it all together. It's grand to watch him work."

"And?"

"And what?"

"Well, is he nice to be around? What do you think of him personally?"

"Well, I uh." Megan heaved a sigh. How was she going to bring this up without sounding completely bonkers herself? "Here's the thing, Mam, he thinks he's being followed around by uh…" But her tongue stuck to her teeth and she couldn't form the words.

"Meggie, what are you saying? He's being followed by what? What are you saying?"

"Oh well, nothing, never mind. He's good at what he does and I suppose that's the best thing I can say about him or anyone."

"Meggie, sometimes I wonder what you are thinking. I have to admit, I did look him up on the Boston Globe web site. He has a good list of articles he's written, and I read the short biography the paper had next to his picture. I must say Meggie, he's quite a good-looking man."

Megan sighed hugely. "Yes, Mam, he is a very good-looking man. I'm sure the little snap you saw does not do him justice. He's very polite, too. It's just that…"

"It's what Meggie? Are you still going on about Richard? The whole relationship has been over for months and months. You must get on with your life and forget that bastard."

"Mam!"

"No, I mean it! It is time for you to get out of this funk you've been in for almost a year and move on. Now, I'm not expecting you to get involved with Jim O'Flannery, but wouldn't it be nice if—?"

"Mother, I am not going to get involved with Jim or any other man for that matter for a long, long time. I need to get this story finished and that is all. Okay?"

"Very well, Megan."

She could tell by the sound of her mother's voice that she'd hurt her.

"I'm sorry, I didn't mean to fuss. It's been a long day and I'm tired. I'll call you in a few days, all right?"

"Yes, dear. That will be fine. Now, in the meantime, do your articles and be the sweetest girl I know you are with Jim O'Flannery. You don't have to put on the attitude with him. The two of you have a hard task, so do the best you can."

"All right, I'll do the best I can. I'll call you when I

get back to Dublin. It may be a few days, but I'll call before then if anything important happens."

"Don't worry about Jim. I'm sure he's sound as a penny. It's probably jet lag. Love you, dear."

"Bye for now, I love you."

Megan rang off, and glanced down at the tub that had filled to the edge. She dipped her toe in and pulled it out in a flash, it was so hot! She'd have to wait it out or she'd look like a steamed lobster within minutes. No, she was too tired. She let the water out while she washed her face and teeth, brushed out her hair, and trudged up the stairs to the little attic room she shared with Jim.

****

Jim unlocked the attic room and found one lamp shining dimly from the old metal desk. He looked to the right and saw Megan—all five-ten of her, gloriously stretched out in a bed that looked as though it might have been a version of a medieval torture rack. It did something to him to see the shape of her wonderfully long legs under the blankets. He shook his head. Nope, he was not going to think about it. He sighed and tiptoed to his suitcase, pulled out a robe and his shaving kit, and went out to find the bath.

Jim tried desperately to act nonchalant when he passed people in the hallway dressed only in his robe. He tiptoed back into the room and sat on the side of the bed after he'd showered. He yawned hugely. He was beat, but didn't think that he could quiet his mind enough to get any sleep. He started to take off his robe and stopped. He didn't own any pajamas. Well, he supposed he'd use the old underwear routine. He'd slip his robe on in the morning before he got out of the bed, and minimize the shock factor. He looked one more time at the long form of Megan Kennedy stretched out under the covers before he turned off the light.

After several restless minutes, he realized what was keeping him awake.

Her scent.

It floated on the air, swirling about his head. It was lemon and sunshine mixed with something else that he couldn't quite put his finger on.

His gaze lingered on the opposite wall. The half-moon window above the desk let in a pool of neon light and filtered shadows and the droplets of rain sheeting the outside. Shadows, light on light, dark on dark, fluttered across the floor and wall. Jim watched the raindrops slide down and spatter, the sound lulling his tired body to sleep. He sighed again, turned over, and put his pillow over his nose. Maybe then he could block out her scent.

The rain battered against the hotel, and the rhythm finally eased him into a restful sleep.

****

Megan pulled her lower lip in between her teeth and chewed and chewed until she tasted blood. *Bother! How can I keep a perspective when I'm mooning over the man? I must be able to do my job without my head spinning from kissing him. Thought I should die from wanting him when his arm came around me like that. I could have quite swooned like some silly schoolgirl. How am I going to be a good writer with a non-compromised perspective when all I can think about are the man's hands and lips? Bollocks, ah bollocks! Grow up.* Megan chided herself. And she knew she'd get it together. She always did. It might take a while, but she'd get it sorted out.

When Jim had come into the room, she'd tensed. She heard him sit on the other bed, and then thought she heard him taking off his robe. She could see him in her mind's eye, all glorious six feet three inches, but she had put her mind's hands over her mind's eye and tried to sleep. She heard the bed groan under his weight and a sigh filtered across the room. She wondered about the sigh, wondered if it meant he was sorry he kissed her. No other sound came from the bed and all she could hear was the sound of the rain beating its steady tattoo against the hotel roof.

Megan turned over trying to get comfortable among the lumps and sadly sagging middle of the mattress. She pulled her knees up to her chest to get around the bumps poking at her and sighed deeply. Miraculously, she fell asleep.

****

Seamus floated into the room on the steady current of air swirling about the landing of the staircase and set the magic box between the beds. A whirring sound emanated from the little machine. Seamus sprinkled some sparkling dust over the two sleeping people. He watched as their subconscious woke and watched the same exact dream.

The movie began with Megan wearing a veil standing before a priest with Jim as they took their vows. They turned and looked at one another, love glowing around them like a halo.

The scene abruptly changed and Megan stood in front of a stove, stirring a pot with a baby on her hip. Jim walked into the kitchen with a small boy in tow. He took the baby from Megan, gave him to the little boy, and swept her back in a huge kiss. They both laughed and then turned their attention to the children. Again, the scene abruptly changed.

Megan and Jim sat facing each other over twin desks working on twin computers. On the top of each monitor sat a funny little leprechaun doll. Megan's hair was streaked with gray and Jim's was completely white. They looked up and smiled at one another, each reaching for the other's hand.

The scene changed, and a gray-haired Megan, still tall, but looking fragile, walked hand in hand with a white haired, slightly stooped Jim. Jim reached for Megan and kissed her.

The movie scrolled to the credits and finally "THE END" written in an ornate old English script.

"Humph," mumbled Seamus. "Cheeky to sign their names on Heaven's creation. Just cheeky. Need to speak to Iggy about all that."

Seamus turned and looked at his charges. Their minds were still very much open and Seamus saw both Jim and Megan smile in their sleep, while he floated to the beds and threw another bit of dust over them. Their minds blinked like open eyes and became once again as one with their physical bodies. He waited and watched until he heard a snore rumbling from Jim and a tiny nasal whistle from Megan. Seamus picked up the magic box, pulled on one earlobe, and disappeared.

****

He paced the floor. Back and forth, back and forth. After hours of pacing, he sank onto the bed exhausted. He looked at his watch. It was near on to midnight, and yet he couldn't sleep. His mind whirled with the sound of his last victim struggling to breathe as the wire pushed against the man's windpipe. Ripples of excitement coursed through him. He tingled with the memory of the man's gasping, and the inept fingers clawing at the vice-like grip around his throat.

He got up again to pace the floor. Thoughts of Megan wouldn't let him be.

Why was she here in Sligo, of all places? Why? Had she followed him? Her and that Yank? It couldn't be possible. He was too careful. They couldn't suspect him. He wasn't ready to be caught.

Not yet.

No, not yet.

He had to prove to Megan that she still loved him. He'd be so famous; she wouldn't be able to help herself. His father would finally come around as well.

Oh, yes, he'd be famous and they'd all be sorry that they didn't love him the whole while. He'd be famous, and then he'd get Meggie back.

He'd have to make a plan; a plan to get rid of that Yank. After all, he was an American, an Irish American. Yes, he'd plan it out just so, and Mr. James O'Flannery would be the next victim. He'd have to wait till they got back to Dublin, though. Only one per city per week. That way it would take them a while to find him.

No, he wasn't ready yet for them to catch him.

No, not yet.

Richard finally staggered to the bed in exhaustion and fell over it into a fitful slumber.

Chapter 13

Someone was after her, chasing her, getting closer and closer. She stole a glance over her shoulder, stumbled and almost fell. They were coming, closer and closer. She ran pell-mell toward the hazy outline of a building shrouded in gray mist. Her breath came quick and shallow. She thought she might faint. The building was within her reach. At last she grasped the doorknob and turned. It wouldn't open. The door latch rattled against the jamb but it wouldn't open. She looked over her shoulder, but there was nothing in the swirling mist.

Then she heard footsteps. Running, running toward her. She wrenched the door, willing it to open. She glimpsed quickly over her shoulder, sure that they were closing in. Sweat dripped into her eyes; her hands were slick with it. She turned and turned the knob, pounding on the door, trying, trying to get it open.

She screamed.

"Jim, Jim."

A hand grabbed her shoulder and shook her. She tried to scream again, and then a soothing voice nudged her consciousness.

"Wake up, Megan."

The darkness and mist receded. Megan opened her eyes.

She was in the attic room in Sligo. She looked up and saw Jim bending over her, his hand warm on her shoulder.

"Are you okay?"

Megan braced herself up on her elbows and took a big breath. She closed her eyes and the dream fled into the background. She looked up into Jim's face. He'd crawled out of bed to save her. His black, black hair stuck up from the back almost straight up. He stood there in his boxer shorts, the white no-nonsense kind, and his hand touched her shoulder and the nightmare was gone entirely.

He was pretty terrific looking, even if he had an indentation from the sheet running across his cheek and his hair stuck up all over his head. Megan's mouth went dry, and she turned her head away from Jim and tried to swallow.

"Yes, thanks for saving me. I'd say you're a knight in shining armor, but you haven't got any clothes on."

"Oh," Jim muttered, looking down. "Well, I'm going to head for the bath. You can change up here, all right?"

"All right," Megan said as she turned the rest of her body to the wall. She heard him moving around, pulling on pants and a shirt, before he grabbed something and headed out of the room.

Sounds of the awakening hotel lulled Megan into a relaxed state. The horrifying nightmare, even now, was fading away into nothingness.

She took a big breath and closed her eyes, hoping the last bit of the dream would vanish. She relaxed into the pillow and another image took hold in her mind.

She and Jim stood in front of a priest. A priest, and wait, she wore a veil. What? There were two little boys, one was a baby, and the other was named…Seamus?

Had she had another dream last night as well?

Megan sat up and quickly hopped from the bed.

"There'll be none of that now. Get dressed, you great dolt," she mumbled as she rummaged around in her suitcase and pulled out a pair of gray wool slacks that weren't too crushed and a white sweater. She would wear her black blazer, and then she would look quite professional with a few strategically placed accessories. But even as she pulled on her clothes, the dream about Jim and the two little boys filled her mind. She pushed her thoughts away and focused on dressing. She'd look quite professional. Yes, quite professional.

She dressed quickly and brushed out her snarled and tangled hair. Now, it was time to find a sink and a mirror. Her mind still filled with the dream, she grabbed her purse and makeup bag and headed out the door. Her head was down as she went down each step, her mind far away. Without warning, the toe of her black pump ran into the toe of Jim's bedroom slipper. She looked up at him, and did her utmost not to roll her eyes. *The man was positively a ray of sunshine, God give me strength.*

"Good morning," he said cheerfully.

Jaysus, was he always so, so, so cheerful in the mornings? No, she would not snap at the poor man just because she felt like. Ah, bollocks, what did she feel like? *Come on, Megan, be nice.*

"Morning. I'm on my way to the bath. Meet you in the restaurant?"

"Sure," he said.

She sensed him watching her as she walked past him.

****

Jim made the bed and straightened his things before taking the computer and following the aroma of coffee and ham to the restaurant located in the back of the hotel. Jim treated his first cup of coffee of the day with a reverence he had for few other inanimate objects. Ah, life was good with a cup of hot joe.

Megan came into the eating area and stood inside the door, looking around. Jim watched her, before she saw him. She was stunning. She wore a red silk scarf tied loosely inside her jacket, and her glorious hair brushed out and pushed back with two ornate combs.

Suddenly, a picture of Megan in a white dress and veil flooded his memory. They were standing in front of a priest and Jim had said, "I do." Jim shook his head. Where on earth had that scary thought come from?

Jim shook his head again, took a drink of his coffee, and muttered, "Seamus."

"What's the matter, O'Flannery, didn't sleep well?" Megan sat down and gave Jim one of her all too frequent smug looks.

Jim sipped his coffee before answering. "Matter of fact, I slept great. That's why me hair was sticking up all over me head," he answered in a mocking Irish accent. "You look very nice this morning."

"Well, thank you. You do, too," Megan said, looking appreciatively at his navy blazer and Kelly green tie. "Nice combination, O'Flannery. Everyone in town will think you're a millionaire."

"Really?" Jim looked down at his slacks and blazer. He didn't get it.

"Lots of people think all Americans are millionaires."

"You're kidding, right?"

"No, it's true. Poor misguided folk. I know better. I've read American newspapers," she said as she picked up her spoon and waved it for emphasis.

"You are one funny woman, Kennedy. Now, after we eat whatever it is that they eat for breakfast around here, have you made a plan for the two of us?"

"I think we should fill out a goal sheet with all the information we know and then start drawing some of our own conclusions. I've done a study on serial killers, their usual psychological profiles. We can use that for some story back-up. The Mighty Flynn loves to see data—lots and lots of data."

"Very good. And if we need something else, we can always Google it. I got Wi-Fi last night in the bar."

"Very good." The waitress brought tea and a plate of soft, buttery buns to the table. "Oh, what shall we have this morning?"

"Don't suppose I could get bacon and scrambled eggs?" Jim wistfully asked the waitress. His breakfast the previous morning had consisted of some sort of fish.

"Certainly, sir. And you, madam?"

"I'll have bacon and eggs as well."

"Right-o. I'll bring them straight away."

Jim crossed his arms on the table and looked long and hard at Megan. The image of her gray-haired and fragile, but still very elegant, flitted through his mind. She'd be beautiful when she was eighty.

"Of course, she'll be beautiful, you dolt, and now is the time to ask her."

Jim sighed and covered his face with his hands. He peeked between his fingers and saw Seamus standing on Megan's shoulder. He was glad she was fishing for something in her purse at the moment and not watching him.

"Can she see you?" He thought rather loudly.

"Of course not, boy-o. Not unless I wish her to."

"You just better wish her to see you then. I'm tired of looking like an idiot because of you. She thinks I'm mad as a hatter."

Megan looked up in time to catch Jim, glaring at her shoulder. "Jim, are you all right?" she asked.

"Sure."

The waitress brought their breakfast, and he started to make a dent in the mountain of eggs on his plate before he looked up. Seamus was on the table, leaning over Jim's coffee cup, slurping away, humming to himself between his very noisy sips. Jim used his thumb and forefinger and flipped the little guy head over butt onto the table. The leprechaun jumped up, sniffed, straightened his hat and jacket, pulled on his earlobes, and disappeared.

"There is something I forgot to ask," Jim said mentally to Seamus as he drank from the cup, wondering if he could get leprechaun germs. *"Were you responsible for that dream last night?"* Jim looked around the room as casually as he could, trying not to draw attention to himself. He thought he saw a flash of green over near the kitchen door.

"Seamus, if you're here, show yourself," Jim commanded silently. There was no answer. Jim decided to give it up. For the time being.

****

Megan glanced up, happy to see that Jim was looking somewhat coherent. Maybe she'd imagined what she now thought of as his "leprechaun look."

Maybe she was the one who was crazy.

Maybe there really was a leprechaun trying to get her to fall in love with this man.

An image of Jim, white-haired and sitting opposite her behind a computer monitor, flashed in her mind. On top of the monitor sat a leprechaun doll with red hair and a curled red beard.

She shook her head. This was getting to be too much.

Chapter 14

"So tell me," Jim said after the waitress had taken their plates and refilled their cups.

"Tell you what?"

"About the profile."

"The profile?" Megan had a blank look on her face.

"You know, the 'average' serial killer," prompted Jim.

"Oh. Well," she said as she leaned forward a bit conspiratorially. "The person is usually very self-assured but tweaked in some way. He; they are mostly men, you know, not many women, if it is a woman, she is anti-social, disorganized, and might be a heavy drinker. Anyway, sometimes the killer is sporadic, and then there is the spree killer who doesn't care who he kills or why. There is the methodical one who kills a specific type of person for his own twisted reasons, like the boy-o we're looking for."

"Yeah, no kidding."

Megan thought of Richard when she'd said the word tweaked and remembered the terror that seemed to radiate from him when there was a mention of his father. Richard's father had abused him, beating him physically, and what was worse, psychologically. The abuse went on until, finally, Richard had moved out and escaped sometime after he was nineteen. Megan had observed "triggers," certain incidents that caused

Richard to withdraw into himself, act very surly and verbally abusive. He'd twisted her arm once and that had been the beginning of the end. After that incident, she'd investigated him and had found that everything about Richard was a lie; his position, his friends, even the car he drove turned out to be one that his father leased for his clients. During the investigation she'd conducted, she'd found out about Richard's mother and all the times Richard had been hospitalized because of his father.

Megan had seen the under-the-surface horror in Richard once. The aftereffect of the physical as well as mental beatings would hide itself behind a wall of bravado and oily charisma. Richard's controlling personality spoke volumes about his fear of his father and his inability to have control over his own life since he'd been a very small boy. Megan's thoughts of Richard played through themselves, taking her in a completely different direction than the topic at hand.

"Many times a trauma of some sort in the killer's life will precipitate the stress, act as a trigger, and that's when he begins killing.

"Sometimes he will kill for a while and then when he's finally caught, the authorities can put two and two together and decide that they have caught someone who's been murdering for years by their *modus operandi*. Of course, all his, 'I killed him because I was abused' blarney doesn't make it with me.

"You remember the story of Cain and Abel," she half-asked, half-stated. "Did you know that not one chap blamed the bloody club Abel used to beat Cain? Not like they do in your country blaming guns instead of the people who fire them off." She quirked a smile at him. "I don't suppose I need to spout any political correctness to an American." She fluttered her eyelashes coyly for a moment.

"But back to the killers. They kill because it is a way of controlling the outcome of their lives. They want to be caught, need to be caught, and in some grotesque sense are doing the killing to feel as though they can facilitate their own destinies. Some killers leave blatant clues. Some write letters to the newspapers spouting philosophy. Remember the Uni-bomber and the Son of Sam?"

"Hey, not all serial killers are Americans, you know," Jim defended. "Remember Jack the Ripper?"

"He was a bloody Brit, thank you very much."

"You mean, amongst all those crazy IRA terrorists there isn't one guy that did it 'cause he got a charge out of it?"

Jim's remark angered Megan so that she took a huge breath and let it out slowly. *Silly girl, of course he's right. Keep some perspective.*

"I don't believe in all that blarney. If the stray, misguided thug up in Ulster bloody kills their own neighbor every time they turn around, then so be it. The IRA doesn't do political in Dublin. Not since the twenties when we became a free Republic." She knew she was stretching that statement until it broke. There were always the fanatics. Of course, Jim boy would know that, him being a journalist. "And another thing, you shouldn't think that all Irishmen are terrorists any more than all people from Florida will kill any European tourist they happen on. Don't you find it incomprehensible when someone has a preconceived notion because you are from somewhere instead of who you are as a person?"

Jim shook his head slowly and leaned forward to pat her hand.

"Megan you are such a firebrand. You should be a 'carrot top' as mad as you get." He saw a storm start to build in her gaze, and the center of that storm was aimed right at him.

He hoped she would lighten up just a little, and soon. He ached to hold her and find out the depth of that passionate behavior.

He almost let a sigh escape. He could let himself slip so badly and fall hook, line, and sinker. He should be much too pragmatic for all of that. Much too sensible. He just didn't fall for any pretty face. It had to be the right pretty face, at the right time, and in the right circumstances.

He'd shelve this whole topic until a later time.

"I think to be on the safe side, we need to drop all the political talk. And by the way, I know that not all Irishmen are terrorists, any more than all Arabs are out to get us. Generalizations can get mighty sticky, don't you think?"

Megan picked up a manila folder and made a playful swipe at his head and giggled. Jim looked up and grinned.

"Point taken. No more political talk. I will become apolitical for the rest of the trip. Now, have you decided about anything for our next step?"

"Yes, let's go pick up Freddy and have him watch out for the bad guys while we do a little sleuthing."

"Sounds jolly good."

"You know, I'll never get used to hearing that."

"What?"

"Jolly good. It sounds like those guys in old historical films with their pinkies stuck in the air while they drink tea," said Jim, demonstrating.

Megan laughed and her silvery laughter rippled through him. Jim braced his chin against his hand and looked on at her with delight. He thought he could listen to her laugh the whole day, and never once get tired of it.

He shook his head to clear the thought and gathered up his things quickly.

Chapter 15

Megan and Jim circled the cordoned-off crime area, but now, to Megan's relief, in the daylight. The two were making an attempt to absorb all the information available. The killer had done a neat job. The murder had been planned down to the last detail and left nothing to chance. The murderer had positioned himself next to an outcropping in the wall, putting him in the shadows. From the look of the footprints, it would have taken him exactly one step to get to the victim.

The Dublin police had ascertained from information from the first few murders that the killer would strike up a conversation with the victim in a crowded bar, walk with him outside, and then ask him to go back in to retrieve something. That much they'd surmised from the various witnesses who had recalled seeing an American come in and look for something and then slip back out again. The killer may have worn some sort of disguise. Perhaps he was so ordinary that no one remembered any distinctive features about him.

Megan and Jim, following the lead from the Dublin police, decided that the killer must be a man because of the upper-body strength necessary to strangle these large victims. It was a man, and a good sized one at that.

Jim had gotten a copy of the victim's statistics

from a buddy in the States via e-mail. His friend worked in forensics in Boston where a copy of the man's ID had been sent prior to his body being flown to the States. The Irish police had released the victim to the family, who in turn were even now sending the victim on to Boston.

Freddy Nolan, their informant, had overheard his father telling his mother that a forensics team from Dublin would be there any minute.

Megan looked over her shoulder for the umpteenth time. She was sure the police would catch them nosing about.

Even though it was broad daylight and the sun was shining, she felt a quiver course through her.

"Jim boy, can't ya see that the lass is frightened out of her wits. Best you go over and kiss her hand or some such."

Jim caught sight of the pesky little leprechaun. This time the little man was sitting in a highly stylized cart, decorated with garlands of flowers and vines, and hitched to a donkey that wore a nosegay of red and pink flowers on his bridle. The animal looked about, idly chewing on a bunch of straw.

"Who's your friend?" Jim asked of the donkey. *"Aren't you afraid he'll let one go right there in midair? Maybe 'it' will come back and land on those pointy shoes of yours."*

Seamus blustered in disgust, snapped his fingers, and he and the donkey cart were gone in a puff of green smoke.

Jim shook his head and then got his mind back on the task at hand. Megan looked at him, and pulled her brows in thought. She opened her mouth to speak, but

Jim cut her off.

"Don't worry, everything's under control. I just want to measure this space between the footprints and we can go back to the room and start making some charts."

Megan looked over her shoulder again. Nerves. She was a complete Nervous Nelly, and uncharacteristically so.

Since last night, much had changed; first the dream, and then Jim saving her from her nightmare. A lot could happen in a short eight hours. Megan shook her head, wondering what would happen next.

"Well, I think I'm finished. We can go back to the hotel. What time is it anyway?"

"Half past three. Jolly good, let's get out of here. This place is giving me the creeps. Well, it's not *here* exactly—it's everything that's giving me the jumps."

At the hotel, Megan and Jim made themselves comfortable in the bar. As they waited for their drinks, Jim took out a legal pad and began to draw a diagram.

"Now, according to my informant in Boston, the victim was five feet eleven inches and weighed around two hundred and five pounds. The killer came up behind him and I was told that there was more pressure on the left side of his throat than the right, so our killer is left-handed. Since there was more pressure placed on the upper part of the throat than down under the jaw, the killer is probably about an inch or two taller than the victim. So we have a killer who's about six feet two inches and left-handed. It's a rudimentary algorithm, but more truth in it than not. It's a sure bet he's a national, so we need to look for all six foot two, left handed Irishman."

"My, is that all?" Megan rolled her eyes and giggled.

Jim cut his eyes at her before he continued. "The problem is there are so many people around because of the beauty contest and the artists' festival that it will be hard to find out if the killer is a local or from another city."

"I'd say he's from Dublin."

"Why?"

"Because the killings started there, that's why."

"Hmm, point taken."

Megan's gaze drew to his mouth and she remembered the kiss the night before. The sound of the rain drumming against the windows. Jim's arms around her lulled her into a very relaxed but very acute feeling of excitement. The thoughts made her shiver. Megan clenched her hands in her lap, opening and closing them again and again. That kiss, soft and pliant, had shaped itself to her as if they were made for one another. It was so right, so utterly right. It was so…

Jim looked up at her. "Are you okay? We can do this after dinner if you'd rather."

"Yes, let's order an early dinner. I say, let's go to the theater tonight and watch a play and get our minds off murder for a short break."

"I can't send any information about the killer to the Times, just those photos you shot yesterday with a description of the victim. The police don't take well to information being spilled before they say so."

Jim continued to shuffle through his voluminous papers, stopping and reading any interesting tidbits along the way. Megan sighed a little. There was certainly a lot she'd rather be doing with Jim than working on a murder investigation.

"Have you written this day's piece for the Globe as yet?" she asked, hoping to get his attention and her mind off other things.

"Yeah, I'll tell you what, in the interest of time, you edit my piece and I'll edit yours and we can wire them. We should finish inside an hour. Want to grab a burger while we're working? Kill two birds with one stone that way?"

"Sure, but there's no McDonalds around here if that's what you're thinking. We'll have room service send sandwiches up to the room, and then go to the theater around seven."

"Sounds good," said Jim. And then he remembered. He remembered that he and Megan shared a room where there was not only one, but two beds, one on each side of that ugly, gray metal desk. He took a moment, closed his eyes, and attempted to wipe his mind clear of Megan thoughts. He had to. He had a job to do.

Chapter 16

She was a rare woman, a rare and beautiful woman. Knowledgeable, passionate about many things, but how could he write and edit while she looked over his shoulder? He looked up at her then, watching as she finished off her whisky and sorted out papers to put in her briefcase. Well, it was mind over other unmentionable parts of his anatomy. He had to put everything in perspective without going crazy over that cute little nose and those deep green eyes?

He wanted her in the worst way. The *worst* way. Keeping his perspective around her had turned out to be a daunting task. But he'd do it. He was much too sensible to let all of this, whatever it was, drive him crazy. They had a job to do, and between the two of them, he knew they could pull it off.

"Ah, boy-o. I knew it. I knew it would just be a matter of time before you fell in love. Now, I do believe that there's a priest still up at St. Ignatius and he's just around the corner. Let's trot on over and speak to him and get the Banns read."

Seamus stood on the bar near Jim's sleeve. Seamus snapped his fingers and a tiny Irish harp appeared. The little elf sat cross-legged, with the harp on his lap and strummed the very out of tune strings.

"Ho ro, my nut brown maiden
Hi ri my nut brown maiden

Ho ro ro, maiden
Who else would I marry but thee?"

As quickly as the harp appeared, it disappeared and Seamus puffed himself onto the rim of Megan's whisky glass. With great slurping sounds, he licked the bits of whisky he'd just dabbed off his fingers. Jim watched all of these antics, tried not to laugh, and then remembering himself, glared at him. But the little man looked back smugly. Seamus hopped off the whisky glass and sat himself comfortably between Megan and Jim. He pulled a miniature Irish harp out of the air, and after strumming a few chords burst into song:

"Oh the summer time is comin',
and the trees are sweetly bloomin',
and the wild mountain thyme,
grows around the bloomin' heather,
will ye go lassie go?"

Seamus sighed, waggled his brows at Megan, turned and waggled them at Jim, threw the harp into the air, and disappeared.

Jim closed his mouth with a snap, watching Seamus's antics and realizing that his jaw had sprung open and his chin was somewhere in the vicinity of his belly button. Jim had to admit that the little guy really had a terrific voice, and obviously a few drops of single malt helped lubricate those pipes. Jim felt like clapping for the performance, but he didn't. He had to keep focused on—wait. What had happened last night while the two of them were asleep in that garret? Did they both have the same dream? He put on a stern face and glanced at the spot where Seamus had been.

"You were responsible for that dream last night weren't you?" he thought loudly. *Can you think loudly?*

"Not me boy-o. It was those ad fellas upstairs. Upstarts, all of them. Why, they made the credits at the end bigger than the title. And by the way, Mr. Smarter-Than-Your-own-Britches, it's all true."

"What's all true?" Jim felt his brows rise up his forehead.

"Why the dream of course. That's what them old goats, pardon yer honor," Seamus said as he bowed toward Heaven and nudged down the rim of his cap, *"have planned for ye and the lass here."*

"Predestination? Have you turned Presbyterian on me?" "Balderdash!" Jim said aloud.

Megan's gaze shot up to Jim; her brows rose in question. "What's the matter?"

"Ah, nothing, just thinking out loud." He knew his face was bright red. He felt the blush get out of control. Jim glanced at the rim of Megan's whisky glass, and let the breath he'd been holding slip slowly out between his teeth. Seamus was gone. Thank goodness!

"Well, we'd best get on upstairs and get to work if we're going to make that show by seven." Megan slid off the barstool looking at him curiously.

She stopped by the desk and ordered their sandwiches and a pot of tea and scones while Jim climbed the stairs to the room. She looked after him quizzically and worried. He had that leprechaun look again.

Chapter 17

Megan and Jim walked out into the clear, cold night. It was only a few blocks to the theater. They were to see a murder mystery. The play was one that had been nominated for the annual award at the Arts Festival, but Jim wasn't too happy about the whole thing. He'd rather have watched a comedy.

He was too obsessed at the moment, thinking about killing Seamus. Perhaps he was afraid that the plot of the play might give him too many brilliant ideas. But then again, he supposed you couldn't kill an angel. If that was what he was and not a demon straight from—

"*Ah, ah, ah, mustn't say that,*" said Seamus. The elf sat perched on Megan's shoulder as they walked toward the theater.

"*Why don't you make like a tree and leaf?*" Jim silently wished.

"*Ha, ha, that's a rip if I ever heard one,*" said the little man, holding his sides in laughter. "*Funny. Is that how all you young people talk nowadays?*" Seamus stopped laughing rather too abruptly and with his arms akimbo leaned in toward Jim. "*Now, you and the young lady here are going the wrong way. St. Ignatius is behind us, laddie.*"

"*I'm not going to see a priest tonight; I'm going to see a play.*" Jim closed his eyes.

"*A play? Saints preserve us. And with all that you*"

Chapter 18

Jim thought about Megan's corporeal body the rest
the evening, successfully ignoring even the suspense-
ed play. He thought about her on the short walk to
 hotel and again when he escorted her to their room
l told her he would be up after he had a nightcap. He
ught about the problem until he felt like his head
s too small for all the thoughts crowding about in his
in.

He could see no way at all for them to be together.
e most obvious and glaring problem was where they
ch lived.

Boston was a real hometown in every sense of the
rd, and he really didn't want to leave there. Not ever.
e lived in Dublin, and he couldn't very well ask her
 move either. He knew she had just as many
achments in Dublin as he did in Boston.

He couldn't ask her to give up her job. He was
rtain hers meant as much to her as his did to him. But
 had a sneaking suspicion that he was getting past the
int of not being able to live without her.

It worried him. It worried him like nothing had for
very long time. What would happen to his heart that
s so inexplicably attached to his brain when he
 that plane in Shannon and left?

He walked into the bar and settled hi
ol before he looked about. He had t

*and Megan lass have to do. Boy-o, listen to your uncle
now and go back to St. Ignatius. 'Tis the only way that
you'll be saved."*

"*My uncle?*" Jim's eyebrows raised in question.

"*Oh, aye. Six-times, that's great-great-great-great-
great-great-great uncle, you being a direct descendant
of my sister Maggie. And didn't I tell ya? I need to tell
you about your ten-times-great-grandmother. What a
lass. Feisty as all get out. Take a fist to any lad and best
him, she could. I see some of that in you, boy-o. Now
your ten-times-great-grandmother—*"

"*Please tell me that my ancestors didn't have
pointed ears and slanted eyes like Mr. Spock,*" Jim
thought in a half prayer.

"*Oh, no, laddie. I just look this way because King
Brian looks much the same. He's the king of the
leprechaun's, don't ya know. And who the devil is this
Mr. Spock?*"

Jim stared at Megan's shoulder trying to imagine
what his great-uncle times six really looked like.

"Why are you staring at me?" Megan's tone was
curt and wary.

"Uh, sorry. Actually, I was looking over your
shoulder at the houses along the street."

Megan liked looking at him with a pretend glare.
She could take her time reveling on his blacker-than-
night hair and his pale, almost translucent skin. His
eyes were the show stoppers. They melted into her right
down to her toes.

She continued walking, staring at him, and
suddenly she pitched forward.

"Ohhhh!"

Jim grabbed her arm as she stumbled. Her toe had

caught on a crack in the pavement.

"Watch yourself," he said as he held her arm tightly. He stilled, looking deep into her eyes. "Uh—"

He searched about in his mind for something to say to break the spell she wove around him. "How far to the theater?"

"We're here. You're standing in front of the bill."

Jim turned his head slowly to see the entryway to a small Broadway-type theater with a lighted marquee.

He shook his head slightly, still holding Megan by the arm.

"Okay, let's go in."

The theater had rows and rows of old-fashioned, wooden, flip-down seats. Jim and Megan walked down almost an entire row before they found their assigned places.

The play was a murder mystery with shadowy lighting and strange voices that occasionally spoke from the wings. Suspense filled the theater and the lighting and acting created an aura of anxiety for the audience. Sometime after the second act intermission, Megan looked over her shoulder, coming halfway out of her seat as she did so.

"What's the matter?" Jim asked.

Megan sat flat again, stared straight ahead for a moment, and then shook her head slightly. She leaned closer to Jim, cupped her hand over her mouth and spoke in his ear.

"Remember last night when I said someone was watching me? Well, there goes that feeling again."

Jim looked around nonchalantly and couldn't be sure that he didn't see a shadow lurking in one of the upper boxes.

"*Seamus, is there someone watching Me*... sent the thought heavenward, hoping Sean... catch it on the way.

"*Can't say, boy-o. Not my departmen... watch after the corporeal body, so to speak... soul.*"

Jim let out a disgusted sigh. The house l... down and the play resumed.

****

He stared at her from the upper box, wil... look at him. Her red-gold hair, hanging lov... shoulder, fell softly around her face as she... looked. Ah, he knew she could feel him. H... Their bond was as strong as ever. He'd prove... she needed him, still loved him.

He had to get rid of the Yank. But if he k... here, they might catch him sooner than he wa... to.

No, he'd have to wait until he got back... Then he'd make plans that included Megan.

He'd keep her in the little flat he'd hi... River Liffy.

If she didn't behave, he'd just have to tie... supposed.

But with time, surely she'd come to her... realize just how much she loved and needed... the little place he'd picked out near the river... just the thing.

his problems.

A man read poetry to an attentive crowd. Jim thought he might be reading Yeats but wasn't sure. Ireland crawled with intellectuals, and sometimes Jim felt a bit like a cultural boob comparatively.

Jim's mind was on the reading and his own morbid thoughts when the barkeep brought his whisky. Some niggling feeling nudged at him and Jim's mind came back into the present. His attention was drawn to a man standing at the other end of the bar. He stared at Jim, only at him. The man was dressed for the weather in a soft-billed cap and a type of slick overcoat. The bill of his cap was strategically pulled down over the man's eyes, hiding most of his features. He continued to stare at Jim, and Jim stared back for several seconds before the man moved away toward the back wall and the kitchens.

Something about the way the man acted, the way he stared at him, made Jim's hair stand on end. A memory nagged at him. He couldn't put his finger on it, but it left an ominous cloud hovering behind. Jim got up to follow the man. He moved quickly, trying to note facts about his appearance rather than just emotional impressions. The man continued to retreat until he was through the side entrance.

Jim ran toward the door and pulled it open. He walked out onto the top step. He stood quite still and scanned the rainy darkness. There was no one there. Who was it? A feeling of apprehension worried him. A sinister, palpable thing, curled down his backbone. There was no one; just the rain spattering against the concrete step and black pavement just beyond the pool of light. He felt it now, hard, Megan was in trouble.

Jim stepped back inside and returned to the bar and his drink. He slugged down the whisky and waited a moment for the reader at the end of the bar to finish the poem. An eerie premonition came over him. He had to go now, quickly, and make sure she was safe. He took the stairs two at a time to the attic room and Megan.

He reached the attic landing and the door to the room in a half dozen strides. With a forceful push on the door he stepped into the room.

He stopped and with an effort just short of shouting spoke calmly. At first. "Megan, this door is not locked. Why isn't this door locked?" He heard his own voice booming off the walls of the little room.

"Because," she said coming toward him, barefoot and wearing a heavy, fuzzy robe. "I didn't know if you had your key."

"Well sh—!" Jim slammed the door, glared at her, and then began pacing the floor. He turned abruptly and locked the door, checked the window above the desk that was so tiny Seamus couldn't have slipped through, and sat heavily in the desk chair.

Megan padded toward him in her bare feet.

"What the devil is going on?" Megan put her hand on Jim's forearm, forcing him to look at her.

"I think I've seen…okay, remind me…what does Richard look like? Does he have a mustache, a beard, a toupee, anything like that?"

"Richard? No-o. Why are you asking about Richard?"

"I think I saw him downstairs. I think he was staring at me. I followed him to the door but I lost him in the dark."

"Why would Richard be here?" Megan frowned.

"My guess is"—Jim got up and began to pace the confines of the small room—"he's following you." Jim stopped short and leaned into Megan, nose to nose. "Now, tell me everything you remember about him."

Megan looked as if she were humoring Jim. She took a breath and sat on the edge of the chair. "He's got dark hair, auburn with black. Dark brown eyes, and no, he hasn't a mustache or a beard or a toupee."

"How tall is he?" Jim wanted to complete the picture in his mind.

"About an inch or so shorter than you, but he's not as well built, he's almost slender. Tell me what's up here."

"You said you felt as though someone's been watching you during the time we've been here, right?"

Megan nodded as she retreated to her bed, sat, and pulled her feet under her. She felt a chill run down her spine, leaving a trail of ice on its way. "But—" she began.

"I know this sounds whack-o, but sometimes well, I just feel things before they happen. You know?" Jim looked down at his hands self-consciously. How he could run on! "Maybe it's just something that happens to me sometimes, I don't know." He *had* to explain, he had to make her understand. "But I just have a feeling that the man I saw was Richard, or someone dangerous…to you. I think we should head back to Dublin and you can stay at my hotel. Maybe we'll change the hotel, and I'll register under my mother's maiden name or something so it will be harder for him to track you."

Megan's mouth opened in shock; she shivered and wrapped her arms around her middle. Jim stepped over to her and drew her into his arms and held her close. He pulled Megan's head against his chest, letting his fingers slowly massage away the tension along her spine.

Her scent enveloped him, and he sighed deeply until he almost lost track of why he was holding her. He cleared his thoughts and focused on why he'd charged into the room.

"Megan, if it is Richard stalking you, I'm not going to let him do anything to harm you."

Megan looked up at him in surprise and he knew instinctively she'd forgotten why she was snuggled up next to him.

She broke from his embrace and stood. "You are too far off the mark there, O'Flannery, too far by half. How can you make outrageous statements like that?" she demanded. She glared at him, and began to pace the floor. "St. Joseph, you're an investigative reporter. You know how to find out facts and make assessments without getting emotions into it. I should think that you'd be ashamed of yourself with all this talk. Really. And no, I won't go to a hotel with you—"

"Megan," Jim said exasperatedly, "you aren't listening to me. I said—"

"Listen to you?" She stopped, leaning toward him and glared with her hands on her hips, and her face flushed bright red. "Listen to a self-ascribed mystic, who has a bloody leprechaun as his best mate? I should think not." Megan marched across the room and grabbed her purse and shoes. Her indignant departure was marred by the stubborn lock, but a second later, she stomped from the room, slamming the door behind her, but not before she let out an expletive that made Jim blush. He winced as the door slammed with a resounding thud and then threw himself back on the bed.

"Jimmy, I think, that is, I know that you're off the track as to why I'm here." The leprechaun floated on air in a sitting position with one ankle braced on the opposite knee. He leaned forward, his brows pulled down in all seriousness.

"Now, as I've said before, I'm here to help you regain your faith. And it looks as the only way you'll be gettin' back to the church is by a good girl like Megan Kennedy. Can't you see, Jim?" he said, throwing his little leprechaun arms out wide. "If you've no faith, no love for God and all around you..." The leprechaun stood, poised near Jim's nose, and pointed at him. "Well, ya know what happens to them."

The leprechaun descended to the bed and began to pace back and forth on the coverlet, climbing over Jim's leg as if it were a hill. Seamus's head was bent down, chin to chest, as though he carried the weight of the world on his shoulders.

Jim braced himself on his elbow and stared at the little fellow for a moment.

"You know, Seamus, it's been a real kick in the teeth to be around you this past week. I meet the most beautiful, talented, plain wonderful woman, a rare woman, and you are constantly trying to screw things up. I mean what was this 'no patty fingers, if you please' stuff? I almost broke my neck stopping that kiss. She thinks I'm loony because I told her about you, and in case you don't remember, I told you that I didn't want to get serious with Megan...or anyone else for that matter. I doubt if I'm going to Hell because I haven't fallen in love." Jim lay back down on the bed with a groan. He scrubbed his face with his hands and took a deep breath before he sat up to make eye contact with Seamus.

"I promise I will see my priest when I go back to Boston, go to confession, and go to mass, okay? Now, lay off. I've got enough troubles. And another thing," Jim said, jutting his face up at Seamus, his nose a scant inch from the leprechaun's. "When we were in the theater, I asked you to help and you said 'no, not my department.' Crap! What if that guy is after her and she ends up in Heaven before her time because you didn't help, huh?" Jim poked Seamus square in the gut with his finger. "I'll bet the guys upstairs won't give you your wings because of that," he added as he bounced off the bed.

Seamus stood up, his forefinger poised in the air.

" *'Oh blame not the bard if he flies in the bowers,*
Where pleasure lies carelessly smiling at fame;
He was born for much more, and in happier hours
His soul might have burned with a holier flame.'
Sir Thomas Moore 1779-1852"

Then the little man bowed from the waist with a "holier than thou" attitude emanating like a halo.

"He was a little after my time, it is, but you get the general notion, don't ye now?"

"Get lost." Jim poked his finger into the little guy's chest and watched as Seamus actually fell, right on the thin air.

Seamus made a disgusted sound, pulled on his earlobes, and disappeared. Jim sat back on the bed, expelling a pent-up breath.

Megan thought he was crazy, a real idiot and that

was obvious. Jim slumped down on the bed again, letting his head fall forward into his hands. Something niggled at his sixth sense, telling him she was in trouble and Seamus sure as heaven wasn't going to help. If he could use the term *heaven* loosely, he thought as he scowled at the air. If his nagging suspicion was correct and this crazy Richard character was following her, then he'd move Heaven, pardon the expression, and Earth to protect her. He realized that he hadn't been in *protector mode* for a long, long while. He wasn't the forever kind of guy, was he? His heart whispered, "Oh yes, yes, you are." Jim scowled at the room, not sure it wasn't Seamus that whispered instead of his heart.

He honestly hadn't thought of forever until he'd met Megan.

Jim got up from the bed and paced back and forth. He scrubbed his hand over his face, stood exactly in the center of the room, and stretched until all of his bones protested and cracked.

Now what? He'd find Megan and make sure she knew that they would leave first thing in the morning. That was as good an excuse as any. He'd have to be very careful around her. He'd already laid it on way too thick. Spouting about premonitions and leprechauns was not the thing to do to make points with Megan.

Jim left the attic room, making sure that the door locked behind him, and went in search of Megan. As he walked slowly down the stairs, his mind raced with thoughts about her and their relationship, as new and meager as it was. If Seamus hadn't been "Mr. Into-your-Face-and-Fix-it," his life would be a lot easier to take right now.

Since he'd come to Ireland, he'd felt his usual, take

me or leave me demeanor slipping. He cared now, cared about what Megan thought about him anyway.

He turned the corner and saw her sitting on the top stair of the third floor. He stopped. Her back was rigid and straight, but her shoulders trembled slightly. Jim took a big breath, trying to calm the turbulent thoughts in his head.

He sat down next to her on the stair and she gave him a sullen look for a moment before she turned again to stare at the wall.

"Hi."

She said nothing.

"I'm sorry if I got you rattled. I was excited about what was going on in my mind. That's something that doesn't happen to me, you know. I'm usually a really cool and controlled guy." He hoped his smile took the sting out of his crazy behavior, if she would look at him and see his smile.

Megan laughed ruefully. "You mean when you aren't conversing with leprechauns."

"Right, when I'm not conversing with leprechauns. Why don't you go get dressed and I'll take you to the bar for a nightcap?"

Megan took a deep breath as though trying to resolve something in her own mind.

"All right, be right down."

"Good, I'll wait for you right here."

She got up and walked with purpose up the stairs and the room door closed with a thud.

"Ya know, boy-o, I popped down to St. Ignatius and lo and behold if Father Smith wasn't there listening to confessions. Now, why don't you and the lovely Miss Kennedy go there and talk to the man and post the

152

banns? What do ya say?" asked the little leprechaun as he made a friendly jab in Jim's arm. Seamus produced a tiny Irish harp and began to sing.

"The time has come to part, my love,
I must go away.
I leave you now, my darling girl,
No longer can I stay.
My heart like yours is…"

Jim turned on his best intimidating stare. "Beat it." His voice growled and bounced off the walls of the stairwell and off Seamus as well. The leprechaun puffed out his chest and brought his chin up high.

"Beat it, smart-ass. I've had it. You're supposedly my guardian angel, but all you've done is make my life very complicated. And when the big stuff comes along like helping me find out if someone's about to pounce on Megan, you take off with the *it's not my department* bullshit. Well, I've had enough. It's not *my* department. So beat it boy-o, and don't come back." Jim took his thumb and forefinger and flicked the leprechaun off his puff of invisible air. The little green clad figure tumbled head over tail and then disappeared.

Jim laughed quietly as he watched the leprechaun's quick descent. He wished he could share that scene with someone—with Megan—but of course, Megan already thought he was crazy.

"Just what are you laughing about?" Megan had returned to catch him in the act of chuckling to the thin air.

"Oh, nothing. Are you ready for that drink?" he asked, eyeing Megan's tight jeans and midi sweater appreciatively. He should be thinking about or doing something else, he told himself.

"You're not too tired, are you?" he asked as they started down the stairs.

"Well, I think I'll survive one whisky." She laughed quietly and her laughter poured down his spine like fingers stroking his bare skin.

Jim turned his head and willed himself to get his libido under control. Things would get out of hand unless he had the fortitude to master his emotions. He could do it. He'd been the strong silent type his whole life and now wasn't the time to change personalities.

Idly, he put his hand at her waist and led her into the bar. He stopped her for a moment and looked around. A new man was reading some really old-sounding poetry, Beowulf or a poem maybe of the medieval era, at the end of the bar. Only a few customers remained, giving the area a quiet, lonely aura. Jim left Megan at a table and after ordering the drinks, he took a moment to look around.

Whoever the man had been, he'd disappeared. Jim nonchalantly went to the side door and peered out for a moment at the dark, ominous rain. He wished he could shake this feeling of dread, but he could smell the danger lurking under the veneer of quietly clinking glasses, soft conversations, and subtle wisps of tobacco smoke floating on the air.

The last victim hadn't been killed in this bar, but the murder was committed within a few city blocks of here.

Jim saw a flicker of light across the dark, rain-drenched street. He leaned against the glass trying hard to catch a glimpse of whatever it was.

"Mr. O'Flannery, your drinks are ready."

"Thanks," said Jim as he took the two glasses and

walked to the table where Megan waited for him.

"What were you looking for?"

Startled at the sound of Megan's voice, Jim looked up. He'd been so far into his own thoughts that he'd almost forgotten her. Almost.

"Just looking for that guy I told you about earlier." Jim took a sip of his drink and then leaned back in the booth to gaze at her. "Look, I'm sorry I got so weird upstairs. I usually don't get the willies like that unless it's founded. Don't look at me like that, Kennedy. It's true. I can get these premonitions of doom sometimes." He sat forward and took her hand in his. He took a deep breath, deciding after a short internal battle that he should come clean. Maybe then she'd think he wasn't too crazy, just slightly nuts.

"I knew something terrible was going to happen the day before my father died. I was eleven years old, and it paralyzed me so that I couldn't leave my bedroom the whole day. My mother had our neighbor, who was a nurse, come in and take a look at me. I couldn't explain to her what was happening any more than I can explain it to you now. I know that it's only happened a few times to me and it happened again a little while ago. That's why I acted like such an idiot."

"How did he die?" Megan squeezed Jim's hand.

He took a quick drink from his glass and released Megan's hand to scrub his fingers across his jaw. "He died of a heart attack in the subway. He fell down and no one even noticed him for a while. He died, away from home, among strangers, and before anyone that knew him, could get to him. It was really hard to take. The police came to the house and told my mother. I was up in my bedroom, and I heard strange voices. That and the 'feelings' or whatever they were scared me so much that I hid in my closet. My grandmother came up and found me. She stood there and gave me the strangest look like I could have prevented it or something."

Megan was quick to comfort him. "Oh, I don't think so. Remember, you were eleven. She was sure to be overcome with grief. I'm sure you imagined it, because you remembered how you felt the day before."

"Maybe."

Jim took another sip of his drink and settled his large frame back into the booth.

Megan noticed the dark circles under his eyes and the skin around his mouth pulled tightly down. "Jim, let's get some sleep. Try not to think of it anymore tonight. It'll all seem brighter in the morning."

"Sure."

Jim threw back the last of the scotch and then helped Megan from the booth. They held hands as they wound their way up the stairs to the attic room. He seemed to draw comfort from holding her hand and Megan was glad of it. The poor man had appeared to cave in when he talked about his father dying. It couldn't be easy for a boy to lose his father, especially when he felt it all too vividly before it happened. That must have scared him into the next century.

"How old are you, Jim?"

"Thirty-two. Why?"

"Just wondered," Megan answered.

"You mean how many years it had been since my dad died?"

"Yes, I guess so."

"Twenty-one years, an entire lifetime. And then, sometimes it feels like it was yesterday. I still wonder sometimes if there wasn't anything that I could have done."

"You mean as an eleven-year-old boy? Come on, you know better than that one."

"Intellectually yes, but…"

"No buts."

"Right."

They'd reached the landing to the attic door and Jim stopped in front of Megan and held both her hands. He looked at her until she felt her toes curl inside her shoes. Those clear blue eyes pierced right to her heart.

Jim cupped the back of her head with his hand and drew her to him.

The kiss was slow and arousing. Then it became demanding. His tongue touched hers and every thought fled from her mind as sensations continued to cascade through her. Her hands pushed under his sweater to feel his broad, taut back. Jim pushed her gently against the wall next to the door, his body so close that she could feel all of him press against her. She clutched at him, pulling him closer. The feelings coursing through her were so new, the territory so uncharted, that they completely overwhelmed her. She broke the kiss. She looked into eyes gone all smoky blue, and the sight of it turned her tummy to jelly.

"Yes." She looked up at him with a burning behind her eyes. "I know. Maybe…no, you're right."

Megan turned toward the door, her hand shaking so hard that the key refused to turn in the lock. Jim leaned around her, his big body still pressing against hers. His hand held hers as he turned the key in the lock. She turned then, into him and wrapped her arms around his neck and pulled his mouth down to hers.

He held her, urging her into the room. He lay on the closest bed, and pulled her down to him. He stroked her back, his hands wandering under her sweater.

She pulled her face away, holding his head in her hands. "Oh, Jim, I want—"

He sat up and pushed away from her. He took a breath and then turned to her. "Megan, if I make love to you I won't be able to leave. I'll—"

"No, Jim tonight…just tonight."

She kissed him again, trying to show him with her kiss all that she felt for him, but would never tell him.

He moved both hands down to her bottom and pulled her against him. She arched into him, pulling him closer.

The kiss seemed to go on and on, the heat building until it crowded out every other thought in her mind.

Again, Jim broke the spell. He turned slightly and pushing himself up, he braced his forehead against hers. He gave her a quick kiss, then, slowly, he sat up and braced his elbows on his knees, holding his face in his hands.

Megan rubbed his back, staring sullenly at him.

"Jim…" she began.

"Don't you see?" he asked as he looked at her over his shoulder, his face wreathed in abject misery. "I'll never be able to leave here without you. I'm already half gone now. Megan, I like my life the way it is, and I can't be pining for you across an entire ocean. And I know me. I'm as big an emotional lush as anyone from the Emerald Isle. I will miss you, but I'm not going to allow myself to. I want this as much as you, maybe a lot more. But I can't do it."

Jim got up, grabbed his shaving kit and robe, and

stormed out the door.

The sound of the slamming door reverberated slowly and faded away. Megan stared at the closed door, willing the doorknob to turn and for Jim to reappear.

After several long moments, she dragged herself from the bed, all the energy gone from her body. She pulled off her jeans and sweater, each movement mechanical and wooden. She pulled the nightgown over her head, and pulled back the covers of the little bed that had so recently held the warmth of both their bodies. She curled herself into a ball under the covers and wept quietly into her pillow.

****

Long after Megan slept, Jim returned to the little room. They both slept fitfully. Seamus tiptoed into the room and threw a handful of dust over Megan and Jim.

Now, they slept soundlessly, dreamlessly. Their tired bodies began to mend and to strengthen. Seamus took another handful of dust from his pocket and threw it over them. As had happened the night before, their subconscious awakened and rose from their bodies to watch. Seamus turned on the projector and the same movie played again.

Jim, in her dream, was a tottering old man, who still kissed her tenderly.

Jim watched Megan cook for him and their two sons. He watched as he kissed her and saw her laughing green eyes smile into his. His subconscious looked carefully this time, trying to decide whether they were in Boston or Ireland.

Megan remembered working at adjoining desks with two stuffed leprechaun dolls sitting on twin computer monitors in the dream. The memory felt so familiar and comforting.

She too looked to see whether she could recognize where they were. Had they stayed in Ireland? That thought nagged at her subconscious until she almost missed the pleasure of the rest of the dream.

During Jim's dream, he watched Megan fragile and gray-haired, but still very erect and stately, holding his hand as they walked together. He didn't know where they were, and suddenly, he didn't care. He knew from that instant that he'd be with her for all time. In the grand scheme of things, it didn't matter where they were, as long as they were together.

The movie ended and Seamus turned off the projector before cheeky credits ran at the end. He tiptoed from the room after he was sure that their subconscious minds were again sleeping dreamlessly.

"We'll see about this tiny locale problem, yes, we shall."

Chapter 19

He ran out into the rain. The cold wet chilled him down inside his bones. He stopped and flattened himself against a large lamppost. There he could still see, but not be seen.

The damn Yank had caught a glimpse of him at the bar and then pursued him. How could he have been such a daft prick? Of course, he had no way of knowing the man would come into the bar after the theater. Since Megan hadn't been there, he'd gotten away with appearing mysterious to the dense American.

They were all so stupid. Americans, it was their fault, their doing, all of it was because of them.

The memories he avoided, that he wanted to forget, crashed about him; memories so abhorrent, so devastating that they paralyzed him. Sometimes with fear, sometimes with a rage so white hot that he shook and could not stop shaking. And still the memories came. They poured through his mind hard and fast. He was powerless against them.

Hadn't his father left his mother for an American? He raged at him, always. But the belittling words, the emotional assaults on his self-confidence—they were much worse after he'd married that American whore. His mother had always tried to protect him by encouraging him to hide. Sometimes it worked and sometimes, because his father had taken his precious time to seek him out, the beatings would be worse still. It was hardly Richard's fault that after only a few months the American bitch had left his father. After she left, the beatings from his father had shown no mercy. His father's uncontrollable anger was aimed at Richard, always at Richard.

The beatings and psychological abuse were nothing compared to Richard's knowledge that his father simply did not love him and could not stand the sight of him.

The thrashings had been ferocious, debilitating, savage, but never savage enough to show bruises, sprains, or broken bones. His father had stopped just short of that. The family abuse was their dirty little secret, kept close to home. He put his hands over his ears, and pushed hard, to block the sound of his father's voice. But it was always there. Always.

"You're no good. You'll never amount to anything, and I shall withdraw my support of you. You're no better than that slut of a mother." The voice would go on and on; asleep, awake; in every moment, he heard the voice.

Not long after the American witch had left his father, his own mother had died of a broken heart. Richard was powerless to do anything to help her.

He'd been forced to live with his father then, a terrible existence until he broke away at nineteen. But now, his father would see soon enough what an important person he was and he'd be sorry for all the beatings and the name calling.

He'd be sorry that he hadn't treated Richard better when he'd lived at home.

Soon Megan would come round as well. Yes, she'd be there waiting for him when he got out, and they'd have a wonderful life together. Maybe they'd move to the Jarro with all the stall vendors and mix in with the working class.

They'd be welcomed with open arms. And the folk there were all Irish. No bloody Yanks there.

A smile spread across his face as he looked at Megan's attic window once again. Then he turned and walked back to his own small room he'd rented over the little Italian restaurant on the next street.

Chapter 20

Megan twisted in the car seat, trying to find some comfort in the hard cushion. She and Jim had rushed around all morning, filed their initial stories, packed, and ate. Jim had said little to her. She'd kept to herself as well, thinking not to disturb his solitude and perhaps help herself into being more aloof.

He'd climbed behind the wheel of the car in that commanding way he had, nodded to her once, and started driving. He'd cleared the city in a very short time, still silent but his attitude somehow reproachful.

Megan agreed last night had been too much for both of them and they needed time and distance from one another after the stories were filed. He was absolutely right about their not becoming physically involved. It could only lead to an emotional involvement, and who had the time and energy for that?

She'd heard him mumbling something to himself and could almost imagine that he was speaking to the leprechaun after she'd heard the words *priest* and *banns*. Perhaps, Jim was attempting to keep himself from getting attached to her, so attached that he'd think about proposing marriage. Ah, bollocks, poor fellow. Megan's ruminations on Jim's feelings came to an abrupt halt. She sucked in her breath and shook her head. Why should she feel sorry for the big lug? Poor fellow my behind! She suspected that her animosity had everything to do with keeping her too-fresh emotions about that certain gentleman at bay.

She peeked at him out of the corner of her eye. He kept his eyes straight ahead, his shoulders hunched, and his chin almost to his chest. He had a gray sort of look about him. She guessed she needn't give him too much grief. Jim looked as though he'd had it this morning. The strain of telling her the story of his father's death and that fellow he'd thought was Richard had taken it out of him all right. She hoped, she really did, that he wouldn't take all these ideas about premonitions too seriously, but of course, to him, those emotions were dead serious.

And then there was their near miss on the staircase. On the staircase, like a couple of teenagers. She'd have to get her own head examined when she got back to Dublin.

And then she remembered...the dream she'd had about Jim flooded her mind. She turned her head slightly, catching a peek of him from under her lashes.

He must have felt her watching him, because he turned his head and gazed at her.

Suddenly, he turned on his blinker and stopped the car on the shoulder.

"Are you ill?" she asked.

Jim put the car in park and put his arm nonchalantly across the back of his seat as he angled his body toward hers.

"No, I'm not ill. But I've got something to say, and now is as good a time as any."

"We're likely to be hit, sitting on the side of the road in this way. Don't you think we'd best get to an exit?" she said a little nervously as a huge truck came awfully close to the little car.

Jim looked out the back window. One truck and then another followed closely and sped past them. The little car trembled in their wake. Their car might be swept away with them. He shrugged his shoulders slightly, not fazed at all by his own and Megan's demise by truck.

"No, I think we'll be fine. Now, about last night," he said in a no-nonsense voice, cocking his brows down at her as though she were a child he was remonstrating.

"We've said all we need to say about that subject." Megan turned her head and looked out the window. She felt her shoulder come up to ward off his glare.

"Not me. I don't think so."

Megan crossed her arms over her chest, raised her chin a notch, and gave him the very best glare she could muster.

"Megan, did you have a dream for the past few nights? A dream about the two of us?"

She felt a flush climb up her neck and settle on her cheeks.

"So you did."

"Well, what of it?" What had he seen? But it was more important now to keep herself tough, not giving in for a second even though she was consumed by curiosity wondering what he'd seen.

"I know you don't want to hear this, but Seamus made the dream come to us. He's determined to see us married. I'm not sure why. I think he believes it will save me from myself. It's sort of his celestial mission." Jim grimaced on the word mission and then took a deep breath. He angled his body closer and bent his head until his lips met hers in a long slow kiss that sent

Megan's nerve endings out of control.

She broke away after a moment, her lips trembling.

Jim shook himself a moment, and then looked at her. He tried to recognize the emotions lingering on Megan's face. He hoped, in his heart of hearts, that she felt as he did.

"Do you realize how serious this is?" he asked, his voice barely audible above the noise from the highway. "I know it's past the time when I can live without you. Like it or not, there'll be a part of me that I leave behind if I go home and you stay here. And the problem is; can I live without the part of me I'll leave behind?"

"Surely, by the time you've gone back to Boston, you'll have changed your mind," she said, gazing out the side window, refusing to look at him.

Jim grasped her chin and turned her face to him.

"No, no I won't. Regardless of what Seamus says or does, I know this is what was supposed to happen. The dream was so real, and both of us had it, as if our life together were ordained. As if it were meant to be. You are a rare woman, Megan."

"But Jim…marriage, children? Wasn't that the last thing on your mind when you got on that plane in the States last week? Hadn't you been hurt by a woman and decided that your poor heart should rest a while? Wasn't that foremost in your mind, to leave it off with women until whenever?" she said, throwing her arms open wide.

"Now, where did you hear all that? Did Seamus tell you, or was I talking in my sleep?" Jim asked.

"I haven't any idea. I know this is too big and too monumental to be decided on the side of the road."

Jim turned and looked out the windshield, cringing

slightly when a huge truck whizzed by. The little car rocked in its wake, in danger of being tossed to the other side of the road.

"This is not the safest spot to have an amorous conversation." Jim drummed his fingers on the steering wheel a moment, then put the car into gear and moved onto the highway. They travelled along in silence for a while, the rain beating against the windshield, the wind buffeting the little car. Jim hummed tunelessly.

Megan's thoughts crowded all of it out until she heard Jim speak.

"Say, why don't you come back with me to the hotel tonight? We could get a nice dinner, a few drinks, and maybe…" Well, hell, it couldn't hurt to ask.

"And maybe nothing, boy-o. Don't you remember all the sound reasons why we shouldn't get involved?" She smiled to herself; now wasn't this just like a man?

"Things have changed since last night," he said as he stroked her hair before his roughened thumb moved slowly across her neck. Megan's breath caught in her throat as the subtle friction sent a riot of chills up her spine. It would take so little to fall into bed with him, so little and her resolve cracked by the second. And if she did, then what? Would she come away with yet another broken heart?

"Jim, I think…"

"Megan, we can't fight against something that's meant to be. I know I'm sounding like Methuselah, old-fashioned, and silly, but can't you see?" His voice was quiet and silky, and the sound of it touched her skin like warmed bed sheets on a cold night.

"Maybe the whole reason that I'm here and that we met is that we are meant to be. No matter how pragmatic you are, you know that things like people meeting and accidents that aren't really accidents happening are the puzzle pieces of the universe fitting together. For all intents and purposes, that is. There are no accidents, no coincidences. What did Einstein say? 'God doesn't play dice with the universe.' "

He moved his hand back to the steering wheel and held on tight, glad for the rough textured cover of the wheel. Pushing over the small bumps and points of the cover gave his hands something to do and helped focus his mind. He stared straight ahead, thinking he'd said too much. Quoting Einstein? He had spoken before his brain was in first gear. Jim saw Megan glance his way. She looked like she wanted to roll her eyes, but was too polite to do so.

Jim stared out the windshield as another huge truck rumbled past. This time, the truck seemed to take the little car along with it. It would be very prudent to move a little quicker in the slow lane. Not only for safety's sake, but it would keep him from feeling like an idiot as he rambled on about the great plan of the universe. As if he knew anything about that. He changed the subject.

"When we settle in tonight, we'll start working on the story, and if anything else pops up, you know, about the two of us; then I guess we can work on that, too."

"Very well." Megan cringed when another truck passed them, but sighed and turned to look out her window. Maybe if she put some distance between herself and Mr. O'Flannery, she could begin to think straight again.

"Would you like me to drive?" she asked as her shoulder came up and her head turned away from the rumbling truck.

"No, that's okay. How much farther do you think it is?"

"About another hour."

"Good, I'm getting really hungry. Is there a place to stop around here to eat?"

"Hmm. Maybe. Let me look at the map and you look for the next exit."

"Right-o, old chap," said Jim in a mocking English accent.

Megan raised an eyebrow at him and gave him a steady look before she turned her attention back to the map.

"Oh aye, let's go to Castle Pollard. It's twenty kilometers or so off the highway, but we can see the Abbey there. It's the one I did a story on."

"I read that," Jim told her.

"My story?"

"Yeah, I read it on the plane coming over. Very well done, I'll say."

Megan felt her face flush. "Thanks. It's very inspiring, that place. You know that the water actually flows uphill."

"Huh?" Jim glanced at her, looking at her lips and remembering what they felt like on his. He straightened in his seat and cleared his throat.

"There's a grand hotel there. They have wonderful food. We'll have lunch and then I can show you the abbey."

"Great, only we'll have to ask someone about our story or we won't be able to charge lunch to the Globe."

"Oh, silly man, I'll pay for lunch," Megan said with a laugh.

"Never. It's not in 'Gentlemanly Behavior 101.' "

Megan laughed again, still looking at the map.

"The next left exit, turn off." Megan glanced up at his profile. Could she ever become immune to those wonderful eyes and that hair? She tentatively reached out and brushed some hair back from his forehead. The silky strands ran through her fingers and refused to stay put.

"I know. It always does what it wants to regardless of what I try to do to it. When I was in college, I used to put that gel stuff on it so it wouldn't get down in my eyes. One summer, I gave myself a buzz cut because I worked for a landscaper. When there was no hair, it couldn't get in my face all the time."

"It's so soft. Well—" *Stop acting like an idiot Megan*, she told herself. "It's not far down this road, less than twenty kilometers to the north."

The silence settled over them in the little car. But Jim felt a prickling along the back of his neck. A prickling that could only mean one thing—Seamus.

"*Ah, yes, Fore Church and Benedictine Abbey. Founded around 650 AD,*" Seamus said as though he were reading from a guide book. "*St. Feichin, an Ascetic Monk, died there in 664 of the yellow fever. A well that has such a powerful current it is said to flow straight up, and the stream is one of what is known as 'The Seven Wonders of Fore.' Not a small wonder boy-o. But I don't believe there are any priests there these days. I suppose you could dedicate yourselves to one another at the church until we get back to Dublin and have a real priest say the words over ye.*"

Jim let out a huge sigh and broadcasted his message, silently but stridently. "*I thought I got rid of you. I was hoping desperately that I'd gotten rid of you.*

So what's the deal, why aren't you gone?"

"Well, I've been back to the old hearth upstairs. Been talking to the chaps about all this goings on down here, and they said—now I have this straight from the big guy himself—"

"You mean...?" Jim asked.

"No, not that high up. My superior. He said that I can help you with your other problems, supernaturally speaking, you know. But only the once. So when you ask, you'd best make sure that it is only the once."

"Cool. Okay, Seamus." Jim smiled, but he continued to focus his thoughts as loudly as possible to Seamus. *"You can stay, I might need you. But when I start kissing this girl, bug off, understand?"*

"Jimmy lad, there'll be no carnal knowledge without the blessings of a priest on my watch. But I may reconsider if you dedicate yourselves at the Fore Church. You have another ten kilometers to think about it." With that, Seamus pulled on both ear lobes and disappeared.

Jim sighed hugely. He didn't know or understand anything that Seamus was talking about. But he did know that he'd fallen for this woman, hook, line, and sinker, and there was no going back. He truly felt a cord had somehow inexplicably tied itself to his heart and the other end was tied to Megan. It was a very odd metaphor. But it was truly how he felt. If they moved apart from each other, the cord might rip out his heart. He knew he wanted Megan, and he needed no convincing to want to be with her forever. The prospect of being without her was becoming more and more daunting.

A step toward commitment and marriage was huge

and momentous and of inconceivable magnitude. How could he be sure that Seamus was who he said he was and that he had Heaven's blessings in this venture? Actually, not analyzing the hell out of it made the whole prospect seem extremely and strangely natural.

"What's the problem?" Megan asked.

"Nothing."

Chapter 21

Megan looked at him for a long moment. He had that leprechaun look again. Sometimes she worried about his sanity, and sometimes, she believed there actually was a Seamus standing there talking to him urging the two of them to get married.

Megan closed her eyes and breathed deeply. Suddenly, fragments of a dream floated through her mind, a tantalizing bit here, an almost remembered bit there. Then all at once the fog blew clear, and she saw herself as clearly as if she watched a scene in a movie. She was standing at a stove, stirring something in a pot. A little boy ran through the doorway of the kitchen. He had coal black hair and green eyes. The boy looked a lot like her father and his name was Seamus. Good God! How had that come into her subconscious?

She clicked her tongue and shook her head before she opened her eyes. She refused to think about what the baby on her hip looked like, even though his wee face peeked at her from around a corner in her subconscious.

Megan shifted in her seat and closed her eyes again. This was too silly by half. She sat quite still for a few moments, letting the rhythm of the tires off the pavement lull her into a relaxed, contented mood. They traveled for a few minutes before Megan opened her eyes and looked around.

"Ah, here we are. Let's stop here at the Moffat Arms and have a meal. I'm done in thinking of food and not having any," Megan said. "I don't think that I can wait till the abbey."

"Sounds good to me."

Jim parked the car, grabbed his briefcase, and opened the door for Megan. She could get used to having a gentleman around to help her out of cars and into rooms.

The Moffat Arms was perhaps eighteenth century, whitewashed, three storied, and with two chimneys. It had probably been built as an inn and remained so to this day. The front door opened into a small foyer that spilled into a cozy room. Huge wooden cross beams hung in the low ceiling, darkened by hundreds of years of wood smoke and tobacco. The floor creaked and groaned under their feet and seemed to be devoid of even surfaces or angles. In front of a fireplace that took up a good bit of the facing wall, tables and benches were placed in several conversational groupings. Jim ducked his head to pass through the door and stood for a moment, appreciating the ambiance of the place.

"And good day to you."

"Good day to you, too. What's on the menu?"

"We've a lovely lamb stew, just from the pot, it is." The man continued to wipe glasses and stare at Jim.

"You're American, are you?"

"Yes, I'm from Boston."

"Ah, home of the late Mr. Kennedy, is it?"

"Right. How about bringing us a couple bowls of that stew and two Guinness?"

"Right you are."

Megan and Jim seated themselves and only a few

minutes passed before a woman brought them their meal.

The stew proved very tasty and Jim had already finished when the barkeep came to their table, wiping his hands on a towel.

"You know there was a man here a bit ago. Had on a big coat and a hat, inside mind you. Wanted to know if there were any Americans in town. Thought he might be looking for you."

Jim and Megan looked at one another for a moment in stunned silence and then turned as one to stare at the keep.

Simultaneously, they spoke.

"When was he here?"

"Oh, been an hour or more. Told him it was the wrong time of year for tourists, but I did send him on to the abbey. Always brings in sightseers. Was he looking for ya? Have you lost him from somewheres?"

"Uh, yeah," Jim lied, nodding his head. "He's my cousin. We did lose him. I really appreciate it, mister." Jim shook the man's hand and then helped Megan on with her coat as they headed out the door. He dashed back to the table to drop some bills and looked at the publican before leaving.

"Thanks, mister," Jim told the barkeep again.

After, Jim turned on the engine and started driving toward the abbey. He turned to Megan. "Are you thinking what I'm thinking?"

She looked at him, her lips so tight they hurt. She gave him a swift nod but continued to grab onto the dashboard.

"I don't suppose you think he's our killer, do you?" Jim asked.

"You mean, do I think that Richard and the killer are one and the same? I don't know, but I do believe this one may be our man. You may have fantasized that you saw Richard. I mean, of all the men in Ireland, you think you saw Richard? Black Irish or no."

"Black Irish or no, my fanny, I told you last night that something big was about to happen. I knew it."

"Jim—"

"Jim nothing. God, I love it when I'm right."

"Oh, stick it," Megan said as she crossed her arms across her chest. "Maybe you are and maybe you aren't, no, turn here. Can you see the twin towers? Very unusual. Now I think we should split up and then we'll cover more territory in case he's about."

"Oh no. We're sticking together. Safety in numbers. You are going to be like a growth on my side." Jim stomped on the brakes and sent the loose gravel under the tires in all directions.

"Oh yuck, what a dreadful visualization," she shuddered.

"I mean it, Megan. We're going to stick together."

"Might I remind you that he doesn't kill women? And he doesn't kill the Irish, either." Megan threw her hands up in agitation, warming up to her tirade. "How did we go from point A to point Z without stopping somewhere along the rest of the alphabet? You see a man you think is the serial killer, kilometers off the beaten track, kilometers away from Dublin or the last place where a victim was killed, and you think it's got to be him. Ah Jaysus, Jim. Are you thinking that this serial killer has followed us to Fore Abbey? We've both gone off it, I say. The two of us have gone round the bend. So he's looking for you. Maybe he's looking for another American, and have you thought of that? St. Joseph, how can you possibly think that the killer from Sligo and from Dublin could be following us?"

"Because I told you, I saw that guy at the bar in the hotel. I know it was Richard. I've been up close and personal with our man Richard, remember? And the barkeep said he had a big coat and hat on in the pub, so perhaps it was his way of a disguise, so no one could say what he actually looked like. So you don't believe me? Fine. Whoever it is, is asking questions, and asking questions like they know I'm on to them. Maybe I want to find him so I can ask a few questions myself," said Jim as he moved to her side of the car, opened the door and grabbed her hand. He helped her out, pulled her to his side, and held on even though she shrugged back a bit. "I realize I'm going off as though I hadn't put all the facts together in a chronological and logical order, but I am telling you, these ideas had to come from somewhere. Maybe Seamus is helping after all. Maybe?" Jim shrugged and pulled Megan around and gave her a quick, hard kiss.

"But if it's Richard, he will be after you, because you're the Irish woman, get it?"

"No, I don't. But I'll play along since I've nothing better to do at the moment." Megan raised the back of her hand to her forehead in mock "saint pose" and grinned at Jim.

"Good, St. Megan. Now that we have that settled."

They turned to the twin-towered church and trudged over the gravel pathway and in through the semi-ruined stone walls. The church and outbuildings were laid out in perfect right angles. It should be quite a sight from the air, but up close it was a jumble of stones of many sizes. Jim thought the monks who constructed the place with fieldstone must have been unbelievably strong if they lugged two hundred fifty pound stones on a daily basis and fit them together.

For a ruin, it was totally original looking. Jim scanned the outside area. There were only a few people in a small parking lot, braving the cold and blustery day. The barkeep was right; the icy January wind did not lend itself to outdoor sight-seeing.

By the time they walked to the doorway of the roofless narthex, they were alone with the howling icy wind.

The church was well known for having two towers, one at each end; very unusual for a medieval church. The church itself was built on a terrace placed above a powerful well that had a current so strong that it gave the illusion of actually flowing upstream. Above the door's lintel, decorations had been etched deeply into the stone; symbols and pictures that must have taken years of painstaking labor and were now so worn away that it was hard to decide what they'd been, except for the shadowed image of a Greek cross.

"The lintel weighs between 54 and 72 stone, or that's 750 and 1,000 pounds to you, Yank." Seamus crossed his arms over his chest, tilted his head back, his eyes closed in superiority. *"There is a myth that St. Feichin actually prayed the lintel into place. Can ya imagine it? Ah, so grand."* The angel was so overcome with the excitement of the moment that Seamus swept his arms out in a grand gesture matching his words, lost his balance, although he was standing in mid-air, and fell backward.

Jim held in a chuckle and then shook his head,

hoping to give Seamus the hint. "The walls are so thick." Jim brushed his fingertips over the roughened stone. There were marks from numerous fires over the centuries.

"Ah, yes. The Abbey was burned twelve times between 771 and 1169. But did the Benedictines give up? I should say not!" Seamus's voice floated on the wind, but Jim caught every word.

Jim tried not to roll his eyes as they walked down a stone pathway.

"That's the well," said Megan. Her voice struggled to be heard above the wind. She gestured with her hand as they passed a stone structure, an enclosure near the ruined church's location.

"You see, the water flows uphill. It's what they call one of the Seven Wonders of Fore. Actually, it is an optical illusion, but I think it is grand if one can believe in things without seeing them. Kind of like faith, you know?"

Jim stood at the wall, gazing at the gurgling water that looked for all the world like it was a movie playing backward. The wind blasted him from behind, and despite his size he felt as though he might be pushed over. The wind's icy fingers sent chills up his backside. He raised his brow. "You mean like believing in Seamus?" He grinned at her befuddled look. "Got ya!" He laughed aloud, watching the expression on Megan's face go from surprised to miffed. "Let's duck in through the doorway. It's getting a little blustery out here."

Megan nodded, her cheeks numb from the cold—and embarrassment. Jim put his arm around her and led her into the nave. The chancel was slightly bigger but also roofless. They left the chancel and took the walk to the opposite towers. They were quite alone. It seemed everyone else had the good sense to stay in with a cup of tea.

"If someone is here, they'll be lurking around those two ruined towers," Jim said, pressing his mouth to Megan's ear so she'd hear him above the wind.

"Right, but if we go to the left, maybe he'll be to the right and then if we go to the right, then he'll be to the left. Do you catch my meaning?" Megan was intent on splitting up. She'd have to convince Jim that it was safe enough for them to do so. She didn't for a moment believe that the serial killer, the one who'd killed five people now and in all the major cities in Ireland, would be on this deserted field in this ruin of a church in the middle of January.

"Right. But safety in numbers." Jim thought a moment. "I'll tell you what, as long as I can see that red hair, then we'll split up."

"Done."

They both walked carefully around the crumbled bricks, trying to make as little noise as possible, but that was a fool's errand that they soon gave up. The wind whipped between the archways and cracks in the stonework, and the wind blew away the sound of their footsteps. They toured the right tower, and then walked together toward the left.

"There's a chapel in the hillside where the last Irish hermit stayed." Megan pulled on Jim's arm and raised her voice, and then gestured toward the small hillock in the back after they'd searched the open area thoroughly.

"Okay, let's go."

They trudged up the hill, bending their heads

against the cold. Megan wished she were back in the little car sharing Jim's body heat. She'd come to the Abbey last July. But the cold in January made it nearly impossible for her to put cognizant thoughts together.

They reached the door of a formidable stone structure. The walls must have been three feet thick and the door looked like one solid slab of wood with wooden and leather hinges. It must have taken a very strong man to even budge the door open a crack. And the interior would have been freezing cold and dark, even on the sunniest and hottest day of the year. Jim stooped to open it. He struggled for a moment and then looked up at Megan. She was practically on top of him, trying to stay out of the cold.

"It's locked," he said.

"Blast. I forgot. We need to get the key from the keep at the Fore Pub."

"We won't worry about it then. If we have to get a key, then so will the killer, or whoever it is that's looking for me."

"Come on. We'll go to the Abbey. It's not far across this field. The priests will give us a hot drink, and you can meet Father Timothy. He's the one I wrote the article about. He may even have something stronger for us than a hot tea." Megan wiggled what she was sure were frozen eyebrows at Jim.

They trudged down the path, their shoes crunching on the gravel and intermittent frozen vegetation. The breeze continued to gust, sometimes so strongly that it seemed to push them back down the path, and effectively slowed their progress to the abbey. Megan wished she had the fuzzy woolen hat she usually wore in the cold months. It was probably in the same place as her fuzzy woolen gloves. She shivered, crammed her hands deeper in her pockets, and pulled her head down into her coat as far as she could.

They moved down the path past a tree, stark against the winter landscape. The tree had only three branches.

"It's the Holy Tree," Megan said above the wind.

"What?"

"See, three branches." Megan held out her fingers in illustration before she crammed her hand hurriedly back inside her pocket. "Father, Son, and Holy Ghost," she said and then crossed herself absently.

"Right." Jim crossed himself as he eyed the tree. They continued to walk, shoulders hunched against the gale and doing their utmost to keep it from blowing them backward. Within minutes, very cold minutes, they arrived at the abbey. Most of the building, or rather the collection of small buildings, obviously built over a period of hundreds of years, were in ruins. Near the center of the area was a small, round two-storied structure surrounded by a curtain wall. Megan found the long string that hung on the outside of the door. She pulled it down with a hard yank. From inside, they could barely hear the faint tinkling of the bell. They waited, huddled in the space between the door jamb and the outside, sheltering a little from the wind.

Megan pulled the bell cord again, and again they waited.

The wind blew colder and a dense gray cloud moved over the tepid sun. Shivers raced down Megan's spine as she eyed the fickle sun in its retreat. A gust pulled at Jim's hat, until he had to grasp the bill with both hands to keep it from flying away.

Megan looked up, trying to shrug between the shivers. Jim looked at his watch. It was almost three in the afternoon. Surely, someone was at home.

Several more minutes of very cold waiting ticked by. Megan knew without looking or touching, that her nose was streaming and bright red. She was too cold to care. Finally, the door opened. It creaked and protested every centimeter of the way.

Chapter 22

The door opened the smallest bit. All Jim saw was one very brown eye staring at them through the crack.

"Aye, what will you be wantin'?"

"Father Timothy, it's me, Megan Kennedy."

"Ah, Miss Kennedy, grand, grand."

The door growled and groaned every centimeter it was pulled, but it opened at last. A priest in a brown monk's cloak, cowl, and hood pulled the door open all the way. Jim could see the man's deep-set brown eyes in his very wrinkled face.

Rain, as well as wind, began to pelt at them fiercely. The old priest only had to signal for the two to hurry across the courtyard and into an enclosed area.

Jim got brief impressions of a courtyard littered with leaves and branches, a few cracked benches, and walls that surrounded a barren winter garden. In the distance, he heard goats bleating below the sound of the wind racing around the corners. The old man stopped once more and put his shoulder to another door off the courtyard.

This door squealed in protest and Jim helped to shove it all the way open.

The trio quickly entered and with an effort, Father Timothy closed the door against the weather. Jim stood inside and dripped onto the flagstone floor while he looked around in amazement.

The cavernous room looked like it had been hollowed out of stone. The mortar covering the wooden framed walls had darkened to a gray-brown over the centuries. The room had a huge wood-burning stove on the farthest wall away from the door. In the center of the room was a marred but highly polished long table that could seat maybe twelve or fourteen. Herbs hung from the rafters and the musty smell of damp and of old men in less-than-clean wool robes overshadowed the woodsy scent of the herbs. Jim shrugged out of his overcoat and then helped Megan with hers.

Megan and Jim stood in the foyer as another priest, his cowl down and his hands tucked securely inside his sleeves, approached from the opposite end of the room and gestured for them to step closer to the stove.

"Ah, Miss Kennedy. I was telling Father Francis the other day how we had delighted so in your visit last summer. Come sit down and have a meal."

"Thank you, Father." Megan stepped into the room tugging on Jim's arm to follow.

They were shown places at the long table with high back chairs on each side. Two more priests hurried about, putting plates and spoons on the table. The priests filled mugs at each place with a beer-like liquid. Jim gave a surreptitious sniff. He'd hoped for something a little more substantial to ward off the cold. The damp, frigid air had made itself to home up Jim's spine, effectively giving him the shivers. He smiled at the priests and nudged Megan.

"Oh, this is my friend, Mr. James O'Flannery. He's come all the way from the States. We went to see the stream and the Holy Tree, and they quite impressed him."

"Mr. O'Flannery, is it?" The priest's eyebrows rose. His brown eyes twinkled, mumbling Jim's name under his breath and then a look of recognition played across his plain face. "A county Mayo name?"

"Why yes, Father Timothy. How did you know?" Jim could do nothing but smile at the little man. He was so personable and open.

Father Timothy laid a finger against the side of his nose and winked at Jim. "I'm a bit of a historian."

"Hardly, Father Timothy." Megan patted the old man's arm solicitously. "I've seen many a library, but none as complete as the one you've amassed."

"So kind, Miss Kennedy, so kind. Now, please pray with us and partake of our simple meal."

The four priests with Jim and Megan stood behind their chairs and Father Timothy blessed the food.

Once seated, they started with the savory soup. It was delightful and hot.

Jim nodded to Father Timothy. "Benedictine, eh? Surprised you're still here. Though, I'm glad you are. This meal is wonderful." Jim raised his mug to the priests in salute. "I read Megan's article. It seems you've had some rough times with the people in the area, as well as the church."

Father Timothy steepled his fingers. "There have been letters written to the head of the order about closing the monastery. 'Waste of money,' they say, 'waste of resources. What good do they do?' they ask. Then our good bishop reminded them that we have started an on-line shop to market our cheeses. We've a webmaster, the whole of it. We've had orders from all over Europe, but we're still in the red, what with two of the nanny-goats dying. It's been something to start the business. It's been a challenge, but no sacrifice is too small for our Lord."

"Right." Jim again raised the mug to his lips. The ale must have a high alcohol content. After he'd consumed only half of it, Jim felt his ears start to buzz. He abandoned the beer for the sampler of cheeses one of the brothers had placed in front of him. The smooth texture and delicate flavors were phenomenal. Jim decided right then and there to get the web address. His grandmother would love some of these cheeses for Christmas.

The abbey was dry and warm and the food first class. They ate companionably, speaking on about every topic when Jim felt the telltale prickle against the back of his neck. It could only mean one thing. He put down his spoon and looked around for Seamus. He could almost smell the little elf's tobacco. Seamus would keep himself under wraps for a while yet.

Jim cleared his throat. Maybe if he asked Father Timothy, he could get an answer that might help him with Seamus.

"Father Timothy, do you believe in guardian angels?" Jim said it plainly. He might as well get some solid professional advice about Seamus, and who better to ask than a Benedictine? If he remembered right, they were known for being quite tough, no-nonsense priests.

Father Timothy looked up in surprise, his bushy eyebrows raised. "Why, certainly, of course."

"Do you believe that they can change themselves into anything to convince you that they are a guardian angel?"

The priest looked at Jim and his expression was hard to decipher. Perhaps the old man thought Jim was as bonkers as Megan did. The lady in question cleared her throat loudly.

"I'm afraid I don't understand," Father Timothy answered.

"Well, say this angel comes to help a person out of a predicament, but when you inform him that you don't believe in guardian angels, he turns himself into something else, say…" Jim looked down into his soup bowl, trying hard to be nonchalant. "A leprechaun, for instance."

When Jim glanced at Megan, he noticed a becoming flush cover her from her eyebrows to the top of her sweater. Seamus harrumphed loudly and Jim was sure the whole room heard him. Father Timothy merely leaned forward, raising his eyebrows again.

"Now, I'd much rather believe in an angel than one of the wee folk."

"See, and didn't I tell ya. Sorry state about your religious training, James boy-o."

Jim ignored Seamus and continued. "But supposing this angel did appear, and the person he appeared to wasn't sure if he was trying to kill him or help him. What do you think?"

"Well, I believe that if the angel was sent on a particular mission that he'd do anything he could to accomplish it."

"Uh huh." Jim slowly nodded his head. He turned slightly and quirked an eyebrow at Seamus who'd appeared on the top of Jim's mug, before the leprechaun pulled on his earlobes and disappeared.

"Would it surprise you, Father, to know that there is an angel in this room right now?" Jim asked.

"Not at all, not at all. There are angels everywhere,

watching over us all the time." The brothers and priests all nodded in agreement.

"What do you suppose they look like?" Jim felt Megan's foot collide with his shin, and he stifled a grunt.

Father Timothy consulted the clock on the wall of the kitchen. "Sorry, Mr. O'Flannery, we can't talk now. We'll bring this up later. But now, it's time for vespers."

The priests gathered up their plates, bowls, and other utensils and dumped them in the old-fashioned sink filled with soapy water.

Without saying a word, they led Jim and Megan through a small courtyard and into a chapel.

It was an ancient place, what had Seamus said— parts of it had been built before the ninth century. There was one stained glass window that looked to have been repaired several times. The cracks in the stonework had been patched with gray mortar giving the walls a sense of impermanence. Some of the ends of the benches were held up with stones and they creaked alarmingly as Jim settled his big frame into one.

"Now's the time, boy-o."

"Now's the time for what, Seamus?"

"To dedicate yourselves. You know you love each other, now don't you?"

"Seamus, I'm about to hear vespers and I want to concentrate, now bug off."

"Jay-sus, always talking about those insects."

Jim choked back a laugh and was rewarded with an elbow in the ribs by Megan. She ducked her head quickly to one side with a "Shh!"

"I know, but my angel's giving me trouble," Jim

whispered in her ear.

She rolled her eyes to the ceiling before she looked down again.

Sometime during the *Agnes Dei*, Jim reached over and took Megan's hand.

She turned and looked at him, a smile trembling on her lips.

She was magnificent. He'd been in Ireland less than a week, but now he didn't know how he could ever live without her. She was a rare woman, indeed. He sighed and continued to hold her hand as they left the pew to receive the Eucharist.

Father Timothy smiled at them knowingly as they knelt before him and he offered them the host and then the communion wine.

He blessed them both and it took no stretch of the imagination for Jim to feel like he'd just gotten married. Slowly he said the words in his mind, "*I, Jim, take thee, Megan...*"

Seamus knelt next to Jim with folded hands. He had the look of one in devout prayer and his expression was very smug.

For a moment, Jim looked at him. He turned his head back to the altar and with the back of his hand, gently swatted Seamus off the kneeler. No leprechaun was going to spoil his imaginary wedding.

Megan looked at the handsome man kneeling next to her and it took so little for her to feel the vows come to her mind. "*I, Megan, take thee, James Xavier...*"

****

It was well after dark when they finally left the abbey. The priests were wonderful and kind, but they couldn't house Megan unless it was an emergency. Jim and Megan decided to travel back to the Moffat Arms to get a room.

Megan let out a huge sigh as they rode along in the dark.

"So what's that for?"

"Oh, I don't know. I've had the loveliest day. Seeing Father Timothy again did me a world of good, and then there was this American that seemed quite taken with our Seven Wonders of Fore."

"Yeah, but what does he know?" Jim said, thinking instead of how he was taken by the lovely Megan. Churning-backward streams be damned. He looked at her out of the corner of his eye and noticed a wisp of that lovely hair flutter about her neck in the airflow of the car's heater. Her skin simply glowed. It occurred to him that it was glowing from the inside, like a candle burning and never going out.

"I wouldn't sell the man short, you know. He seems quite on the bright side to me, he does," Megan said in her singsong lilting way.

"Glad you think so."

He wanted to tell Megan how he'd felt kneeling before the priest in that ancient little chapel. How he'd heard the marriage vows rumble through his head. But then again, perhaps not. One can't rush these delicate matters. She'd probably throw something at him if he brought up Seamus or marriage or anything more serious than buying a Guinness.

"I suspect we can have separate rooms this night," Megan said.

"Gosh, Megan, I was getting used to you snoring."

Megan promptly whacked him with her purse. "I think staying away from each other and temptation is what we should do."

"Now who said I was tempted by you?" Jim's face was of a complete innocent.

"You did, you silly man."

"Oh, okay." *Tempted* did not have the right connotation for the way he felt about Megan. He'd have to get out his thesaurus and try to match a word about how he felt. His feelings for her raged like a wildfire that he didn't want to quell.

The wind and the rain battered the little car as they slowly drove down the rural, one lane road. They were alone in the car; so alone that Jim felt that he and Megan were the last people on earth. It was as though this little city on the Atlantic was at the ends of the earth.

Chapter 23

The drive back to the Moffat Arms was smooth and uneventful. Even the rain that had pummeled them mercilessly for the past ten miles began to cooperate. For once it came straight down and not sideways. Neither of them felt the need to speak, wrapped in a soft cocoon of silence punctuated only by sudden gusts of wind and the rain on the roof.

Jim took the next curve in the road smoothly, when he noticed someone coming up behind them. The car following them accelerated until its bright blue LED high beams pierced the darkness of the one-lane road. He frowned; he and Megan were not the only ones on this lonely, desolate bit of country byway.

The other car swerved to the right, almost colliding with their rear bumper before it moved behind them. Jim jerked the car to the left and lay on his horn. Maybe it had all been a terrible mistake. Maybe the other guy would leave them alone. But their pursuer rammed into their rear bumper with tremendous force. Megan was thrown back against her seat and then forward with the impact. She gave a sharp yelp, righted herself, and then clung to the dash and door handle.

"My God, what is happening?"

"I think somebody's trying to kill us." Jim had to get them away from the other car. He stomped on the accelerator, but he couldn't outrun their pursuer. On the attack, the assailant rammed into their rear bumper, throwing them back against their seats. Megan grunted in pain as her shoulder hit the door frame.

"Megan, hold on!"

Jim had nowhere to go. He glimpsed the front and the side in the small periphery of the headlamps. On either side of the narrow lane was at least a five foot drop, a sheer fall into gullies that ended in piles of rocks and mud. If their car was forced off the road, they could easily be killed. Jim's mind flashed through scenarios and possible resolutions. There were damn few.

Jim glanced in the rear view mirror. The lights from their assailant very quickly inched closer and closer. He floored the car, urging the small engine to go above and beyond. He took the next curve so fast; it felt like they'd gone up on two wheels. But the car's rear stayed on the road.

There was no time to be afraid, no time to do anything but work the problem.

The road straightened and the lights from their attacker shone brighter and more intensely. Jim saw nothing but the lights almost blinding him.

On the straight of the road, the more powerful car gained speed and again inched closer and closer. Jim stomped down on the accelerator and they pulled away, but only in feet, and then only in inches. The next turn came up fast. A sharp curve to the left. Jim tried to tap the brakes before the turn. But as he slowed, their pursuer accelerated and crashed into them. Jim and Megan were thrown back in their seats and then forward into the dashboard. Jim pushed down on the accelerator for all he was worth. This time he slid sideways into the sharp curve in the road and he began to spin. The front end whipped around, just missing their assailant's front bumper. Jim tapped on the brakes and turned the wheel sharply to the right. They floundered and continued to slide sideways. Seconds ticked by. Each second stretched out, feeling like years before Jim was able to get the car pointed forward. The other driver struggled to maintain control on the muddy road. He wasn't giving up.

Megan jerked her head around for that split second, and tried to see who was in the other car.

"Who the bloody hell is it? Why are they doing this?" She yelled above the rain and the tires squealing.

Suddenly, the next sharp curve emerged in front of them. With slow, smooth movements, Jim slowed the car into the turn and then hit the accelerator, tearing down the road, attempting to outrun the other car.

The rain poured down, sheeting the windshield, but he had no clear line of sight. Jim pushed the wipers on high over and over but rain blurred across the windscreen and obstructed what little he could see. He strained forward and stared through just the few square inches to the left of the steering wheel. His breath came in a quick, sharp tattoo and oxygen was a commodity he could not bargain for.

He slowed his breathing. *Don't lose focus. Keep us in one piece until you can find a way to escape.* He had to save Megan.

The rain lashed down. Where was the curve? Was it left or right?

The headlights from the other car flooded the inside of the cabin with harsh glaring blue light. Their tormentor was still gaining on them. Jim hit the accelerator again. Maybe his little box of a car could still outrun whatever was behind them.

Jim could see so little. All of his concentration, all of his energy focused on one task; he must stay on the road. The thought flitted through his mind; *we are going to die right here. We are going to die before...* but he put the thought away.

He glimpsed it ahead through the sheeting rain; a little grassy area on the right-hand side of the road. Sensing the shoulder was wider than it appeared, he raced onto what he hoped was grass, and slammed on the brakes. The car skidded. The rear end whipped out and a portion of the left rear tire spun in the air at the lip of the gully.

Their assailant flew past in a blur of water and mud.

The engine sputtered and died.

Rain lashed at his face from the half opened window. He laid his head back. He had to slow his breathing and heartbeat; he had to think.

He leaned forward and with stuttered motions, closed the half open window. He laid his head back again, trying to control his breath and clear his mind.

Two seconds passed and then three. He opened his eyes.

The rain beat against their roof and hood, drowning out every other sound. He didn't hear the other car and he could see nothing in the blacker-than-black rain.

He put his hand on Megan's shoulder and shook her gently. She turned her head but said nothing. He squeezed her shoulder briefly, letting his arm fall back down into his lap.

"We have to leave. He may come back looking for us. We have to leave."

She nodded and said nothing.

Jim re-started the car and with a little bit of persuading, the still-spinning tire made purchase with the ground, and the car slowly pulled out onto the one-lane road.

Chapter 24

It was another twenty minutes before they reached the Moffat Arms. Jim parked, pulled on the emergency brake, killed the engine, and laid his head on the seat back for a moment of peace. He turned in his seat to face Megan.

"Are you okay?" He waited for her to respond, but she only nodded.

"I don't know who it was, or why. All I can think of is, well, I don't know."

"Maybe the killer knows we're getting close, or thinks we are," Megan replied. "We'll have to head off to Dublin tomorrow. Maybe something has happened on the city front that we've not learned about. I'll have to phone in to the night desk when we get in."

Megan's voice sounded distant and reedy. The impact of the attack, like a thing, crowded through their minds. Her voice trailed away in the swell of the gusts battering the car. Leaves and twigs rustled and scraped against the tarmac of the parking lot. They waited, each lost in their own thoughts. The weather began to calm: the wind seemed to blow itself out, the rain slowly stopped, and a heavy mist clung to the windshield in great drops and rivulets.

The intermittent gusts whined and pushed between the cracks of the doors and windows. Still, they didn't move, but looked at one another, just visible in the street lights outside the hotel.

Their breathing had slowed to normal when Jim leaned toward Megan and their lips met. His tongue followed the curve of her mouth and she trembled at the intimacy of his touch. His hand came up and stroked the side of her face. She slowly moved her arms around his back and pulled him forward.

"Megan—" Jim broke off the excruciating kiss. He sat back, his head against the seat.

"No, it's all right." She touched his cheek once and then turned, opened the car door, and got out.

Jim slammed his hand against the steering wheel. It was getting to be too much. Frustration mounted each and every minute. Not only frustration, but the attack, Seamus, seeing the priests, and all the dreams; it was too much to digest.

In that split second alone in the silent car, he realized that he need not be torn by indecision. No, he knew now more than he ever had that he would stay with her and make her his. Maybe it was the terror of their close brush with death, or maybe Seamus had finally gotten to him. But he knew as well as he knew there was a backward running stream, that he loved her and wouldn't be able to return to his old ways, back to his old safe life with no complications and no commitments. Megan was his commitment now.

He had to convince her of that.

He left the car and retrieved their suitcases from the back before slamming the door.

Megan walked so quickly toward the hotel that he had to sprint to catch up with her. She was already at the desk checking in before he reached her side. She turned, and with a too-bright smile, held out a key to him.

"You've got room 3B, and I'm in 2C."

"Does that mean we're not even on the same floor?"

"It does."

"Megan," he said as he pulled her toward him and away from everyone within earshot. "Are you all right? I think we need a strong drink to ward off the shock we had."

"I think you're right. Let's leave the suitcases here and we can pick them up when we're ready to go to our rooms."

"Okay, sounds good." Jim didn't like the way his hands trembled and the way his legs felt, as though they might fold right under him, but Megan managed to turn smartly and walk to the pub.

They sat at the bar and Jim ordered. He took off his coat and looked at the mud on his right sleeve, shrugged his shoulders, and downed the whisky as soon as the glass touched the bar in front of him. He ordered another.

They drank in silence, not looking at or touching one another. The close call and their close proximity began to overwhelm them both. They left the bar, not touching, but walking close together. When they reached the desk, Jim retrieved their luggage and they walked the two flights of stairs to 2C.

Jim took Megan's key, unlocked the door, and ushered her in.

He turned to her, helping her with her overcoat and then her blazer. He took off his tie and jacket and with trembling fingers, took the combs from her hair and pulled her into a close embrace.

"To think I almost lost you," he murmured into her hair. His kiss was long and slow, filled with desperation and promise.

She was more beautiful than he could ever have imagined. A rosy flush tinted her almost translucent skin; the veins below her ear pulsed rhythmically. He would never tire of the sight of red-gold hair falling across her white shoulders.

He looked deeply into eyes that never wavered from his own.

"I know I love you. I'll always love you," he said, his lips barely touching hers as he pledged his love, as his hands moved to caress and honor her.

She sighed and ran her hands gently down his face, into his hair, and down his back.

He pulled his head back to gaze at her and watched as her eyes fluttered open. "Megan," he whispered. And the name was a pledge more than a plea.

"Oh, Jim," she breathed the words, her sweet breath coming out to flutter on his cheeks. His kisses drifted between the valley of her breasts.

****

A niggling thought pushed and prodded to the front of her mind. She pushed it aside, but still the thought took hold and would not let go; *he will leave, go to America, and you will be left behind*. But the all-encompassing emotion, the passion, and the pleasure that filled her soon pushed the thought aside.

Chapter 25

Megan slept deeply, her breath puffing out rhythmically. Jim rested on a pillow, inches from hers and watched her sleep for a very long time.

Quietly, he got up to go to his room. He had to think. The relationship with Megan, the stories they were writing, their near miss in the car; it was all happening too fast.

He unlocked his room door to find a double bed, dresser, and a sink with a mirror flush against the far wall. He threw his suitcase and jacket on the bed and crossed to the window. There was little available light to see anything distinctive, but the impressions were of a road in front, a field, and tiny lake on the other side of the road. Jim could see the unmistakable outline of a wooded area that flanked the building on either side.

The cold and the urgency to get to the church had kept him from even looking at the lake that afternoon. Maybe he'd have a chance before he left the next morning.

He couldn't really care less now. His lips curved in a smile. He hadn't thought he'd come to Ireland and get a bride to go along with his newly acquired leprechaun. His heart felt light and warm. It had been so long—no, he'd never experienced this contentment before. The elation bordered on giddiness. It was Megan. Megan—and he'd never tire of her. It was as though they were made for each other. She was a rare woman, a rare woman, indeed.

Wait...Seamus! It had to be. Seamus had told him from the beginning that he needed to fall in love, to settle down, and then all would be right with Jim's world. But even if it was Seamus's doing, the end result was the same; he loved Miss Megan Kennedy and intended to wed her as soon as the law would allow. He already believed he was married. The Vespers service at the abbey had been the real thing between him and Megan, a dedication, a marriage. Was it only a week ago that Jim would have railed against such a notion? How did that old song go?

"What a difference a day makes;
twenty-four little hours."

Wasn't it the truth?

Jim washed and changed into a pair of gray sweats and heavy socks; regardless of all the extra clothes, he still shivered. The dampness went right through him on this island nation, and chilled him from the inside out. A boy from Boston chilled, who knew? The feeling was as strange as seeing a backward running stream.

After a sigh and a shake of the head, he decided that it was time to get to work and quit thinking so vividly about what had happened in the abbey and stop sighing over what happened in Megan's room. It was almost eleven p.m. and he hoped she'd sleep through. She needed the rest so he could go back to her room and they could pick up where they'd left off. He shook his head abruptly. *No, you nitwit, give the poor girl a chance to get used to you, after all.*

****

Jim hurriedly looked back over his notes from the

forensics people in Boston. No fibers, no fingerprints, and the determination that the murderer was six feet two and left-handed.

This killer was smart. Very smart.

Jim bundled up his paperwork and put it away.

Why was the guy after Americans? Why? If he could determine a suspect with a hatred for Americans, then maybe he could find the motive. Right now, there was no motive except for the one in the killer's head.

He needed to find the killer's motive. That is, if the killer wasn't a six foot two, left handed Irish loony.

Was there a motive?

Chapter 26

Megan awoke before midnight and stretched like a contented cat. She was sorry Jim hadn't stayed, but glad he'd gone as well. If she were by herself, it would be far easier to make some decisions. Maybe she could make up her mind about what had happened and about what she wanted. It would be far easier to do that thinking without those wonderful blue eyes staring at her right through to her toes.

She threw on her robe and made her way to the bath at the end of the hall. The hotel was very quiet. What patrons there were on this cold, blustery night were sleeping. The heat from the shower warmed her considerably, but couldn't wash away the wonderful, fulfilled feeling she had that had taken up residence inside her since early that evening. She smiled to herself.

She'd never imagined that having...well, that having such emotional sex with someone, loving and passionate could be so, so...what was the word she was looking for? Ah, satisfying. She giggled at herself as she wiped the condensation from the mirror. She pushed her fingers through her hair, over and over again, holding it off her neck and toweled the ends dry. Then she opened the door and peeked out; hmm, no one in the hall, so she hurried back to her room and unlocked the door.

Not feeling at all sleepy, she hummed tunelessly to herself and paced the confines of the small room. Something was bothering her. Some thought she couldn't quite put her finger on. She stopped in front of the dresser mirror and stared at herself, and then looked down at her left hand. What was it? She couldn't quite—

She felt married. To be honest, she didn't know what it was to be married, but there was something in her that was akin to commitment to Jim.

It all boiled down to that. She'd said vows that afternoon in the chapel, perhaps they'd been to herself, but still, they were vows that wove around her heart, the bonds even now tightening, but in a very pleasant way. Did Jim feel the same? It seemed so funny now, remembering the dream, and remembering how it was to kneel beside him.

"Oh bother," she muttered as she threw herself face down on the bed. "What the bloody hell am I supposed to do? Love the man until he goes back across the water, never to return? My heart wouldn't survive. No, it wouldn't." She pushed her face into the pillow, breathing in the feathers and dust and sat up and promptly sneezed.

A loud pop reverberated and a puff of smoke swirled about the center of the room. Megan gasped and stumbled across the floor until the door pressed against her back.

Her ears buzzed loudly and her heart hammered. The buzzing grew louder and she put her hands up to cover her ears and squeezed her eyes shut. She curled up into a tiny ball. Her eyes opened and stared at a strange apparition appearing inside the swirl of smoke.

It was a *whateverthehellitwas.*

"Now, now, colleen. None of that."

She heard a voice, but it was not speaking to her inside her head. It was as audible as—she'd heard that voice before, but there was a voice in a puff of smoke. She squeezed her eyes closed; maybe if she didn't see it, whatever it was, then she wouldn't have to believe that *it* was actually there.

She made her mind go blank. All this confusion—it was all the emotions crowding her good sense out of her head; she was hallucinating. The need for air burned her lungs and she drew in a large breath. She opened one eye a tiny crack. Something moved on the bed. Her body turned rigid, and she felt she'd faint at any second. She'd awakened as the star of a bad horror movie.

"And why don't you open your eyes and have a look at your old Uncle Seamus?"

"Because I don't believe in you, that's why." The words came out in a croak.

"Ah, but your heart tells me different, young lady. Now, now, open your eyes. You can see me in your mind anyway, don't you know."

Megan's heart thudded painfully against her chest. And still, she squeezed her eyes shut tight and held her breath. Her oxygen-robbed lungs tried to open and contract. She made herself inhale and heard the sound of her own breath rattle in the quiet of the room. Could she open her eyes? Would she lose her mind if she did, like that fellow in mythology who'd looked at the monster and went stark, staring mad? Crap, if there was really a leprechaun standing on her bed, she'd have to apologize to Jim for all those things she said to him about being crazy.

She opened one eye. A man, the size of a school child's ruler, dressed in a green suit, stood in the center of her bed, leaning on a cane with one foot crossed over the other.

"St. Joseph," she whispered more to herself than to the little fellow waggling his eyebrows at her.

"Come sit down, lass. We've a bit of talking to do."

Slowly, Megan uncurled from her place on the floor until her legs spread out in front of her.

"Now, I think it's high time we introduce ourselves. I had to wait for the proper time, don't you know. The proper time when your mind would be open to the possibility of meself."

The leprechaun began to pace back and forth across the coverlet. Megan raised her hand to her face and pushed her slackened jaw shut with her fingers.

"I'm an angel," he said, standing very tall, and then bowing at the waist with great formality. "I may seem not to be, but I am. You see, yon man's religious training was so distant in his past that I had to choose to be something that he could believe in."

"But one of the little people?"

"Aye, sad state of affairs," he said, taking off his cap and scratching the thick red hair behind his left ear. "Now, accordin' to what I've been told upstairs, my territory, don't ya know, the two of you should be married and live happily ever after. I'm not saying that it will be easy, no, I'm not. Life on this planet is hard for any who lives here, I should know. 'Twas two hundred years past and I lived here meself," he said, emphasizing his statement by leaning toward Megan and nodding his head.

"Yes, I lived in a terrible place near Ballycastle. Terrible, terrible. Children dying of starvation and sickness of the potato famine, men dying in the ditches for want of food." He shook his head again and Megan saw sadness from the little man's downcast eyes. His obviously painful memories made her forget for the moment that she really didn't believe in him at all.

"Yes, but what's it all got to do with Jim?" Without thought, she got up and crossed the room to sit on the floor at the foot of the bed. Seamus came near her and sat down, swinging his legs back and forth as he stared off at an invisible place across the room.

"Well, ya see, the poor boy had lost his faith in God, in the Church, in all of it. So I was assigned to help him to come back into the fold, as it were, and I decided that what he needed was a lovely Irish lass and that should do the trick, right enough. But he's been resistin' my suggestion right along. Stubborn. It's the Black Irish, don't you know. A good many of 'em are like that as well."

"So I'd heard," Megan commented dryly.

"Now, your job, my dear, is not to worry about a thing. Your Uncle Seamus will see to all of it, I will. Remember what it says in the Good Book—He even knows every lovely red hair on that head of yours. According to the boys upstairs, your hearts were in the right place when you were at the abbey and you've been dedicated to one another. Good thing, too. Didn't come a moment too soon, if you know what I mean," said Seamus, waggling his eyebrows at her. "They demand a lot less rigmarole up there than they do down here. The ways of man get much too complicated whereas the ways of God are simple and direct. It's the humans, don't ya know, trying to think like they think God wants them to think."

"So we are dedicated?" Megan faltered with the question. She felt her jaw slacken again, and she snapped it shut. Married? To Jim?

"Aye, so ya are. Now, I think I'll pop into Jimmy's and see how he is. Ta-ta." With that the leprechaun pulled on both earlobes and disappeared.

Chapter 27

After the last of the green smoke cleared from the top of her bed, Megan finally managed to stand. Her legs held her up only because they were pushed against the mattress. She went to the tiny sink against the wall and washed her face and ran a comb through her hair. They were dedicated to one another, as good as married, as good as—what?

Things could get out of hand. Yes, definitely out of hand. She had to get herself together. Did the man love her enough to stay in Ireland? Did she love him enough to move to the States?

Things were most decidedly out of hand.

She couldn't give up everything for him. Could she?

But, said a little niggling voice in the back of her mind, *how are you going to live without him?*

Megan walked to the door with every intention of going to see Jim. She stopped, her hand on the knob, a half turn before the latch clicked. She moved back to the sink and brushed her teeth.

Chapter 28

She deliberately made her mind go blank on her way up to the next floor. She wasn't sure what she was going to say to Jim, or even why she was going, but she had to see him now.

Maybe if she spoke to him, all of this turmoil in her head would sort itself out.

Slowly, she walked to the stairs and took them to the third floor, each step dragging, half in dread, half in anticipation. She traversed the hall, looking at the door numbers until she came to number three.

Her heart thudded almost painfully, and she wondered about the possibility of a twenty-seven-year-old woman having a heart attack. Her hand lifted to knock, and she stepped back. She raised her hand once more, and finally knocked.

Almost immediately, the door swung open. Jim stood with his hand on the knob, but his attention was locked on a sheaf of papers in his hand.

"Yes," he said, and then he finally looked up. "Oh, Megan, honey, how are you?" His look warmed as he regarded her. Megan felt the heat in his look travel down to her toes and she knew she'd melt into a big puddle if she let herself. Could she ever get used to those eyes? She certainly hoped not.

"Come on in." Jim reached out and pulled her into the room, buzzing a kiss against her temple. His hand held hers tightly like he was loath to let her go.

Megan didn't move, and she clasped and unclasped her hands behind her back. She felt unaccountably shy. Jim stopped in mid-stride and turned to look her full in the face.

Megan's expression perplexed Jim. This shy, coy girl seemed quite uncharacteristic to Megan's usual go get 'em personality, too much so.

He stood for a moment and watched her. She shifted from foot to foot, her gaze locked on the floor. Megan had changed from charging female journalist to virginal nun. In thirty minutes, no less.

"So, what gives?" he asked. He reached for her and planted a kiss on her lovely compliant lips. He held her close and his touch wandered up and down her back. She reached around him and pulled him to her. He felt her hips connect with his solid parts. Too solid. She finally looked up at him and her flush deepened.

"What is it Megan?"

"I...um...I..."

"Yes?"

She pulled away slightly as she continued to clench and unclench her hands. She pursed her lips for a second, walked to the window, looked out, and sat on the edge of the bed. She cleared her throat, took a deep breath and spoke.

"I had a visitor."

"Is it Richard? Is he here? Where is he? Don't worry Megan, I'll make sure you're safe. I'll kill him if he's hurt you."

"No, no, not Richard."

Megan looked down again and heaved a big sigh. "It was Seamus."

She said it simply, only the name. This time she did look up at him; waiting, watching carefully to see what he would do or say.

"Seamus?" Jim sat down with a plop on the bed. He reached for her hand and squeezed her fingers before he brought them to his lips in a quick but tender kiss. "Jeez. You'd think that little *thing* could bug off and leave us alone."

"Are you supposing that he is what he says he is?" She looked at him now more than she had since she'd knocked on the door.

"You know, I thought about that. What if he's some demon from Hell or from another planet, or—?" Jim ran his fingers through his hair and then braced his elbows on his knees, steepling his fingers under his chin in thought.

"Demon from Hell is it? I'll be thankin' ye to read the parchment I have before me." Seamus popped into the room on a puff of smoke, with his arms akimbo. He was a mere fraction of his usual size, which made his voice sound like he'd inhaled helium. He held a huge scroll in his right hand, abruptly snapped his wrist, and the scroll rolled open. The parchment was filled with bits of sparkling dust and written in gold lettering.

"To all those present.
Bear witness that the bearer of this
Identification is:
Seamus, Angel Second Class
With all the rights and duties thereto presented."
Michael, Archangel

Jim grabbed the parchment from Seamus. He had to see this. The parchment had a strange feel to it as though it were made of spun glass. He looked carefully at both sides, running his fingertips over it and feeling the edges before he turned to smile at Megan, gave her a wink, and then said to Seamus, "Great, Seamus, but how do we know that you didn't pick this up at a second-hand shop somewhere?"

"Me? Try to be foolin' ya?" The leprechaun's usually squeaky voice rose at least an octave. The little man's already flushed face turned even redder. "Really lad! And didn't I tell you that I'm your six times great uncle? And wouldn't an uncle be helpin' a poor lad like yourself and not be trickin' him?"

Seamus's voice grew louder, his face redder as he paced quickly up to Jim and Megan and threw his arms out wide.

"And I might as well be a-tellin' ye that Michael the Archangel doesn't look a thing like that Travolta fella in the movie. He's redheaded like the lass, here. Irish, he is."

Seamus's face had turned such a vivid, bright red that Jim was afraid he'd have a stroke. *Wait, can an angel have a stroke?* Before Jim could think another fraction of a second longer on this dilemma, Seamus nodded once with vehemence. He grabbed the parchment from Jim. Again, he snapped his wrist and the parchment rolled shut like a roller blind. Then the little angel plunked down on the tiny bit of grass spread out in front of the very tiny church that had conjured itself up. Seamus sat with his nose stuck high in the air and his arms crossed over his chest.

Megan's eyes grew large and her jaw dropped in surprise.

The performance could have won Seamus an award while at the same time flabbergasting Megan. She

216

turned to look at Jim who wore a cynical expression. His cynicism, surprisingly, stunned her more than Seamus's recital. Hands on hips, she turned to Jim, nose to nose.

"Now here, O'Flannery, you can't be hurting his feelings, surely. Now, now, if the...er...man has told you that he's your great uncle—"

"Six time's great, love," Seamus corrected as he gave a sketchy little bow.

"Aye, six times." Megan put her hands on her hips and gave Jim a frosty look. "Then why can't you believe him?" Megan's brogue grew broader with each word only adding to Jim's confusion.

"Ah, he's an American, colleen. And they don't seem to make notice of such things," said Seamus, heaving a great sigh and then speaking conspiratorially behind his hand.

"Oh aye, so I've noticed." Megan rolled her eyes to the ceiling before she again sat on the bed.

Jim looked from Megan to Seamus. This turn of events had him bamboozled.

"Now the two of you are on me? Great, just great."

"Now, now—none of that."

"Listen, Seamus, bug off, will you? Let me and Megan work this out for ourselves, okay? And no peeking, got it?"

"Very well. I think it's a wonderful idea. Now, you two have a memorable honeymoon. We needn't be going back to Dublin for a few days, aye? Such a lovely place, Castle Pollard. We might be visiting the abbey again before we leave. Such a magnificent place, reminds me of me own church in Ballycastle."

The leprechaun smiled with self-satisfaction,

bowed deeply from the waist, pulled on both earlobes, and he and the church disappeared in a cloud of smoke. Jim heard a tiny laugh waft through the room like a wisp of fragrance. He turned to Megan. He felt like he'd been sucker punched. He walked to the wall looking carefully at the place Seamus had disappeared. Then he turned back to Megan, his nose a fraction of an inch from hers.

"Hon-ey-moon?"

The word was drawn out in a heavy croaking sound reminiscent of summer bullfrogs in rural Massachusetts. He felt a little weak in the knees, but decided sitting next to her would be a mistake. Because if he sat next to her, well, could it be true?

Megan turned those green eyes on him, only peeking at him through her thick lashes.

"What's this about a honeymoon?" he asked again, sure that he'd heard wrong. Hadn't he?

"Um." She cleared her throat, and then she cleared it again. "Seems at the abbey, according to Seamus that is, we dedicated ourselves to one another and that's all that is required." The last of the sentence came out in a little breathless gasp.

Chapter 29

"Whoa! Are you telling me that in the eyes of the Almighty, we are now husband and wife?" Horror piled on top of horror and the word *wife* came out of Jim's mouth with a decided but unwarranted squeak. "Now, who said we were getting married? At the abbey, I mean."

Something in Megan's eyes and furrowed brow told him that he'd stepped in it, all the way up to his knees. He actually sounded like he didn't want to get married, that he was sorry that it had happened. But when he took a breath and slowed down a moment, he wasn't, he really wasn't. Then why was he acting like he'd been shocked by a cattle prod?

"Listen, Kennedy, are you ready for this? I mean, is this what you wanted—I mean when you wanted it?"

He knew he was making a mess of it, the explaining, but somehow he couldn't seem to stop himself. He was like a lamb following the leader off the cliff's edge. He couldn't shut his big mouth. He did want to marry her. Hadn't he been thinking about this for days, with or without Seamus? He'd said too much. Too much. Megan's face crumbled and a tear coursed down one cheek. Quickly, she dashed the tear away with the back of her hand. Her face changed and glowed with anger. She doubled up her fist and let him have it right in the breadbox.

"You cretin, I thought it was what *you* wanted. I'll find my own way back to Dublin." She strode quickly to the door, jerked it open, and slammed it ferociously. Jim staggered back, fell on the bed, and held his stomach.

Oh brother, had he done it now. He had the distinct impression that there'd be no more honeymoon for him.

Chapter 30

"I'll give you fifty euros now and another hundred at the end of the week. Will that suit?" he asked, pulling the large, brown raincoat about him. He looked as though he were warding off a chill; or asserting his anonymity.

"Oh aye, 'tis lovely." The old woman looked at him shyly, her eyes, the color of mud, peered up at him. She looked as though she hadn't washed in days, and her dress smelled to high heaven. He didn't really care, as long as he could get the place fixed up in time for Megan.

"Where's to buy a bit of bread and beer about?"

"Oh, down to the corner, it's O'Grady's, though I'll be telling you to watch the place. Grimy it is, oh, aye. Not as clean a place as I'm thinking ye should have for food and such."

"Well, hmm, yes, I suppose," he said, looking again at the woman's fingernails as she combed her fingers through her clumped, greasy hair.

"I'll be bringing my wife back here in a few days. You'll have the place cleaned up by then?"

"Oh yes, sir. She'll be spick and spangled by then." The woman gave him a slight curtsy before he turned to leave. The smell of the room was beginning to intrude on the well-being of his stomach. Perhaps he'd better come back the day before and check it out, make sure the place was clean and there were a few bottles of stout in the tiny fridge.

"Cheerio, we'll be seeing you right enough, then."

"Oh, aye, sir," the woman said again with another half curtsy.

He walked outside as quickly as possible, breathing in great gulps of fresh air when he reached the alleyway.

Even standing near the dumpster, he felt cleaner. He'd have to come back and clean it himself. He couldn't bring Megan to such a place.

Chapter 31

Jim tentatively knocked at the door before he looked at his watch and noticed it was nearly one thirty a.m. He had spent the past hour trying to figure out what had happened. Reliving and recounting every word, he decided that he'd blown it big time. He knew he'd hurt her, he'd spoken too quickly. And as usual, he'd spoken without thinking. That seemed to be his usual *modus operandi* these days. Speaking without thinking. It seemed that he'd picked up some bad habits since crossing *the pond*. When was he going to turn his brain on? He couldn't risk losing her, now that he'd found her, and he knew in his deepest self that if he lost her, he'd lose what was left of himself as well. He could be such an idiot.

She opened the door, holding it open enough to admit him. She looked as though she'd been crying. He didn't think Megan cried very often, not with her personality; she was not a weepy female. That knowledge made him feel lower than low. He looked about the room, noticing immediately that she'd begun to pack. Was she going to make a fast getaway?

"Listen, Megan, I'm sorry. Please forgive me for speaking so quickly, but you've got to admit that the whole thing was so overwhelming. It threw me off guard. I mean, didn't it throw you as well?" He held his hands out in a gesture of submission, wanting very much for her to fall into his arms, kiss him, and tell him it was all right.

"I'm leaving."

"Yeah, I noticed." He glanced around. Her clothes, normally so neat and well-cared for, were rumpled into balls and stuffed willy-nilly into the suitcase. "That's what I wanted to tell you, I'm sorry. Do you forgive me? You wouldn't leave a poor defenseless American to fend for himself in a strange land, would you? Please forgive me, Megan. I love you more than I can say. I promise." He knew he was rambling and sounded like a real idiot, but he had to tell her everything so she wouldn't leave and never speak to him again. He'd almost lost her once tonight and he wouldn't risk losing her again, physically or emotionally.

Megan took a deep breath, turned away from him, and paced the small confines of the room. She looked so wonderful in her shabby, fuzzy robe and too-large slippers. She was the most beautiful woman in the world to him.

She stood for a moment, looking out at the black night, watching the rain mist against the window. She shivered and Jim saw the tremor all too clearly play across her shoulders.

"I think it best that we don't see each other again. I'll get myself back to Dublin, somehow."

"Oh, Megan, stop being so silly." The frustration in his voice was evident, even to him.

"Silly? Silly, is it? I won't ride in a car with a man who doesn't want me." The hurt in her voice came through loud and clear.

"Megan, honey," said Jim, trying to put his arms around her. "You know I want you. Ah, come on. It was just a shock that's all. Can you blame me? I mean here comes Seamus like he's the Almighty himself, and he tells us we're married? Do you remember saying anything to Father Timothy? Out loud, I mean? Come on." He was finally able to get his arms all the way around Megan without her pushing him away.

She looked at him and the look spoke volumes. She was ready to spit in his eye. Her red hair had somehow turned even redder, like she was blushing from the tips of the roots. Or was it the way her face flushed so hard that she looked like she might turn purple at any second?

"Megan," he said, trying his best to sound convincing, because he really did believe that he loved her. He knew it. "Sweetie, please forgive me. I do love you and I do want to get married. But if we're married now…well, couldn't we keep on having our honeymoon? Hmmm?" Jim said with every bit of cajoling and oozing of love that he could muster.

Megan stopped struggling and looked at him long and hard. His smile was warm and seductive and it made her shiver. Oh yes. He made her shiver. There was no doubt at all. And shiver in a good way. But this would have to stop right here and now or her heart would not survive. Everything between the two of them was moving at lightning speed, so fast that it was hard to process it all; the abbey, Seamus, the dedication, the sex. She would have to work at untangling all these emotions if it was to make sense enough for her to understand and embrace.

The light caught the sparkle in his eye, making them change to almost an azure. She had to be very careful or she'd be swept away only by his looks.

"Do you mean it, James Francis Xavier O'Flannery? Do you mean it? Do you want to marry me, good and proper this time?"

Jim reached down and kissed her. Her lips, so soft and pliant, melted into his and he felt there was such a rightness about it, such goodness about it. He raised his face from hers and sighed.

"Yes, Megan Elizabeth Kennedy, at this point there's no going back. There's no trying to do what I did yesterday, live like I did yesterday. I want to be with you for the rest of our lives."

Megan heaved a great sigh, rather melodramatically.

"Oh, neat-o, I quite like that." She reached up and kissed him, long and hard. The feelings for her pulsated through him and his heart sang with it. Megan was his and he'd show her in every way possible that he meant that he really loved her. He drew her closer, tracing his fingers along the underside of her breast and his hand found its way to stroking her back and hip. She pushed herself away and he stilled. Her eyes were sultry and steamy, and a deep, deep green. His pulse quickened. She straightened her fuzzy robe, folded her hands together with a very proper demeanor, and gave him a little smile.

"I think you should go to your room. Now!" She was completely full of herself. She had him, and she knew it. She'd call it *cheeky*.

"Go to my room? But I thought we were going to have our honeymoon." Jim felt like he'd just been run over by a large, fast moving truck, a truck with red hair and green eyes.

"Not now, lover boy," she said as she patted his

cheek and led him by the arm out the door into the hall. "We must get back to Dublin, you know."

"But, Megan—"

"Ta, ta, get packed so we can leave first thing in the morning."

The door shut and Jim was left standing on the other side, his arms held out beseechingly. He slumped against the wall, staring at Megan's door.

What had happened anyway?

Jim was left with such a plethora of confusing thoughts coursing through his mind that he felt he had to call his grandma, and not to say hello. Maybe she could put him straight. And then again, maybe she had some information and had actually found something out about Seamus. There was a guest phone at the end of the hallway, and Jim did a quick calculation of the time difference. He hoped he wouldn't make her miss her favorite quiz show again. But she loved him, she really wouldn't care.

"Hi, Grandma, it's Jim. How are you? Is Mom okay?"

"Jimmy, how are you? Where are you?"

"We're in a place called Castle Pollard. There's a Benedictine Abbey near here, and we went to visit the monks today. And by the way, Ireland can feel colder than Boston. I almost froze today touring this old dilapidated church from the seventh century. I took lots of pictures, so we'll have a great time going over them when I get back. Now, please tell me what you've found out about you know what."

"Ah, well. Deacon O'Boyle did ask his friend in the Bishop's office. The man said he'd like to speak with you when you returned. He'd like some information, but as it is, they can't really decide what the thing you're seeing is. And here's the strange thing, no one has doubted for a moment that you are conversing with an angel. They can't understand the leprechaun transformation though. That hasn't ever been heard of."

"Well, tonight I was in Megan's room and Seamus was in there with her, and he looked like those pictures of King Brian of the Leprechauns. I was half baiting him, so I asked him was he really an angel, and Megan said—"

"Oh, Megan can see him?"

"Yes, as of tonight."

"Well, that's grand. Two people can't hallucinate about the same thing at the same time, now can they?"

"Yeah, I told Seamus he could be a demon just as easily as an angel, and he was very put out. He flipped open a piece of parchment that looked like it was made of spun glass. The parchment read like a 'to whom it may concern' document, and get this, it was signed Michael, Archangel."

"Holy Mother—"

"Yeah, no kidding. You can tell the deacon and the man in the Bishop's office all of this. It should keep the whole lot of them up for a few weeks." Jim chuckled, thinking of the repercussions his little angel problem might cause for decades to come. "So I was only checking in, thanks for the info. Good night, Grandma, love you."

"I'll pass on the information. Night, Jim love. Call me as soon as you get back, love you too."

Jim rested his head against the receiver, trying to get his brain from spinning out of control. He had work to do.

"Get to work, stupid. The articles won't write themselves."

He was able to get a cup of coffee from a coin operated machine in the lobby. The caffeine revived him, and he sat on the bed in his room, drawing a diagram on a piece of paper to pinpoint all the murders.

There had been three in Dublin. The first one had made the New York Post because the victim had been from Manhattan. The next two victims had been from the Boston area. The third, murdered in Sligo, was a displaced New Yorker; a man that had recently moved to Atlanta.

All the victims were male, loud-mouthed, pushy, Irish Americans, and approximately five feet eleven to six one in height. Jim imagined that the Irish forensics team had made the killer to be about six feet two inches. It had been easy enough for him to do it. And he had that confirmed by his friend who worked in the forensics department in Boston.

There were never any fibers found on the victims, no fingerprints anywhere around the murdered man, or any clear footprints that could lead them to the killer. It was as though the killer wore a slick garment that would keep fibers from rubbing off, a slick garment. Maybe a waterproof coat, like a raincoat?

The hair on the back of Jim's neck stood up when he remembered the man in the bar in Sligo. The man wore a huge brown raincoat, and the coat had covered him almost to his ankles. The man's hat had a wide brim that he judiciously kept pulled down so that Jim, or anyone else who was looking, wouldn't easily recognize him. It was the man that the barkeep downstairs had described to a T.

Could it be Richard? No, it couldn't possibly be. Logically maybe, intellectually maybe, but Jim couldn't emotionally believe that someone Megan had been close to could be a serial killer. Richard had a screw loose—there was no question. But—a serial killer? No, Jim would have to look elsewhere.

Chapter 32

The next day, the silence inside the car was ominous. Megan nodded to him as he'd placed her suitcase into the trunk. Megan had neatly avoided him and had her breakfast before he could make it downstairs. Her persona as the very correct and very capable Miss Megan Kennedy had arrived and taken up residence loud and clear. No more the hurt little girl of last night's thwarted honeymoon.

Drat. He was so glad she felt better, but he craved their unfinished honeymoon.

Jim looked at her from the corner of his eye. *Cool as a cucumber this one. Not one hint of self-consciousness or embarrassment.* He felt embarrassed enough for both of them. What a situation. Seamus had been conspicuous by his absence as well this morning. *That little, creepy, redheaded so and so. Angel Second Class. Second class, for sure, but angel? Angel, my ass. Am I being uncharitable? Of course I am, but he's earned every bit of un-charity there is.*

He'd have to get Megan to warm up to him again, and then maybe they could get on with their honeymoon.

"May I come see your apartment when we get back?"

"Huh? Oh, uh, sure."

"Where do your parents live? I need to go meet

them, right?" If they were *married*, then he'd have to get busy with all the usual polite modes of social acceptance; like meeting the parents, finding out about siblings, and all that kind of stuff. And then they'd have to go talk to a priest and get all of those modes of accepted, when you were a Catholic, behavior accomplished.

Megan quirked a look at him from under her brow.

"They live in Limerick."

"Could we go see them on the weekend? How far away is that from Dublin? I mean I can't very well Shanghai you to Boston without meeting them first. Right?"

"Yes, I suppose so," she said absently and then turned quickly, her brows pulled down in question. "And who said anything about going to Boston?"

"Ah, come on, Kennedy, I thought we were as good as married."

"Oh, indeed, and why is it you're still calling me Kennedy?"

"Force of habit. Journalist to journalist, okay?"

At least he didn't think she was just another pretty face after all. Of course, she knew that all along, intellectually if not emotionally.

Oh, Megan, you know he's always been the best, the most considerate, the nicest, oh crumbs, cut it out, she thought to herself. Most of the morning, between coffee and eggs and packing the car, she'd almost forgotten the whole weirdness of the dedication and Seamus, and her outburst at Jim. But she would never, never forget her "honeymoon."

"Thanks," Megan finally said.

"For what?"

"For putting me on the same footing as you."

"What on earth should I do? Consider you some kind of hack stringer?"

A bubble of laughter caught Jim off-guard. Her laughter reminded him of silvery bells and he loved the sound of it. He thought he'd like hearing it every day from now on. Yes, every day.

"And didn't I tell ya, Jimmy lad."

"Take a hike, Seamus," Jim thought loudly. *"For once, Megan and I are getting along fine and I don't need you hanging around messing things up. Now, since you've earned your wings, why don't you take off and go back up where you belong?"*

"Ah, glad you asked, Jimmy lad. Seems there is something else that needs doin', although I'm not quite clear on it all."

"Something else that needs doing?" Jim projected his mind to shoot the question to Seamus. What on earth could that mean, "something else that needs doing"?

"Aye, so it is. Do you remember the time you asked me to see who it was that was watching the lass here? And I told you it wasn't my department? Well, it has something to do with the promise I made to help you with one thing that might come up, don't you know."

To help with one thing? Jim's mind turned over all the possibilities of that "one" thing.

Megan glanced at Jim, then turned fully in her seat and looked at him again. "Jim, you have that leprechaun look about you," Megan began.

Jim tried to ignore her comment as he thought about what Seamus had said—that he could help with one thing.

"Listen, what did you think happened last night?" Jim asked Megan.

She flushed and looked away.

"No, no, not that," Jim said and then amended his question. "Although that was really terrific, but you know, what about the guy in the car?"

"I hadn't thought of that. I suppose everything else was pushing it from my mind. Do you suppose we are still in danger? Who could it have been?"

"Seamus seems to think we are in danger."

"Seamus?"

"Yeah, that's what he told me, something about being able to help with 'one other thing.' I'd say that's pretty ambiguous."

"Right. Now why doesn't he appear to me, as well? Or did I imagine the whole thing last night?" Megan was curious.

"No, you didn't imagine it. But according to Seamus, we were married in the abbey, or dedicated with all the broad definitions of what that word means. Then we almost got killed going back to the hotel. We consummated our *marriage*, broke up, and got back together again."

"It was rather a full evening. Something you would read in a novel, but it wouldn't happen in real life."

"That's true enough. Do you have any ideas about who it is, this would-be assassin? Or what Seamus means by, 'one more thing that needs doing'?"

"No. Oh, wait. Remember when we were having lunch and the barkeep told us there'd been a man asking about Americans? He thought the man was asking about you. I wonder."

"Yes, we both thought the same thing, and that's

why we left in such a hurry to get to the abbey. But if that was the killer, he had no idea that we were looking for him. How could he?"

"I don't know. Do you suppose whoever it was went back to the pub and asked the keep about us again? Maybe the keep told the man you were an American and looking for him as well."

Jim turned and looked at her for a full second before he pulled his gaze back to the highway.

"Don't you have a cell phone?"

"Yes."

"Call the keep at the Moffat Arms and find out."

Chapter 33

He prowled the banks of River Liffy, blending in with the crowd of blue-collar workers. He pulled his coat collar up and ducked his head. The bridge was crowded with people, some going to work at this hour of the morning, others coming home from the bars. He looked at his watch. It was five thirty.

He would go to the pub on O'Connell and see if any Americans were still about. Probably not, but he had to get in one more before he and Megan got married.

He'd seen her last night with that Yank and he'd almost killed again. Killed them with his car, and killed them both. His rage had gotten the better of him. What if he'd hurt Meggie in his rage at the American? That would never have done. But then again, he'd not have hurt her. The angels would make sure of that. Of that he was certain. He'd narrowly missed them on that last turn. He'd had the advantage. He was going forward. The Yank had to look back to see who was in pursuit and try to keep his car on the road around the hairpin turns at the same time. That last turn had almost sent them off the road. Maybe Meggie would have survived, and he'd have put everything on hold to nurse her back to health. It wouldn't be too bad. He could do it. She'd love him even more then.

But now—now, the pressure had built inside of

him until he thought he might burst. The pressure always built up until he released it with—

He needed one more.

He walked into the pub, the dim light barely illuminating the interior. The smell of sour, stale beer and soggy cigarettes was the aroma he'd become used to over the past few months. The floor was littered with napkins, toothpicks, and an occasional glass that had fallen off a table. The keep leaned against the bar and eyed him as he came in through the door.

Several patrons were resting their heads down on the bar. A few tables still had people drinking, some whisky, and some tea. Richard looked around, trying to find a viable candidate. A man stood and scratched his thick whiskers, a woman in the corner laughed raucously, another man made toward the back knocking into a chair and upending it.

The barkeep looked Richard up and down, as though he were trying to remember Richard from somewhere.

"Good day, chap." The keep scratched at his cheek again.

"Good day."

"What would you like then?"

"A whisky."

The barkeep poured him a jigger of scotch. Richard took the glass, saluted the bar, and downed it in one gulp. He put the glass down solidly on the bar top and spoke quietly to the man as he leaned in and looked away to the interior of the pub.

"Are there any Americans about?"

"Americans?" The man expelled a short, quick burst of laughter. "In here? I hardly think so, lad.

They'd be on the Southside mucking it up with the high muckity mucks."

Richard nodded to the man and quietly made his way from the bar.

Chapter 34

"What did he say?"

Megan had spent fifteen minutes consulting with the keep at the Moffat Arms about the mysterious character who had asked after Americans the day before. Megan turned her head toward Jim and her face was ashen.

"He told me that the man had come back to the pub. He asked about you, and then, the strange thing is, he asked about me as well."

"About you?"

"Aye. It seems he described me down to the clothes I was wearing last evening. Which could only mean one thing."

"Yeah. That he'd seen you in the abbey or the church. So we can safely assume that whoever saw us together at the Moffat Arms may have tried to run us off the road last night."

"Right." Megan sat quietly for a moment, chewing on her lip. Her mind circled the questions. The idea, the question that always popped up before all the others was, why? And for that matter, who? They'd spent the last hour getting to Dublin, parking the car, and making their way up to Megan's desk at the Irish Times. Megan, with Jim in a chair next to hers, had finished a follow-up call to the barkeep at the Moffat Arms.

"I can think of only one explanation. This guy is

the killer and we are following him around trying to find out who he is, okay? We are on his tail and he doesn't like it. Maybe he wasn't trying to kill us last night—maybe he was only trying to scare us."

"You could have fooled me. I felt like we were about to die both times he rammed into us. I'm so sore this morning," she said as she rubbed the back of her neck and her shoulders.

"As long as other more important parts of you aren't sore," Jim replied as he buzzed her lips with a kiss.

Megan felt a blush and she smiled when she saw Jim blush as well. They stood quietly for another moment outside the editor's office, pulling together their turbulent thoughts before they went in to report to the editor of the Irish Times.

****

"We have a possible scenario that we've worked up, Mr. Flynn."

"Aye?" The editor of the Irish Times looked at Jim over his half-moon glasses.

What hair the man had was white, and several sprigs sprouted at odd angles on the top of his head. He had one very large vein that started at his forehead and moved toward the crown of his head and pulsed rhythmically with each breath the man took. The pulsing would become erratic when he was angered, and this oddball bit of anatomy was a stringent warning to any writer who came into the office to confer with the editor. His starched white collar, cashmere suit, and blue tie done up in a Windsor knot were at odds with his coarse working man's face. "The Mighty Flynn," as the journalists at the Irish Times called him behind his back, inadvertently, perhaps from habit, intimidated anyone who walked across the threshold of his office.

In Jim O'Flannery's case, Jim was more confused than intimidated. Jim had spent till mid-morning driving into maniacal Dublin on the wrong side of the road. It was a sure bet that the other drivers were out to get him. And after last night's escapade, he was really convinced of it. Luckily, they had all missed.

After Flynn's authoritative summons, Jim pulled his notes together and made his way into the editor's office with Megan at his side. There was no doubt in Jim's mind that he was a good writer, but Jim also knew he wasn't always a good speaker, especially under pressure. Jim cleared his throat; alert for any telltale signs from the pulsing vein. Megan and several of the other journalists had clued him into the phenomenon, as fair warning.

"Yes, we think the killer is from Dublin and for some strange reason he hates Americans." Talk about dumb one-liners.

Jim felt like smacking himself in the forehead, but refrained from that particular bit of self-chastisement.

Flynn heaved a great sigh, took off his glasses and tossed them with a flourish onto the desktop.

"Yes, O'Flannery. I believe every child above the fourth form knows that." The editor steepled his fingers, leaned his head against the chair back and waited.

"Well, sir." Jim cleared his throat. This could be harder than he'd bargained for. Did he have trouble with editors as a whole, or was it the hard-nose boss types that made his tongue seem to tangle into knots?

"You're too much of a free spirit, Jimmy lad.

That's all. You're a fine hard-working man. Not enough time with your dad, that's the trouble. Just think of 'em as your dad, and you'll get along right enough."

Jim looked at Flynn and almost burst out laughing. He shook off the momentary hysteria and got his mind back on the subject matter. He cleared his throat roughly and again addressed Mr. Flynn.

"Forensics have determined that he's left-handed and a little under six two. He is wearing a raincoat that is rubberized or waterproofed in some way because no fibers were ever found and neither were any definitive footprints. In Sligo, it looked like something was used to obliterate any boot prints that were left in the soft dirt where the victim fell."

"Perhaps he wasn't wearing a coat at all. How about shoes now, what type would you say?"

"Don't know. Something soft-soled, but if he wasn't wearing a coat, someone would have remembered. Too cold without a coat. He blended right in. We've got to find somebody who hates Americans, specifically Irish-Americans."

"And since you've gone to all this trouble to size this fellow up, suppose you can finish by telling me who he is?"

"Can't say yet. We know he'll strike again soon, though. I'd thought of putting myself up as bait, but I can't get the police interested in the scheme. Kennedy tried as well, but her accent is Irish, too, and besides the guy doesn't kill women." Jim looked at Megan, oh so grateful that she was indeed a woman.

"True enough. Well, the piece is good. I've conferred with your editor. You did a good job, Kennedy. Let's you and O'Flannery here finish this up so's the young man can go back home."

"Yes, Mr. Flynn. We thought we might wait for a day or so to see if he strikes again or if the police catch him, and then we can finalize the piece and write our separate exposés."

****

Megan turned and looked at Jim. Would he really be going? Actually hearing someone say that Jim would soon leave left a lump in her throat the size of a boulder. She'd been thinking about it since he'd arrived, but she didn't really fancy thinking about it. Hearing Flynn say it though, almost made her stop breathing. Megan looked up at Jim, noticing, and not for the first time, how his eyes crinkled at the corners, even when he was listening, as though he wore a perpetual smile.

Jim spoke again and Megan snapped her attention back to Flynn, still mulling over some papers on his desk. He looked up at them over his glasses; his blue eyes looked first at Megan and then at Jim as though he really didn't know who he wanted to look at first with his most intimidating stare.

"And we have a bit of additional information. We were almost run down last night. The guy that did it might have been the one that was asking the barkeep at Castle Pollard about any Americans in the area. We called and confirmed that the man who had first asked about Americans—the one we went looking for at the abbey—had come back to the pub and asked again. The barkeep thought he was looking for us so he told the man where we were. The fellow was so ordinary that the barkeep had no description except that he was dark-haired and tall."

Flynn sat back and shook his head slowly. "You two stay close by the office. I'm going to call the police and tell them what happened, just to let them know, mind you. I think these things need to be reported because they may lead to more information, and to perhaps thwart the bugger from killing the two of you."

Jim and Megan both nodded in agreement. Jim pulled his papers together, ready to leave the office.

"The Globe wanted a follow-up if no more murders occur in the next few days. I'm good to stay until the fourteenth of February unless, of course, you have anything else you'd like me to do," Jim said.

"Not at present. Well done. The two of you may leave. Kennedy, see that you bring your next piece into the night desk this evening. The editor at the Globe wants to run your piece as well."

Megan gasped and turned quickly toward the door. Her piece? At the Boston Globe? All thoughts of the would-be killer vanished from her mind. She looked at Flynn quickly and nodded before turning to leave with Jim. Her excitement was intense and she felt her heart flutter. Jim closed the door with quiet care.

Megan turned to him. "Did you hear what he said? They're going to run my piece. And they've sent it to Boston for The Globe. I'm so excited."

"Yeah, I guess you did a better job than you thought you did. See, I told you to have a little faith."

"Right." Megan reached up and gave him a quick kiss. "I must go. I've got to finish that article."

"Okay. I'll come over tonight. How about a romantic dinner for two at your place?"

Megan gave him a smug look. What she wouldn't do for a quiet, cozy dinner for two with him.

"I'll have to let you know. You work at the desk near the window and come see me before you're off." The knowledge that he'd actually be leaving sent Megan's heart into a spin. If she was smart, she'd steel herself against the hurt his leaving would cause.

"Hey! I'm not going anywhere without you, you know. Now, about that dinner?"

"Jim, I'll see you at lunch and we'll discuss dinner then. There's a lot of food talk about here, now isn't there. I am convinced I'll gain weight from the sound of it. Let's get our minds off this societal eating ritual. Didn't civilization evolve far enough not to talk about eating? Sorry," she said with a sigh. "Let's slow down a bit, shall we?"

"You? Gain weight? Why you, my dear, are about the prettiest thing, and you happen to be the most slender woman with curves in all the right places that I've ever seen."

He pulled her to him as he leaned the two of them against the wall. His mouth came down on hers in a demanding kiss full of promise and pent-up frustration. The kiss went on and Megan felt every part of him pushing into her very compliant body. Jim's kisses excited her like nothing ever had before. His kiss led her further and further into a world away from the office, away from life with its contradictions and frailties, away from everything but Jim. The friction and urgency of their bodies drove her to utter distraction.

They were shielded in a little alcove, but it was still too open to the central floor. The thought, the reality pushed its way into Megan's mind. The thought of getting caught crashed down on her like a bucket of cold water. She shoved away.

"Jim, enough! We can't be doing this here. What's come over the two of us anyway?" she asked as she ran a shaky hand over her lips and then pushed her fingers quickly through her hair.

Jim leaned against the wall, seeming to concentrate and slow down his breathing.

"Newlyweds, I guess," he answered with a cheeky grin after he took another deep breath. He straightened his sweater and sauntered back to the vacant desk against the outside wall.

Megan stood quite still for a few heartbeats. Her turbulent thoughts about Jim pushed everything else out of her head.

Jim.

She had to stop all this nonsense. She had to stop it now before something inconsolable happened. She knew she loved him, but to actually think they were *married*, because they said the words in their minds? Because they'd made the most incredible love she'd ever thought could or would exist in the real world?

You are too silly, my girl. Ah, bollocks. He'll be leaving soon. Even the Mighty Flynn said so. She knew that he would go back to Boston and he'd leave her here with a broken heart. She couldn't suffer that fate twice in one lifetime. She was too smart a woman for that. Her heart had already been broken into little bits by that bastard Richard, and she wouldn't suffer the indignity, the worst hurt that she'd ever felt. No, not ever again.

Right here and now, Megan Kennedy, say goodbye to the charming Yank and send him out of your mind and across the Atlantic.

Chapter 35

He stood outside in the cold drizzle, staring at the gray granite of the building, trying to figure out which was the window near Megan's desk. He knew which floor she was on. But it was harder to pinpoint her exact window on the massive floor. No, this was not the time. He had to think. He had to plan.

He walked to the corner and waited for the bus. He took the second bus that stopped in the gloomy afternoon rain. He knew where he could go to think. There was only an hour or two of daylight left, and it was important that he think.

The bus moved across the capital down the Finglas Road to a suburb that once was the countryside, out of the city to Glasnevin Cemetery.

After thirty tedious minutes of stop and go traffic, the bus finally let him off at the cemetery.

He looked about, half expecting someone to tap him on the shoulder and ask him why he was there on such a dismal afternoon. Dodging behind a mausoleum for a minute to catch his breath, he moved back onto the path and walked quickly to the Republican section.

It was a great place to think among long rows of grassy mounds, all neatly placed headstones and monuments that were inscribed with the names of martyred and venerated patriots.

He saw the grave of Maud Gonne MacBride, a

pretty woman with dark, soulful eyes. She was the founder of the Daughters of Erin, and had been dead a hundred years and more. There rested the Countess Markievicz. An Irish lass married to a Polish count. She'd fought alongside the men in the 1916 Rebellion. And of course, the great patriot O'Connell, a distant relation, and the one who'd brought the English to their knees and had freed his beloved country.

He wondered what they would think of him and his devotion to duty. And his patriotic zeal to kill all the loudmouthed Irish Americans he could.

He heaved a great sigh, filling his lungs with the loamy smell of melting snow and newly-turned earth. He walked quietly among the headstones, his thoughts in turmoil—racing, racing, until he put his hands against his temples to slow the thoughts down. He shook his head, trying to clear his mind. With a deep breath, he finally fixated on one thought.

It was time to do another one, and then he could go get Meggie.

Chapter 36

Megan wore a dark bottle-green velvet dress that fitted to perfection across the bust and hips. The low neckline and sleeves were edged with a light, frothy lace. Stunned into silence for just a moment by Megan's beauty, Jim swallowed hard and then gave her a peck on the cheek. She blushed prettily and introduced him to her roommate Teresa. Teresa's personality and looks were the complete opposite from Megan's. She was voluptuous and brassy but sweet. She was the kind of woman that loved to share a dirty joke and smoke a cigar with a guy. Not his type but he respected the fact that the two women got along like sisters.

He couldn't believe the beautiful Megan was here with him. He was the luckiest man in the world. Now, if he could convince her that she was the luckiest woman, everything would turn out great. But something had been troubling her all night. What it was and when it started, he couldn't be sure.

Megan had been pulling away from him emotionally all day. It started in the car on the way to Dublin. She was putting up a wall, brick by brick, with him on one side and her on the other. He'd hoped that a wedding supper in this quiet, elegant restaurant would help lighten her mood and ease her into married life with him.

He'd asked around and found out this was a prime place for romance. The restaurant was rather more subdued than anything he'd seen yet in Dublin. The bars and places where he'd eaten since arriving were on the rollicking side. Those were not the type of place to have an intimate, quiet dinner with the woman he loved.

The waiters were dressed in tuxedo shirts and vests, and bow ties that fit right in with the dim lighting and the barely audible classical music in the background. They bowed a little from the waist each time they came to the table and hovered about like mother hens.

Jim looked about appreciatively; a wedding supper, that's what this was, a wedding supper. Now, if he could get her to lighten up and convince her about the honeymoon.

Jim reached across the tiny table for Megan's hand. She had spent more time looking at her plate than at him, and it had frustrated him to no end. When would she look at him with those smoldering deep green eyes? When?

Something was going on inside that journalist's brain of hers. Something that was not positive about the two of them, and it didn't look good.

"Megan, I was thinking."

"Hmm—charming, glad you took it up."

"Huh?" Jim sat back. He was confused.

"Thinking." Her mouth quirked up in a smile.

Jim refrained from rolling his eyes and got right to the point. "Listen, I've got to go back to Boston and get my affairs settled. Why don't you come with me? You could meet the family and the guys at the Globe. Then we could come back here, if Flynn will hire me, and find a nice apartment."

He'd done a lot of thinking about this move. He knew he'd miss Boston and the family, but it would be a whole lot harder on him if he didn't stay with Megan.

It wouldn't be much of a hardship. He kind of liked it here, and the Mighty Flynn could grow on him. He paused a moment, studying her quick intake of breath and wide-eyed look. Then she ducked her head.

"What do you think?" Jim asked.

Megan looked up at him slowly and stared at him. He couldn't read her thoughts, although he'd been able to see inside her mind all too easily over the past few days. She took a deep breath before she started speaking very softly.

"Jim, I think it better that you go back alone. We can see each other from time to time, if you like, but I can't think that it should be a permanent arrangement."

"But why? Come on Megan. You know what Seamus said. We're married." He quirked that smile at her. "You know you can't get a divorce in Ireland. At least that's what Grandma used to tell me. I suppose that was over fifty years ago, though." He looked up at her, grinning for all he was worth. When he saw the look on her face, he felt like a balloon slowly deflating. What if she changed her mind? What if she didn't want him after all? Both of those thoughts sent a cold chill up his spine.

"Look," he said. He had to play his cards right. He had to be convincing and *not* shoot off his mouth before he could settle her down, until he could settle *both* of them down. He spoke to her very quietly, leaning forward and stroking her hand. "Why won't you give it a try? I know you have feelings for me. You can't tell me otherwise. I love you, and I want to spend the rest of my life with you. Don't you remember that dream? We had the same dream, together, every night we were in Sligo. Every night. Don't you remember what happened last night? We're made for each other," he said, expansively holding out his arms, enjoying the fact he had her complete and totally embarrassed attention.

"Jim, the whole business is too strange for words. Really, can't you see?"

"So you want a church wedding to do it up good? Okay by me."

Jim pushed back his chair, rose, then dropped to his knees in front of Megan and grasped her hand. He suppressed a grin at the chagrined look on her face.

"Megan, will you marry me?"

Megan turned every shade of red as a chorus of, "good show," "right on, my man", and a flurry of applause was heard from every corner of the restaurant. Megan gestured for Jim to get up as she looked about seeing the smiles, the raised glasses, and the applause from the other patrons.

"Will you please get up?" she said from between clenched teeth as her gaze darted about the room again. Jim sat back down, still holding her hand. She pulled her hand away and took a quick drink of her wine. Jim cradled his chin in his hand, gazing at her adoringly.

"Sorry if I embarrassed you, but you've got to know, I'm crazy about you, and I want to marry you—again."

Megan heaved a great sigh and shook her head slightly, looking down at her plate. She was quiet for several long moments before she looked up again, and shook her head once. Megan looked overwhelmed, as though she'd just come from some dear departed's funeral. A lump formed in Jim's stomach and that ominous lump grew larger by the second.

She was going to turn him down.

"We can't disrupt our lives like this. Weren't you settled before you came over? I'm just beginning to make it as a writer. People are realizing that I'm something more than a silly female looking for a husband and that I can actually do something besides smile and giggle. And I'm enjoying being alone. I'm just fine, and I know you are."

Jim sat back in his chair and crossed his arms over his chest. Jim took a rather long moment before he spoke, hoping against hope that he'd say the right thing. He leaned forward, and made sure Megan alone heard his words.

"I was miserable before I came to Ireland and met you. I haven't felt alive in a very long time. Alive and aware that there has been something else out there besides just me." He leaned across the table and placed his hand on Megan's.

"Megan, I can't go back to the way it was. I love you, you've changed the way I feel about everything. I can't go back to Boston alone. I want to be with you."

A lone tear edged down Megan's cheek. She quickly dashed it away as the waiter came up to the table.

Jim stared at her for a moment. He had to do something, anything, to keep her from feeling that they were better off apart. Seamus had brought them together. Yes, brought them together. So if he'd brought them together, they were meant to be. Why was

Megan fighting their getting together? Why was her level-headed common sense getting in the way?

****

"And what is it you'll have me do, Iggy? You said yourself that the Head Man says they're as good as married."

"Aye, 'tis true enough, but you know we must stand on ceremony. 'Tis the only way the lass will feel done good and proper."

"Och, and then what? The Holy Father himself saying the words over 'em? I tell ye, 'tis a bad thing when the Man Upstairs says they are, and the puny little humans say they aren't."

"Now, Seamus, what needs doing needs doing. Ye must convince the lass to go to America and—what?" Iggy stared off into space for a moment. "Oh, Glory be. There's trouble down there. Ye can go and do your good deed, Seamus. You'll be remembering that you can do one thing for Jim-lad; to help him save the lass."

"Save the lass, but I—"

"Seamus, they'll be needin' you right enough. You can grant Jim one wish to help him in his earthly endeavors, but only one wish. Now, off wi' ye. There's trouble brewin', and he'll be needin' his great uncle times six to help."

****

"May I bring you anything else, sir?"

Jim gave the waiter a cold look. "No, just leave. We'll be done in a minute." The waiter faded into the background. The subtle clink of china and silver were heard just below Megan's sniffling.

Jim let out a pent-up breath. "I just don't see it. Nothing is worth losing this—this relationship that we

254

have. Nothing! If God Almighty says we're married, who are you to say we aren't? Come on." In exasperation Jim stood and threw a wad of bills on the table.

"I'm taking you home."

Chapter 37

They walked out into the night, trudging through the newly fallen snow. Jim said nothing, but Megan could feel his anger radiate from him so hotly the snow should have melted under his feet. They caught a cab, and an ominous silence shrouded the back seat.

At the door to Megan's apartment, Jim took her hand, his voice as soft as the night outside and asked, "Why are you fighting this?"

"Because I just can't grasp it. And when I think I do, all I see is you on your merry way, without a look back to see where you've been."

"You are so wrong, Megan. I'm in it for the long haul. Think about it tonight. Try to see it the way Seamus has it planned."

Something in Jim's voice, something in the sound of his words, startled Megan into looking up into his face. He turned away from her quickly, but not before she saw the hurt in his eyes. She'd hurt him. She'd been working so hard at not getting hurt herself that she'd hurt him.

"Oh, Jim—"

"Good night, Megan. I'll see you in the morning."

He stalked away, each long stride carrying him farther away from her. She shut the door and leaned her forehead against it, tears coursing down her face, silent sobs shaking her shoulders.

He was gone. She'd pushed him away. He was gone and she'd never see him again, and it was her own fault.

Why, oh why, had she done it?

A shell of misery closed about her. Tears ran down her face and dropped onto the lacy collar around her throat.

She stood at the door, she didn't know for how long, when she heard a knock. He'd come back! She just knew it! He'd come back and she could make amends and they'd live happily ever after and—

Megan dashed the tears from her cheeks, straightened her skirts, hoping she didn't look too awful and threw open the door.

"Oh Jim, I—"

There in the open doorway, sheathed in his massive brown overcoat, stood Richard.

Chapter 38

"Coming, coming." Teresa turned one groggy eye on the clock. "Bleedin' 7:35! Who is it bashing down my door at 7:35 in the morning?" She bundled the bathrobe tight, scuffed into her slippers, and opened the door. "God! O'Flannery, you handsome devil. Do you know the time? Come in, before you wake up the neighbors."

"Sorry, I know it's a little early, but I had to see Megan."

"You look like hell, O'Flannery." His clothes were rumpled and it looked like he'd slept in them all night. Well, maybe not slept considering the circles under his eyes were almost as dark as the man's baby blues.

"You don't mince any words, do you?" Jim rubbed his hand over the stubble on his chin, and by the look she was giving him, realized he probably should have showered and shaved before coming over.

"Never have. Have a seat. I'll get some coffee started. The noise of my making the first pot always wakes up Meggie, and then I don't get yelled at for waking her up."

Jim settled onto the overstuffed, flowered couch and stretched out his legs. He felt better just being near her. He knew they could iron out all these differences. He knew it. He just had to work on her a little longer. These feelings she had must just be wedding jitters. He could understand that well enough. Jim also knew that she'd have to be placated with a ceremony. Placated wasn't the right word.

When he gave ceremonies by and large any thought, he realized that there was a great comfort for the average person in societal continuity. Maybe it was a girl thing. But that wasn't right either, because he wanted a church wedding, too.

So maybe a guy thing would be to get rid of the hideous couch he was sitting on. Yeah, a guy thing, he thought as he looked at the grotesque piece of furniture. Maybe they could give it to Teresa.

Teresa came into the room with a tray of cups, coffee pot, and condiments. She'd dressed in a pair of dark purple sweats, Jim was glad to note. No more body parts peeking out that he'd have to ignore.

"She's not up?" Teresa looked toward Megan's bedroom door.

"No, I guess I dozed off for a second, but I haven't seen or heard anything."

Teresa set the tray on the table, and Jim, in his near comatose state, reached for a cup and poured. Teresa shrugged her shoulders, walked to the back of the apartment, and rushed back into the room just as Jim set his cup down again on the tray.

"She's gone."

"What?"

"Her bed's not been slept in, and I found this." Teresa held up a much-used hairbrush and a purse. "She'd never leave without these. I can't think what has happened."

Jim felt the blood drain from his face. She couldn't have been that upset. He walked to the doorway and took a cursory look about her room. Neat and tidy, just like Megan herself. No sign that she'd ever lived there at all. He looked quickly in the closet and on the hook on the back of the bathroom door.

"She's either stark naked or still got on the dress she wore last night."

"Well, we can leave out the naked bit. I know Meggie. Besides, it's January and freezing. She'd wear a robe into the bath if it served a purpose. What on earth could have happened to her?"

"It can't be anything good." Jim struggled to get the panic rising in his throat under control. He wiped his sweaty palms on his trouser leg.

"What time did you get home last night, Teresa?"

"About one in the morning. I thought she was asleep in here. She usually is."

"I left her off around nine thirty. Ten hours, ten hours, where the hell could she be?"

"I'd bet my knickers that she just didn't wander off. Megan would never leave without her bag and a coat. And she certainly wouldn't have gone off with that dress on. She loves that dress, and she's only worn it once before when she and Richard—" Teresa looked at him out of the corner of her eye and cringed just a bit hoping she hadn't said too much.

Jim blew out a disgusted breath. "Then why the hell did she wear it last night?"

"Because she knows how you love green, and that's the only green posh frock she owns. And Mr. O'Flannery, she's as superstitious as the rest of us, and she thought that the wearing of it with you would negate any bad karma from Richard."

Jim raised his hands in surrender and sat abruptly

on the couch, rubbing his eyes with the heels of his hands.

He looked up at Teresa.

"Where could she be? Where? I've got to find her."

Teresa looked at him, and all too clearly Jim read her anxiety. She moved to him and laid her hand on his arm. "She told me Richard had tried to contact her several times, and she'd told him to piss off. You don't suppose—?"

Teresa turned her horrified gaze on Jim.

"Crap! Where does he live, do you know?" Jim stood quickly and began to pace so he wouldn't grab Teresa and shake her in his frustration.

"No, but I know who his father is. He's a big muckity muck in the stock market. Finish your coffee while I get dressed, and I'll take you. We'll be off in a short bit."

Jim went back into the living room. He could do nothing but pace and wear a hole in the carpet.

In ten short minutes, Teresa came into the front room, her hair up, wearing a deep plum, low cut sweater, and skin tight pants, with perfume wafting from every pore, and carrying a make-up bag. Jim looked at her inquisitively.

"I may have to do some womanly convincing, and I'll put this on in the taxi," she said holding up the make-up bag.

"Ah." Jim nodded in understanding.

Chapter 39

Jim and Teresa arrived at the large stock brokerage firm within minutes of leaving the flat. But they had to wait in the outer office for over a half hour. It was too early and no one had yet arrived for the work day. Jim had taken the time to wash and comb his hair in the nearby restroom and shave with the rechargeable razor he always carried in his briefcase. He pulled out a tie he had in his case and was grateful that it matched his coat and sweater well enough. He needed to look reputable. He needed to make sure that anyone he talked to would take him seriously.

He was angry, so very angry, and when he found that bastard Richard, screw loose or no, he'd pull his throat out of his neck.

What if something happened to Megan and he hadn't been there to keep her safe? What if he never saw her again?

He couldn't stand thinking about it and not being able to do something. Thinking about it made it all that much worse. He kept tying his tie to busy his mind, but it didn't work, and the Windsor knot ended up looking more like a granny knot. Finally, he gave up and asked Teresa to tie the damn thing.

They sat and waited and waited. Jim's inability to do anything immediately to save Megan ate away at him like acid.

Soon after nine o'clock, a man in a gray, formal suit led them into a large, plush, paneled office.

The man sitting behind the huge mahogany desk looked like the Richard Jim had seen. He was austere, and each movement he took seemed contrived, as though he planned each second of his day, each movement, and each emotion.

Jim wondered how far they'd get with him. Teresa held out her hand to him, practically leaning over far enough for him to get a good view of her cleavage.

"Mr. O'Connell, I'm Teresa, Megan Kennedy's flat mate, and this is James O'Flannery, here from America to do a story for the Times."

Something flickered in the man's eyes when Teresa said "American" but Jim wasn't sure what it was. The man looked them up and down, doing his utmost, it seemed to Jim, to keep his face impassive, but underneath probably wondering what the hell these two were doing here.

"Mr. O'Flannery is a journalist for the Boston Globe, and he and Megan wrote articles for their respective papers about the murders here of Irish Americans."

A flash of something crossed the man's impassive expression again.

"American, are you?" Mr. O'Connell's accent was more British than Irish, Jim noticed. Mr. O'Connell rubbed a hand across his brow, for just a second, as though he'd had a lapse in his concerted effort to stay austere.

"Yes, sir. We were wondering if you'd seen Megan recently."

"Miss Kennedy? Hardly think so. She saw the error

of her ways some time ago and told my son she'd have naught to do with him. Can't understand what took her so long to see what a know-nothing ne'er-do-well the boy is. But that's neither here nor there. Why have you come to see me?"

"Well, Mr. O'Connell, to tell you the unbridled truth, Megan's gone missing, and we wondered if Richard had anything to do with it."

There it was again, that tiny, twitch-like movement that told Jim an emotion had registered and then been squelched or dismissed.

"Hardly think the boy had anything to do with it."

"Do you know where your son is at this time, Mr. O'Connell?" Jim watched for telltale signs. The man turned his impassive brown eyes on him, staring for just a moment as though to size him up.

"Don't know, haven't seen the boy in quite a while. Have to check with my secretary to see exactly when the last time was. Now," he said as he rose slowly from behind his desk. "If you'll both excuse me."

"Thank you ever so, Mr. O'Connell," said Teresa, once again giving him the benefit of her cleavage. "We'll call you if we have any more questions." She turned to leave as Jim shook the man's hand.

"American, eh? Like Americans. My second wife was American. Liked her well enough, but she and Richard didn't get on."

An alarm bell loud enough to wake the dead went off in Jim's head. Richard didn't get along with his American stepmother. Richard had been physically and mentally abused by his father. Not an excuse, but maybe a reason for...

When they'd made the street, Jim turned to Teresa.

"Tell me everything you know about Richard and his real mother."

"Don't know much," said Teresa, pushing through the door to a café on the corner. "Let's get a coffee and something to eat, and we can decide what to do next. We can't fall down from hunger before we find her. I must call to my office and tell them I'll be late this morning.

"Oh, cor," she said, consulting her watch, "already quite late, I see. Ah well." She shrugged out of her coat and signaled a waitress. "You order, and I shall make that call."

Jim ordered breakfast while he waited for Teresa. Every minute that ticked by could be a minute that Megan was in trouble, in danger, and he was sitting around drinking coffee. He was slowly going out of his mind, but he needed to keep cool. Going over the deep end wouldn't help Megan now, and going without food wouldn't help him think straight.

She could be anywhere in the city. He had to make a methodical study to find her. If Richard had taken the opportunity to kidnap her, then he probably wouldn't hurt her.

Yet.

"Took the day off. Now," Teresa said as she sat down. She paused to sip her tea. "This is what I remember Meggie telling me. Richard's real mum went off after years of abuse by the father. Left Richard there at ten years of age to fend for himself with his da. One lovely woman, eh? Then the father, ol' sour puss we met this morning, meets this American witch and marries her. Then Richard has the two of them abusing him. He runs off a few years later, but Megan says he

265

blamed the American witch for sending his own mum off, and she died before he could get to know her again properly. Screwy, if you ask me. And he didn't like me much because I'm from Liverpool. Made snide, left-handed remarks, if you catch my meaning. Real biased one, him."

"Very screwy. So Richard hates Americans? And anyone else that doesn't fit in with his exalted idea of the pure race, huh? No wonder." Jim took a long swallow of coffee and munched for a minute on a roll the waitress had brought with a plate of some kind of fish that Jim decided to forgo. He looked at Teresa solemnly. "Does he hate Americans enough to kill them?"

"Wha'?" Teresa's red mouth turned into a perfect O.

"Yeah, it's just something I've been toying with. See, I thought I saw a man that fit Richard's description in our hotel in Sligo. And the last murder happened in Sligo. The man I saw was wearing this over-sized brown raincoat, and Megan said he's got an overcoat just like that."

"Not much to go on, just because someone's got a coat like the one you think you saw."

"Yeah, I know. But listen to this; Megan said she thought someone was watching her in Sligo. That started me thinking. The first day I was here, in Ireland, Richard came to the Times and practically accosted Megan. He knew I'd throw him out if he didn't leave, and since then, on and off, Megan has told me that she feels as though someone has been watching her."

Teresa shook her head slowly, making conciliatory noises.

"Still not enough for the police to go on. If you told them you felt as though someone was watching you, you'd probably be the one they'd lock up." Teresa wiped the crumbs from the table near her cup. She kept wiping, thinking, her mind not on her task but on the problem they had to solve.

"Yeah, you're absolutely—hey, I know who can help me. And he owes me a favor."

"Right-o!" exclaimed Teresa sitting up with excitement. "Who?"

"Seamus."

"Who?"

Chapter 40

"Who the devil is Seamus?"

"If I told you, you *would* have me locked up. Let's just say he's...a psychic."

"Oh, cor, really? Too very cool. Well, when can we see him? I fancy a séance now and again." Teresa quivered with excitement.

"Teresa, it's not like that, you see, well..." Jim heaved a big sigh. He had to contact Seamus and trying to explain about him would take too much time.

The Lord only knew how long he had before Richard became violent and hurt Megan. *Would Richard kidnap her just to hurt her? Would he*? With each moment that passed and with each methodical thought that went through Jim's mind, it did look as though he had her. It was that *Black Irish* thing kicking in again. He knew in his gut.

But how much time did he have before Richard's mental state overwhelmed him, he lost touch with reality, and hurt Megan like he did the rest of his victims? And right then and there, Jim prayed that he was wrong about Richard. But something deep inside his gut told him he wasn't. He closed his eyes for a moment. He could see her there just beyond his reach. He—

"I think we've got to go to the police, too," Jim added as he opened his eyes and stared at Teresa's worried expression.

Teresa took a long sip of her tea and then brought the cup down quickly so that it rattled on the saucer. She snapped her fingers and began to shrug into her coat.

"I know—Frankie."

"Who?"

"A fella I used to see. He's a ruddy detective with the Metropolitan. We'll go see him straight away. He'll know what to do, and then afterward, we can get in touch with your friend. What's his name? Oh yeah, Seamus."

"That's the first good news I've heard all morning. Is his office near here?"

"No, we'll take a cab, my treat."

****

Jim and Teresa ran up the long flight of granite stairs into the bustling Dublin Metropolitan Police Department.

Jim looked at his watch. It was 10:45 in the morning. Megan had been missing for over twelve hours. He shook his head in disbelief. If he couldn't rescue her, how would he ever forgive himself?

Teresa leaned toward the man behind the shoulder-high front desk.

"I need to speak to Detective Inspector Devon, please. Frankie Devon."

"Yes, Miss. I'll call him down."

"How come you can't just go to his office?" asked Jim quietly as they waited, leaning against a large granite column that stood in the huge lobby.

"You mean you can just go in and bother the coppers in your country?"

"Sure, public access and all that."

"Jay-sus, I think I like that better than being always waiting and waiting. That's how come we split. Always waiting for him to do this or that and always getting calls from the desk. Too dull by half, I can tell you. Don't know how many dinners I ate cold waiting for that bloke."

"Ah, well, duty calls."

Teresa made a disgusted face just as a very handsome blond man came up behind her and put his arms around her.

"Hello, sweet. Miss me so you couldn't stay away?"

"Oh, Frankie, you are too much. This is Jim O'Flannery from America."

Detective Inspector Devon held out his hand to Jim with a slight frown on his face.

"Detective, we are at a loss and we've come for your help."

Jim saw concern replace the frown and Devon immediately gestured for them to follow him to his office.

Chapter 41

"Meggie, you must hold still, or I shall have to wrap you up much tighter." Tremors raced up and down her arms and body. Her teeth clacked together involuntarily despite the gag inside her mouth and the electrical tape covering the lower half of her face. Richard chided her in a singsong voice that sounded hollow and mechanical. The sound of it, the feel of his breath on her face, frightened her more than being tied up in this strange place.

Sharp burning pain shot through her arms and shoulders when she pulled at the electrical tape around her wrists. She made herself move her hands, scrunching her fingers in and out. Pins and needles coursed up her arms. The pain it caused almost made her stop, but she had to keep the blood flowing.

Richard used something, some drug in a cloth he shoved over her mouth. When she awoke a short time later in the smelly, vermin-infested room, she'd tried to keep herself awake and alert; she had to find a way to escape. She was totally exhausted, her mind so befuddled, she was hard pressed to remember her own name.

She was doing everything: talking to herself, reciting the multiplication tables, praying to St. Jude, everything to keep from passing out.

A few hours before daybreak, Richard let her lie

down on a sofa against the inside wall of the little room, but he kept her gagged and her arms tied behind her back. She imagined things crawling all over her. The thought and distinct possibility that it was indeed true had kept her squirming and thrashing around.

Last night, when Megan had heard the knock at her door, she was sure Jim had come back for her. When Richard saw Megan in the green velvet dress, his eyes lit up. She prayed that he wouldn't remember any time soon that she'd been out with Jim a scant hour before. He went on and on about the dress. His demeanor was so strange. He sounded insane. So she smiled and nodded until her face felt like it would crack and crumble to the floor. Then he'd slapped the cloth over her mouth. She couldn't remember anything after that.

Now, he rambled on without stopping and said something about his father loving him, because Richard would soon be famous. His abstract ramblings and his one-sided conversation sent chills up and down Megan's spine. Jim had been right. His sixth sense had been spot on; now it was easy to believe listening to this madman.

Near dawn, Richard's monotone, one sided conversation became hard to follow. She ignored him, focusing on her task of freeing her hands. A cold chill made her shiver when she heard something about the damned Yank and how easy it had been.

Easy? What was easy? Then it dawned on her. Jim told her and she hadn't believed him. Could it be true that the lunatic that had kidnapped her, Richard, and the serial killer were one and the same?

Megan's heart beat so hard her chest felt like it would explode. She squeezed her eyes shut and held her breath, hoping she could vanish like Seamus. Her stomach clenched and an overwhelming wave of nausea sent her face down to the floor.

"Meggie, Meggie, what is it, love?"

Richard picked her up and sat her against the edge of the couch, then took the gag from her mouth. She dry heaved and the contents of her stomach threatened to come up. She laid her head back on the cushion, closing her eyes, willing the room to stop spinning.

"Richard, could I have a sip of water?"

"Why sure, love."

Richard went to a cupboard and withdrew a thermos bottle. He poured Megan a drink and helped her to sip it.

The early morning sunlight poured in through the window, and Megan's head cleared a little. She looked around the room for the first time since she'd been brought there the night before.

The room was sparsely furnished with a table, chair, small cot, a sofa, and cupboard. The flat reeked with odors she didn't care to recognize.

There were several spots on the floor and the table that looked like Richard or someone had wiped them down. But overall the place was exceedingly dirty. Megan could hear the noise of traffic right outside the window. She knew she was still in Dublin, but she could be anywhere in the city. She didn't think they had traveled far enough to be anywhere else. The smells from beyond the wall of the little room made her stomach heave again, and the tiny bit of tea she'd just swallowed came back up onto the sofa.

Enough, her mind screamed. *Get hold of yourself, girl, and find a way out.*

Megan smiled at Richard, but he was standing in front of the wall swaying rhythmically from side to side and talking to himself.

"Dear," she began tentatively. "Dear," she repeated. "Richard?" Finally, he stopped his chattering and turned to look at her. "I must go to the washroom and clean up." She kept the smile in place and she felt like her face would split open at any moment.

"Now, Meggie, no tricks." His hand shook a little as he pulled off the electrical tape. The hair and top layer of skin on her arm came off with the tape. She swallowed her groan of pain and rubbed furiously at her arms.

Holding on to the wall, she stood and walked slowly into the tiny bathroom and shut the door behind her.

The sink was almost black with grime, the toilet had a reddish rim all around the water line, and the seat hung on by one bolt. Megan turned on the tap, waiting for the water to come out clear. She looked about the tiny room, pinching her nostrils together with her fingers and breathing through her mouth to avoid the smell.

Quickly, she washed her face and rinsed out her mouth. She continued to run the water as she lowered the lid of the toilet and sat, working to marshal her strength.

There was a towel rack bolted to the wall to the right of the sink and a mirrored medicine cabinet above it. As the water ran down the sluggish drain, she opened the cabinet and looked inside.

Rust, dirt, and dead bugs were on each of the four shelves. There was a blackened toothbrush and an old bottle of medication. Megan reached in, trying to avoid touching anything but the bottle. The bottle contained an over-the-counter sleeping remedy.

A plan began to formulate; she would put some of the capsules in Richard's tea. If the medicine wasn't too old, perhaps it could work. When he nodded off, she could escape.

She looked out the tiny window to try to assess just where Richard had taken her. She craned her head all the way to the right and caught a glimpse of a vendor's stall.

So she was near or in the Jarro, where all the sidewalk vendors hawked their wares. She could make it to a neutral place in just a few feet from the front of the building, and then she could call Jim and...maybe he wouldn't want to see her after she'd hurt him so badly. But maybe...a tear trickled down her cheek.

"Meggie, you all right, love?"

She dashed the tears away and straightened her clothing. She could get herself out of this. She was a smart and resourceful woman. She could get herself away from Richard and find Jim. And then she'd be the one on bended knee and beg him to marry her. She took a deep breath, ignoring the smell, and with her head now clear, she began to formulate a plan.

"Yes, give me a moment."

Megan grabbed all the pills in the bottle and put them in her pocket. She replaced the bottle, dashed more water on her face, put the smile in place, and opened the door.

"Thank you, Richard, I feel much better now."

"That's my girl. Come have a beer, eh?"

"Right, but I won't drink alone. You must have one

as well."

"Sure." Richard's face lit up, and he grinned at her. He seemed much more lucid and Megan was hopeful that he wouldn't chop her up into little bits just yet. First step of the plan.

"I shall pour," Megan told him. "Why don't you go and clean up a bit, and then we can talk over our drinks."

"Jolly good."

Richard went into the bath and closed the door firmly behind him. He seemed to think better of it, and cracked the door open a little and peeked out at her before turning back around. As soon as he'd stepped all the way into the bath and his back was turned, Megan reached for the glasses.

With shaking hands, she opened six of the capsules, spilling the tiny round balls into the bottom of the glass. She heard the toilet flush and water running in the sink. Some of the beer sloshed over the edge and a few of the tiny medicine balls came with it in the foam. Megan wiped off the beer on the table and the outside of the glass with the skirt of her dress just as the door opened.

With the full beer glass in hand, she turned to Richard as he came into the room.

"Here you are." Richard took the glass and waited while Megan poured some for herself in another glass.

"Cheers," she said and drank quickly, hoping Richard would mimic her and finish off his.

He gulped the beer down greedily, set the glass down with a thud, and opened his arms for Megan.

Chapter 42

"Seamus? Seamus? Where are you when I need you?" Jim leaned against the counter in the men's room at the police station, his head cradled in his hands. His mind rambled on and on, with each thought hitting a wall and fizzling out like a computer game.

He and Teresa had talked to her old boyfriend, Frank Devon, and he in turn, had started the paperwork on both Richard and Megan. Frank had ordered some of his troops to stake out Richard's apartment and to canvass his known haunts. All of the investigative policemen had the information, and were told especially about the raincoat.

But where was Richard? And was Megan with him?

Jim looked up at his reflection in the mirror. What would he do if Richard hurt her? What would he do if she was already dead? No, she couldn't be. Even in the short time he knew Megan, he felt such a connection with her that he would know if that connection were no longer there.

He stood upright and walked from the room, letting the swinging door nudge him a bit out into the hallway.

Teresa sat calmly at Frank's desk. She looked into a compact mirror fiddling with her hair while Frank talked on the phone. Jim looked around absently. The Metropolitan Police Station resembled closely one of the precinct houses in downtown Boston, complete with the derelicts and lowlifes who always seemed to reside there.

Jim was relieved that Frank had taken them seriously about Megan's possible kidnapping. Now, they just had to find her. Jim walked back into the bathroom and once again leaned against the counter.

"Seamus. Seamus, I need to see you right now. You promised that you'd help me with one thing and this is it.

"Please, Seamus, will you—?"

The door swung open and a man walked into the bathroom. His eyes darted about, looking for whoever Jim was talking to. When he saw no one, he frowned, looked at Jim, and backed out of the washroom.

Jim smiled tightly at the man, watching as the door closed soundlessly.

"Enough, already. I give up. Holy Mother, please send Seamus to me now," he mumbled under his breath.

Maybe if Seamus wouldn't come on his own, one of his superiors could nudge him into action. Jim counted to twenty and when the little guy did a no show, walked back to Frank Devon's desk.

"Ah, Mr. O'Flannery, come sit down." Frank stood and gave Jim his seat while he grabbed a chair from a nearby vacant desk.

"I've been talking to Teresa. She's given me as much information as possible about what Miss Kennedy was wearing and what she might have had with her. You say you left her at the flat at nine thirty?"

"Yeah, that's right."

"She's been gone a neat thirteen hours, then. I'll

have T fill out a missing person's report. Paperwork is the boon and the downfall of many a loyal copper. Now, Mr. O'Flannery—"

"Why don't you call me Jim?"

"Right, Jim, tell me again why you think she's been kidnapped."

Jim blew out a frustrated breath, but complied with the directive. "Because, Richard O'Connell has been following us all over the country; I mean all over, from coast to coast. The first day I was here, he told her, in front of me, that it would never be over between them. He practically accosted her on the main floor of the Irish Times. Don't think I'm overreacting when I tell you I think the man's a lunatic."

"Jay-sus," Frank said.

"And another thing, he hates Americans. I have that from his father. Now, I know you think I'm going off on a tangent, but hear me out. What if Richard O'Connell is the serial killer and he's done it in some warped way to get Megan's attention? He'd kill two birds with one stone, pardon the pun. He decidedly has a screw loose. Richard's just under six two and is left-handed. Another tidbit: he always wears a shiny brown raincoat that reaches down to the tops of his shoes and no fibers were ever found on the victims. Get me? He hates Americans. It's his mission in his warped brain to kill all the Irish Americans he can find, and he does it to impress Megan, too. We have very little to go on with the physical description of the killer except that he is just under six two," said Jim as he ticked off the traits on his fingers. "He is wearing a garment that doesn't leave any fibers, and he's left handed. I know this isn't a lot to go on, Frank, but you can see my reasoning."

Frank stared at him, never so much as blinking while Jim spoke, and Jim was sure that the man thought he was as loony as Richard. After Jim finished, Frank picked up the phone.

"Get a picture of Richard O'Connell from his father, the stock broker on Grafton and Flanning, and then circulate the photo all round. Yes, Sergeant, do it now. He is wanted for questioning and only questioning at this time."

Jim shoved his hands in his pockets and walked away from the desk to quietly beat his forehead against the wall.

The subtle pain helped keep him awake and focused.

He could have saved her; he didn't know how at the moment, but he could have. And when he found out how he screwed up, then he'd really knock his head against the wall.

"Now, don't be doin' that, Jimmy-lad."

Jim looked up to see Seamus standing on thin air, his knee bent and one foot crossed over the other leaning slightly on his cane.

"It's about da—"

"Ah, ah, ah. None of the language now."

"I'll give you language, you, you..." Jim looked around hurriedly, afraid someone had heard him talking to the wall. The hustle and bustle of the police station had masked his small outburst.

He turned around to lean against the wall, hoping to look nonchalant.

"Do you know where she is?" he asked quietly, looking everywhere but at Seamus.

"No, not yet. I'm *your* guardian angel, and hers has

told me that she's working to free herself, that much I know.

"And the man, Richard, is it, is not a threat...yet."

"Oh, great, and when will I know if he's become a threat? After she's dead?" Jim slammed the flat of his hand against the wall in frustration.

"'Twill not come to that. I know it. We're a bit short-handed or I'd take ye there meself. Like I've been tellin' ye. I can't see exactly where she is unless she calls me specifically. I'm your angel, not hers. But we'll have it all straightened out in a bit. I'm workin' on it, Jimmy-lad. Be patient."

"You'll forgive me if I don't jump up and down just yet. Find her, Seamus. Find her, please." Jim stared at the leprechaun. Seamus gave him a jaunty grin, pulled on both earlobes, and vanished.

Chapter 43

Richard drank deeply from his beer and wiped his mouth with the back of his hand. Megan smiled at him again in her shy way, and he knew she'd come around. They could be married. He just had to do in one more. Just sitting here quietly with her like two old married people eased his always-turbulent mind.

He was filled with lethargy, like none he'd known for a very long time. He looked up at her again and her face looked fuzzy and out of focus. He shook his head sharply, trying to dispel the fatigue. He was so tired. So tired. Perhaps he'd have to lie down for just a bit.

"Think I'll rest for a bit, Meggie. Clean up, won't you? I shan't be but a moment or two."

Richard staggered to the couch, unfastened his coat, and lay sprawled, his arms and legs out every which way.

Megan held her breath, her hands clenched together in a death grip, almost afraid to make the tiniest of sounds, afraid to breathe.

Seconds later, a soft snore blew out of Richard's mouth.

Megan stood rooted to the floor, afraid to move. Slowly, she turned, her eyes never moving from Richard. Inching her way, she reached up and unlocked the deadbolt.

It snapped with a resounding thud.

Megan held her breath. Richard could awaken any moment and grab her. She readied herself to run if he moved the tiniest bit. Quietly, she turned the knob. It opened slowly, making very little noise. When the crack was wide enough for her to slip through, she squeezed herself around the door. She pulled it to her, holding the knob until the door shut completely.

She gave a quick look around. Which way, which way to run?

There was a window on the far side of the long hallway and she ran to it and looked down. The view looked like she might be near the river.

She found the stairwell at the end of the hall and ran down the steps, trying to keep her relief at bay until she was truly out of danger. She looked over her shoulder, alert for any movement from the second floor. She made it to the outside door, when a hand reached out and clutched her arm.

Chapter 44

"We should know something soon. Can't very well send out so many men and turn up nothing." Frank Devon stood and rubbed his hands over his face. Too little sleep and overwhelming anxiety for Megan's safety hung over Jim like a blanket.

Teresa sat sprawled in a hard wooden chair, first stretching one side and then the other. Jim watched Teresa and Frank for a moment before he continued pacing the floor near Frank's desk.

"Heard from Seamus?" Teresa asked as she stretched both arms over her head, giving all the men near Frank's desk quite an eyeful.

Jim shook his head and then continued pacing.

"Who's this Seamus?" asked Frank.

"Oh, he's a psychic or something, an acquaintance of Jim's," Teresa answered.

Frank lowered his brows in thought for a moment. "A psychic?"

Jim stopped his pacing. "Well, kind of." He rubbed the back of his neck, ducking his face down. He could feel a flush rushing to his cheeks, and he turned away from the desk and continued to pace. Minutes later, he stopped abruptly.

What the hell was he doing? Why wasn't he out there looking for Megan? Had he ever left the doing up to anyone else, ever, even when he was a kid? No, never. So why was he starting now? Just because he didn't know the first thing about Dublin didn't mean he couldn't go look for her himself. Just because the city was as big as Boston, Cambridge, and Quincy all rolled into one, didn't mean he couldn't wear off a little shoe leather looking for her. He didn't have to wait for Seamus or the damn Metropolitan Police, no siree.

He could just—

"O'Flannery, you've lost it for good," he mumbled under his breath. "Where the hell do you start looking?"

Jim grabbed a chair and pulled it up next to Teresa's. He stared at her, and kept on staring until she squirmed.

"If you were Richard, where would you be? Come on Teresa, you know this guy and we don't."

"Well, I don't really know him; I mean we did have a conversation upon one occasion."

"See? That's a lot more than me and Frank had. Now, rack that pretty head of yours and pull on this guy's skin and tell me what you think."

"Oooh. That's quite nasty, pulling on his skin, don't you think?"

"Never mind, just think."

"All right, all right, now. Well...uh...oh, well...maybe."

"Maybe what?" Frank asked in exasperation.

"Well, he's quite a fanatic, this one is. A national. Thinks the IRA are all living saints and he'd bow down and kiss their feet if he could. Always talking about the good old days, you know the Rising of 1916, like it was the ruddy second coming of Christ. Oh, one time he took Meggie to the cemetery, where the Republican plot is, where all the rebels are buried. Meggie said he went on and on about it, and it fair made her skin crawl. Talked like they was saints."

"Could he be at the cemetery now?" Jim asked as he turned to Frank.

"Don't think so. There are night patrols and the place is too open; there's nowhere for them to stay the night out of the cold. No, he'd go somewhere he'd already arranged, I'll warrant. But where?"

"Is there a place considered more Irish by the Irish than any other in the city?" Jim wanted to know.

"Well, I don't really know, maybe the Jarro. The vendors' stalls there are supposed to be uniquely Irish, but I hear they have much the same type of thing in the States. I'm sure they have the same type of outdoor vendors just about everywhere else in the world. There are lots of places like that in London.

"But if O'Connell is as crazy as I think he is, he may just forget that outdoor vendors are common, and he's parked himself at the Jarro.

"Delusional, I'd call it. Have to be to be a serial killer, if that's indeed who he is. Daft, completely daft. I'll call over to that district and have some men look around. I'll stay here in case any information comes through. Teresa, why don't you show him where the Jarro is? Beats sitting around here waiting until you go crazy."

"Great idea, let's go, Teresa." Jim grabbed Teresa by the arm and hauled her out of the station house, barely giving her time to shrug into her coat.

Chapter 45

"Where ya goin', deary?"

Megan's gaze jerked down to see a dirty hand with cracked nails clutching at her forearm. The hand was attached to an equally dirty woman of indeterminate age. She could have been thirty or fifty. The shabby stained dress that hung on her gaunt frame suggested only that the woman was undernourished and obviously lacking convenient plumbing.

"You be the newlyweds, eh?"

"The newlyweds?"

"Right enough, yer man come down some time back and set up getting the place and all for you."

"Ah, my husband?" Megan's mind moved feverishly over the information. Richard had come here before he abducted her. Or was the woman even speaking of Richard?

"Tell me, are you sure you're speaking of my husband?"

"Ah, love, he describes you to a tee, he did. Brought the food in meself, I did. Where is that handsome man of yours, eh?"

"Well, uh...he's...uh...taking a nap."

"Ah, you newlyweds, ya going at it so hard, makes the men tired, ah yes, it does. Now, let old Molly give you some advice. Love 'em hard and they'll never stray, they won't. And where are you off to?"

"Ah, I need to get some...uh...uh, some soap chips, for the dishes. Can you tell me where a store is?"

If the woman would only let her go! Megan was sure Richard would wake up and come rushing down the stairs to re-capture her. The woman's croaking voice was loud enough to wake the dead.

Megan schooled herself to act nonchalantly, like a new wife out to get soap chips, yes, nonchalant. Megan forced a smile to her lips and looked directly at the woman, trying not to shudder.

"There's Kelly's down the street to the left, and then there's O'Grady's on the other side of the street. Go to Kelly's. He's got the most of anything yer heart desires, he does. You tell the old brigand that Molly sent you and he'll do for you right enough."

"Why, thank you, Molly. You're most...kind. Ta ta." Megan literally pried the woman's grasping fingers off her arm and ran the rest of the way out the building.

The wind bit into her. Chill after chill after chill coursed down her spine. Her nose ran, her teeth chattered, and the goose bumps on her arms were as big as mountains.

She kept running as she glanced over her shoulder. Richard would reach out and grab her at any moment. She glanced down quickly at her dress and shuddered. Her favorite was torn along the seams and there were stains all over the crushed velvet. She didn't care, she couldn't care, as long as she could get away and then the damn dress could go into the fire.

A thought flitted across her mind. She'd end up looking like Molly in no time. She shuddered again as she pushed open the door to Kelly's Emporium.

Every surface in the general store was covered by a

thick layer of dust, and the odd little place smelled of perfume. Perhaps the smell was masking another, more pungent, odor. A grizzled old man wearing a once-white apron stood behind the long wooden counter.

"And what can I do for you, Missy?"

"Mr. Kelly?"

"Aye."

"Have you a telephone? I must call someone. It's an emergency. Oh, and Molly sent me."

"Molly? Molly? Why that old crone, I wouldn't give her the teats on a cow."

"But Mr. Kelly, might I use your telephone? It is quite important."

Something in the look on Megan's face prompted the old man. He went around the counter and patted her hand before leading her to the back.

The room was an office filled with filing cabinets and clipboards hanging on nails around the dirty walls. Papers in stacks littered the top of a desk that stood in the center of the floor. On the desk sat an old-fashioned desk phone in a cradle with huge number buttons.

"Take all the time you need, love. I shall be out front." Before he left, he patted her hand, closing the door soundly behind him as he left.

Megan's hand trembled as she dialed Jim's hotel.

"No, Mr. O'Flannery hasn't been in since early this morning," the desk clerk informed her.

"Do you have any idea where he is?"

"No, but his bags have been packed, so I suppose he'll be checking out soon."

Megan's heart plummeted to her feet. Checking out? "Thanks."

She rang off and called the emergency police

number.

"State the nature of the emergency," a cold, dispassionate voice said on the other end.

"My name is Megan Kennedy, and I've been kidnapped. I'm somewhere in the Jarro, I can see the river from here."

"Can you be more specific about your location, Miss Kennedy?"

"No—yes, I mean I'm in a store called Kelly's Emporium. Can you send someone now?"

"Kelly's Emporium. Yes, Miss Kennedy, stay there and we shall have a policeman over as soon as can be. There is a report out on you. We've been looking for you all day."

Megan heaved a great sigh and leaned against the desk as she hung up the phone. Weariness almost overcame her. She shuddered for a moment, but stiffened her backbone. She couldn't turn into a pile of jelly now.

If only Jim were here. If only…but he was packed to leave. What if he left before she could make it up to him?

What if he left before she could tell him how much she loved him? What if—?

Megan hung up the phone. "That's enough, Megan. Just get away from the lunatic before he chops your head off. You have a passport and a credit card, that's enough to get you back to Jim after you're safe. Stop being an idiot and get on with it." She took a deep breath and looked around the office for another exit. It was too risky to leave by the front.

At least the police were on the way. Teresa had probably noticed she was gone this morning and called them. No, that didn't sound right. Megan covered her tired face with her hands. Where was Jim? Where? Get on, Megan. You've no time to mope.

"Seamus! I know I'll call Seamus; surely he can help me get out of here. Seamus, uh…Seamus, dear, if you can hear me, will you come?"

"Right-o, lass. And didn't I tell you that your Uncle Seamus would make sure every little thing was all right?"

The leprechaun stood in front of Megan, floating on a bit of invisible air.

"Now, let me state the rules, if I may. According to the Angel Second class Compendium," he said as he pulled an inch thick book from his breast pocket, "no angel shall interfere with another angel's operation of his assigned duties."

Megan's teeth ground together. *Stuff the 'Angel Compendium,' just get me out of here.*

"Now, I know for a fact, I do, that your own angel is working hard at helping you himself. 'Twas himself that made sure the pills were available and 'twas himself that told you to put them in the beer, although I think 'twas a terrible waste of good spirits. I can't be helping you directly. Only indirectly, if you know what I mean, your angel is near."

Megan tried not to roll her eyes. The two angels were arguing about who knew what, and she had to escape from crazy Richard.

"Ah, there he is, right behind you. Nice looking chap. What?" said the little leprechaun, cocking his head listening to something Megan couldn't hear. "Ah, all right then, I'm off."

The little angel scowled at the air and Megan

couldn't begin to imagine what they said to one another.

Could there be jealousy and competitiveness between angels? She just needed to get out, never mind the silly spirits showing off in front of her.

"Seamus, I need…"

Seamus bowed slightly to Megan. "Your angel, his name is Michael," he said conspiratorially behind his hand, effectively cutting her off.

"Not *the* Michael, mind you. He got you to this place and now we have to wait for Jim-lad. He's on the way."

"Oh, thank the Lord, but what about…?"

"Yes, you can be thanking Him, but don't forget that you should thank us as—" The leprechaun looked quickly over his shoulder and then turned to gesture to the air behind Megan.

"And what time do you suppose you can start with helping the lass, eh?" Seamus said with a little heat in his voice. It was obvious Seamus was speaking to Megan's angel, Michael.

"Uh-oh, now, lass, he's going to take over and he's just told me that you must leave by the back way." The little leprechaun looked anxiously over his shoulder again, pulled on both earlobes and disappeared.

Megan stared at the closed door for just a second before she sprang into action. She glanced about, frantically looking for a way out. She ran to the back wall, pushing on each seam, hoping one would open and reveal a door. There were footsteps outside the door, an angry voice and—

"Megan, love, now why did you run off like that?"

Megan turned slowly to see Richard, groggy, but

quite coherent. She watched in horror as he reached out to grab her.

Chapter 46

"It's bloody cold, O'Flannery. I just need to button up my coat."

"Sorry, Teresa, no time. You can button it up in the cab."

"If we ever get a bleedin' cab."

After the fourth cab had passed them without so much as looking, let alone stopping, Jim turned to Teresa.

"Which way is it?"

"We can't be walking, surely."

"I guess we'll have to. Is there a bus?"

"Should be. Haven't the foggiest clue which one though."

"Great."

Jim looked around with such a menacing expression that anyone near him prudently stepped out of the way.

"Come on, we'll go to the corner, and the next bus that stops, we'll ask."

A few seconds later, a bus rumbled to the corner. Teresa talked briefly to the driver, who in turn, gestured grandly with his arms to another street corner across the busy boulevard.

"This is just ridiculous," Jim exploded. "Which way, Teresa?"

"Listen, O'Flannery, it's miles from here, and we

simply can't walk."

"Well, if it's simply miles from here, I guess we'd better get started." Jim gestured for Teresa to go on ahead.

She let out an exasperated breath and trudged on with Jim close at her heels.

They walked heads down against the wind, not speaking, elbowing their way down the street. Ten minutes later they managed to catch a cab. Jim looked at his watch.

"She's been gone sixteen hours."

Teresa put her hand on his sleeve. "Don't worry, we'll find her."

Chapter 47

"Oh, Richard, I...uh...I came to buy some soap chips. I had to clean the dishes and the uh...place." Megan looked over Richard's shoulder to see Mr. Kelly's worried expression. The old man knew something was up.

Megan's mind worked feverishly. What could she say or do to alert Mr. Kelly about Richard.

"Oh, Mr. Kelly, this is Mr. Richard O'Connell."

Richard's cold gaze moved from Megan to the man who stood directly behind him. He stuck out his hand in a move to shake. Mr. Kelly grasped his hands, successfully pulling him out of the storeroom and into the store.

"Mr. O'Connell, is it? Wonderful. I've just the thing to show you, lad. Stamps commemorating the rebellion. Have you seen them then?"

Mr. Kelly raised his brow at Megan in a subtle signal.

"Stamps?"

Richard moved unsteadily toward the counter and blessed Mr. Kelly pulled Richard farther into the store and away from Megan.

Megan took a tentative step across the threshold of the office. She took two more steps, never taking her eyes from Richard's back. The sleeping pills had obviously affected him, but not enough to knock him out. Richard was groggy, swaying slightly, and his speech was slurred. Whether it was because the pills were too old or because he hadn't ingested enough, the outcome was the same.

Megan moved slowly and silently past his back, looking at him out of the corner of her eye, but focusing all her attention on the door that led to the street.

Mr. Kelly was talking a million miles an hour, trying to keep Richard occupied. Mr. Kelly was a small, slight man. He wouldn't be able to keep Richard from harming her. His arm was braced around Richard's shoulders while his other hand gestured unobtrusively to her to hurry out the door.

Megan was but two steps from the door when Richard spun around. She gasped. He broke from Mr. Kelly and moved toward her in slow motion. She stood transfixed for a heartbeat, then two. His movements were strange and somehow surreal. He teetered a little, and then lunged forward to grab her.

Terror gripped at her heart and riveted her to the floor. A voice screamed in her head, *"Run, colleen, run!"*

She turned and dashed to the door and threw it open wide. Heavy, stumbling footsteps sounded close behind.

Too close. Tears coursed down her face from the cold and terror and blurred her vision as she raced down the street.

She made it to the tenement she'd just left, but she heard his heavy breathing and footsteps behind her.

She wouldn't look around. It would slow her down. She must keep moving. She ran up the stairs, her feet thundering on the wooden steps. Molly stood on the landing, her mouth agape. Megan shoved her to one side.

She could hear him, his footsteps running. Running to catch her. What would he do? His breath sounded like grating gasps; like an automaton, like a machine.

She heard a voice, *"The roof, colleen, the roof."* It was Seamus.

Megan ran to the end of the hall, jerked open the door to the roof, slammed it shut, and fumbled with clumsy fingers to try to lock it.

The hem of her dress caught on her shoe and she stumbled on the bottom step. She tried to breathe, but cold fear made her heart hammer and black spots crowded around her sight, a sure sign she would pass out and then it would be all over. Like hell! She'd fight that maniac until there was nothing left inside of her. By God, she'd fight him.

She heard the doorknob rattle behind her. She took a huge breath, pushing the much-needed air into her lungs, and ran up the steps, not looking back.

The top door to the roof creaked and squealed in protest. It was warped shut from humidity and lack of use. She pushed until she thought she'd die trying. Finally, the bottom began to move and it swung open wide as the wind grabbed it. It flew open with such velocity that it almost jerked her arm out of the socket. She stumbled past the door frame, catching the wind full face. Tears stung her eyes; wind and droplets of rain whooshed in her face as she lunged forward.

He'd get her. He'd come behind her and grab her and...she groped for the edge of one of the chimneys, the roughened brick tearing at her hands. Her hair whipped behind her and lashed into her eyes, blinding her. She had to look for a hiding place away from the relentless wind and rain. And Richard.

Black soot covered every surface of the brick. The wind blew particles into her mouth, and mercilessly burned her eyes. Tears streamed down her face. With the hem of her dress, she wiped the soot and wet from her eyes. She stopped for a moment and tried to think. She crouched down behind a chimney farthest from the door and glanced around. She was now, at least, hidden from the door to the roof. She ignored her eyes, the two lumps of ice that were her hands, and her chattering teeth. She tried to quiet herself, tried to still her cough so Richard would not hear her.

The door to the roof flung open and crashed against the opposite wall.

"Meggie, I know you're here." His voice was filled with rage. "Show yourself." He howled like a wounded animal. And then there was silence. Seconds later an ear splitting cry tore through the air, and the wind paled in comparison to it.

Megan huddled closer to the chimney, while the floor of the roof vibrated under Richard's heavy footfalls. Then she heard it; a siren above the wind and not too far in the distance. Megan heard Richard turn and his shoes scraping against the tiles. He staggered near the edge of the roof and peered down at the street.

Megan peeked around the chimney. He looked first one way and then the other as his huge brown raincoat billowed out around him.

The sirens grew louder until they stopped directly in front of the building. Richard ran away from the street side of the roof, his feet thundered past her hiding place, and then she lost sight of him. Where was he?

The wind howled around the chimney, drowning out the sound from the street, drowning out even her shuddering, chattering teeth. She had to stay ahead of the madman. She was so cold. She'd never get warm again. Her head came up. She forced her breath to slow. She heard a car door slam, feet running, men calling out. She thought she heard Teresa's voice.

She had to stay quiet! Slowly she stood and flattened herself against the brick as she crept around the edge of the chimney. The air rang with the sound of men shouting from below. She was sure she heard Jim's voice.

Jim! Oh, God he'd come to rescue her!

She glanced right and then left and didn't see Richard. She ran to the edge of the roof, straining to see the sidewalk. Was he there? Oh God, please be there.

"Jim." She stuck her head over the side, waving her arms frantically. "Jim," she shouted again.

A hand, like a vise, grabbed her from behind.

"Now, why are you doing this, Meggie? I told you, I'd be famous and then Father would come around." His hand was squeezing, clutching her upper arm, wrenching it slowly, methodically, causing so much pain that she couldn't think, couldn't react. Megan jerked back and forth frantically trying to loosen Richard's grip, but he stood like a statue, his hand like a hawk's talon gripping her arm and the only thing that moved was his eyes, quick and harried. Richard looked at her, leaned forward, and screamed in her face.

"I'm not ready yet. Why are you calling to him? You are mine; you can't call to him. You can't. I need to do one more…"

His voice pitched high above the wind and the

noises from the street.

She looked at him, stared at the frantic man she'd been so terrified of just moments before. Something inside of Megan snapped, and her mind became clear and coherent.

All during the night, terror had successfully paralyzed her from action. When Richard had shown up on her doorstep, terror had put her will to escape in a straightjacket. But a straightjacket was where this lunatic belonged, not her.

Anger bloomed inside her and overwhelmed the nauseating terror. There was so much anger; everywhere she looked was shrouded in a haze of red. Her blood pounded and raced into her temples and a surge of adrenaline moved through her veins until her hands felt warm and her eyes were clear.

"Shut up, you idiot," she growled at him and felt her lip curl into a sneer. Megan thrust her face to within an inch of his. She watched with great satisfaction as his glazed look sharpened and he cringed back from her.

"Let go of me, you—you—you blithering idiot!" She rose up on her toes and screamed into his face.

She jerked her arm down with a hard, wrenching turn and loosened his grip. Richard was stunned, flabbergasted, and shocked all at the same time.

"But, Meggie—"

"But, Meggie, nothing. Let go of me. Get off of me, you—you—you murderer."

Megan shoved him, pushing her upper body against him and away from her as hard as she could. At last, his grip loosened. He stumbled backward and tripped on the hem of his coat. His arms flew out, flailing about as he tried to catch himself. He lurched forward to compensate for his movement backward. The wind blew his oversized coat out around him and it wrapped it around his legs. He lost his balance in the tangle of his coat and the wind. He pitched backward. His hands grasped the empty air, but not finding purchase, he pitched forward. In slow motion, his hand reached out to her, flailing, trying to reach her. His eyes, huge with terror, bore into hers beseechingly.

He fell head first over the side of the building and Megan heard his scream above the roaring wind.

Megan squeezed her eyes shut, crouched down, and covered her head with her arms. She knew that she would never forget the sickening sound of Richard's body hitting the sidewalk.

Someone's hand was pulling her up. A kind, soothing voice spoke to her and strong arms wrapped around her comfortingly.

Jim. It was Jim. Megan took a long shuddering breath and tears flowed down her face. It was Jim. He never let go, as he led her from the roof.

When they reached the sidewalk, Teresa raced to Megan, hugging her fiercely before a policeman ushered them into the back of a patrol car.

Chaos reigned outside the safety of the small, insulated shell of the police car. Sounds overlapped and blended and turned into noise. Whistles blew, and sirens sounded as an ambulance tore up and stopped at the corner. Onlookers yelled, adding to the cacophony of the insanity all around them.

Megan shook her head, trying to clear away shock. She wiped the tears from her face with her dirty hand. Teresa pressed a tissue into her palm and then squeezed her on the shoulder. Megan took another shuddering breath and shut her eyes. It was over. Jim was here. It was over and she could go home and take a shower and...she looked down at the ruined dress and her tears started anew.

"It's okay, honey, it's all over." Jim kept his arm around her.

Megan looked up at him and touched his cheek. She sniffed loudly and wished she had more tissues.

"Jim?"

"Yes, dear?"

"If you still want to, I'll marry you." Her voice trembled, and a sob caught in the back of her throat. She didn't think she could stop crying.

Jim didn't answer. He folded her in his arms and held on tight.

Chapter 48

"Megan you must hold still, my dear."

"Yes, Mother."

Megan looked up to gaze at her reflection in the mirror. The heavy white satin gown set her skin aglow. The lace that edged the long sleeves hung down to almost cover her finger tips. The scallop-necked bodice encrusted with tiny pearls fitted tightly from her bosom to her waist.

Megan was almost afraid to breathe, sure that the ancient material would split, even though her mother had assured her it wouldn't. The gown had belonged to her great-grandmother and had been worn by her grandmother.

Now it was her turn to wear the beautiful gown.

Her mother pushed her gently into the chair to rearrange the veil over Megan's hair. The swept-up hairstyle was layered on the top of her head with tendrils hanging loose to soften the effect.

Valentine's Day. She was getting married on Valentine's Day. It was so romantic, and it was completely Jim's idea.

His mother and grandmother, some uncles, and cousins had traveled from America to attend the wedding. She loved her in-laws already.

Megan's mother and father had been at her flat for more than two weeks making the arrangements.

Jim's family was ecstatic to find out that he would marry Megan.

Jim's grandma had talked to him for hours after her arrival, something about Deacon O'Boyle and someone from a Bishop's office. Megan couldn't be bothered to ask about it. Her feet hadn't touched the ground since Jim had rescued her. But he told her over and over that she'd done the rescuing. Maybe when the horror of the whole affair was behind her, she could look at the events of that morning pragmatically. Who was she kidding? When she was ninety, she'd still think about it.

Last night, all twenty-two of their party of wedding goers, including Frank Devon and Teresa, had descended on the corner pub and practically closed the place down.

They still hadn't decided where to live, Ireland or the States, but that seemed like a small decision to make after the hell they had passed through to get to this point.

Their final article on the serial killings in Ireland, written as Megan Kennedy and James O'Flannery, run by both papers, was finished and published. The series, in its entirety, had been nominated for the prestigious MacGillicuddy Prize for outstanding journalism.

Everything had happened so fast her head swam with it. Megan had not completely recovered from her close call, because she could still see Richard falling from the rooftop many times during the day. When would she get over it? She shivered; with Jim's help, she would get past it. She'd think about it again after she was ninety. Megan opened her eyes and looked at her mother in the mirror.

"Are you quite all right, love?"

"Yes, Mama; just remembering, you know," she said as she shrugged her shoulders.

Her mother took Megan's hands in hers and looked at her steadily. "Megan, he's a fine man, this James Francis Xavier O'Flannery, and he'll make you a fine husband. You must let the other go. Remembering will only bring you pain. You mustn't have pain on this day, love."

"Right, Mother. You're right."

She stood and turned slowly, examining her image in the waist-high mirror.

"It's a beautiful gown."

"Aye, it is," said her mother with a touch of envy in her voice. "It's a shame that I'm too short and too broad in the hips to have worn it myself."

Megan turned again, watching her reflection in the mirror. She stopped suddenly, the wisp of a memory niggling at her mind.

Yes, it was the same gown as the one in the movie/dream she'd had at the hotel in Sligo. The same gown she wore in the movie/dream that Seamus had shown them of the future.

"Oh, crumbs," she gasped. Her face had gone quite pale in the mirror. She sat quickly, afraid that she might fall down. She hadn't thought of Seamus in weeks, but now everything he'd done or said flooded her memory. She glanced quickly about the room looking for the elusive little man in Kelly green.

"Meggie, what on earth is wrong my dear?"

"Oh, nothing, Mother. Perhaps a bit of wedding jitters."

Her mother patted her hand and then led her out of

the room to wait with her father in the narthex for the music to signal her entrance.

Megan looked about in all the corners, on top of the holy water font, even on top of all the marble columns, looking for Seamus. He was nowhere to be seen.

Her father kissed her on the cheek and adjusted her veil to cover her face. Megan saw the tears in his eyes and returned a watery smile.

But where was Seamus? He'd worked so hard getting them together, making sure she was safe. Could he not show up for the finale? She took glances about for the elusive little man in green.

The strains of Mendelssohn's "Wedding March" began. It was time.

Teresa, as maid of honor, walked down the aisle looking stunning in her deep green velvet dress with the low décolletage.

Jim had asked Frank Devon to be his best man. Frank had jumped at the request, stating that he hoped Teresa would soon come around, and then Jim could return the favor.

Megan walked down the aisle on wobbly legs, leaning heavily on her father's arm. When she finally reached Jim, and her father had patted her hand and taken his seat next to her mother, she started to relax.

The priest began saying the wedding mass, and Jim and Megan glanced up simultaneously behind the priest to the crucifix. It was as if they'd both been summoned. And there to the left, stood Seamus on a bit of invisible air, leaning on his cane. He winked at them, and waggled his brows.

Slowly, the leprechaun began to change. His face

first lost its beard and leprechaun-like characteristics until it became eerily similar to Jim's features. His bright red hair became a dark auburn brown, long and tied back as in the style of the eighteenth century. He was garbed in a golden floor-length gown that puddled about his feet. A gigantic pair of silvery, almost translucent wings unfurled behind him, and a white light shone around him, filling the nave with such brightness it hurt Megan's eyes.

Jim and Megan stared and gasped as the same time. The priest stopped for a moment and looked at them oddly, but then cleared his throat as though to tell them to pay attention. Megan and Jim glanced quickly at each other, then at the priest.

Seamus floated to the left of the priest's head and laughed softly. He waggled his eyebrows at them again.

"I'll be joinin' Saint Patrick's choir now. And you've made that possible, Jimmy me lad. I'm thankin' ye, I am.

"And you, Megan lass, such a wonderful time I've had. It was a grand ride ye both gave me. Ah, a grand ride.

"May the road rise up before you, may the wind be always at your back, and may you be in Heaven an hour before the devil knows you're dead."

He laughed soundlessly and a glass appeared in his hand. He saluted them, drank quickly, and tossed the glass into the air where it disappeared. The tiny harp appeared and Seamus sang.

"She wears my ring to show the world
That she belongs to me
She wears my ring to tell the world
She's mine eternally

With loving care
I placed it on her fi-inger
To show my love
For all the world to see!"

He laughed, a great, gutsy, bellowing laugh, obviously thoroughly enjoying the amazement on both their faces. He hovered a bit, like he was waiting for the priest to make the final pronouncement.

"Hmm, Mr. James O'Flannery, will you take this woman…"

Again the priest cleared his throat roughly, and Megan and Jim brought their gaze down from the top of the ceiling. While they'd watched Seamus ascend to his just reward, they hadn't been paying attention to their own wedding ceremony.

"Oh, of course, and so does she." Jim turned and nodded to those in the church.

The angel rose up slowly, moving like vapor through the high vaulted ceiling. He looked down from his high vantage point and smiled at Jim and Megan. But they were too busy looking at each other to see.

Jim reached over and took Megan's face in his hands. The happy congregation laughed when Megan kissed Jim soundly.

A word about the author...

Kathryn Scarborough grew up as a "Navy junior." The turmoil of changing schools and friends, almost yearly, led to making up a lot of stories or making new endings to the ones she read in school. She went to music conservatory and spent the next several decades singing, teaching, and directing. She has a master's certificate in Special Education. She now writes fiction full time.

She has four grown children, three grandchildren, and lives in central North Carolina with her husband and two crazy dogs. You can reach her at www.scarboroughbooks.com